BU

UNIVI

Elizabeth Randall

Crossing Lives

europe books

ISBN 979-12-201-1619-0
First edition: November 2021
Distribution for the United Kingdom: **Vine House Distribution ltd**

Printed for Italy by *Rotomail Italia S.p.A. - Vignate (MI)*
Stampato presso *Rotomail Italia S.p.A. - Vignate (MI)*

Crossing Lives

I dedicate this book to Rick and members of my family and friends who have supported me in this project

She closed the door behind her. The chilly night air immediately made her gasp. She needed to walk, to think. It was hard to believe what she had just read. Her mother's solicitor had posted her the letter her grandmother had written. It all made sense now, the hostility, the arguments. She hadn't had time for it to sink in. She was fighting back the tears, she felt weak and defeated.

She passed a man, crouched over, pausing to cough. What secrets did he hide in his heart? She wanted to reach out to this stranger in the night. To tell him that secrets could heal as well as harm. He shuffled away. The moon had risen, and the cold wind made her shiver. Her shadow gave her comfort. Quietly, she walked past the entrance to a graveyard. The austere headstones leaned as if buffeted by the horror of death. Her step quickened. The street was deserted, the silence broken by a scurrying in the undergrowth of a big oak tree. A fox ran right in front of her and away into the bushes. She would walk round the graveyard and up to the hill. Lights from the houses beckoned her, she should really turn back to her family, but something compelled her to walk on. She thought of her mother and her life, her illness. A fountain of sadness erupted in her soul. She pulled her coat around her tightly. She needed to be held, she had never felt so alone. Clouds raced across the moon, the light from the streetlamps danced on the pavement, the trees rustled in the wind. She felt breathless as she walked up the hill, her pulse rising in her neck. At the top of the hill there was a bench, she could look down on the city with all its sparkle. Sitting down she felt in her pocket. The letter was still there.

She couldn't bring herself to read it again, but she knew she had to keep it safe. One day she would share it with Mat, he was dependable and discreet. Until then she would hold it herself. No one would be hurt, no one would need to know. What did it matter?

But it changed everything for her. How could she face her father? She suddenly felt an impulse to destroy it. That's what people do isn't it? she told herself. They hide from the truth, facing their children knowing they have deceived them. Secrets like this one should be hidden. Anger rose in her chest. She would take one last look. By the light of a streetlamp she opened the letter. It had been written just before her grandmother's death four years ago:

10th July 2001

My darling Helen,

Now that your mother has passed you have the right to know the truth. She and your father were always close but, early on in their marriage, your father became very depressed. Your mother sought solace and found it in Uncle Jack. Jack, as you know, also suffered from depression- it is a family failing. I shouldn't say 'failing', I feel I have failed as it comes from my side of the family. The closeness that developed between your mother and Jack led to more than just a platonic relationship. Many years later, you were around nine I think, your mother confided in me. She told me that she was certain Jack was your father. Jack's sudden death brought great sadness to the family, but the strain on your parents was immense. Fortunately, their bond was strong and somehow, they pulled through. Your mother made me promise that on her death you would receive a letter explaining everything. I know that this will upset you and for that she and I are deeply sad. Your father knows nothing of our intention, and I will place this in the hands of your mother's solicitor for the attention of you alone. How you will deal with this I have no idea, but you are strong. My mind is going and by the time you read this I will be long gone. Your mother and I love you dearly. Have courage. Do not weep. Take time to think. Don't rush to talk.

Farewell my love,

Your loving Grandmother Rose

She folded the paper and placed it in her pocket. Tomorrow she would phone her father and arrange to meet. Until then she would try and decide whether to tell him or not. Right now, she was sure she wouldn't. He had suffered enough. No one deserves the blackness that descends, and she couldn't risk this happening to him again. She was sure this was the right decision. She turned to make her way back to the warmth of her family, a heaviness in her heart. She felt the sobs rising. Then, suddenly, passing a rubbish bin, she took out the letter again. Painstakingly she tore it into tiny pieces.

Autumn 2005

He saw her get on the train again. Smart shoes, neat figure, clutching a briefcase; she cut an efficient image. For three days he had been thinking of her since he'd noticed her first. There was something about her he couldn't quite place. Did she remind him of someone? It was difficult not to stare. She found a seat diagonally opposite his as the train pulled out of the station heading for the city. He had no plans for the day, just looking out for someone. Someone to follow. Someone to get close to. But he must keep a distance. He felt a nervousness permeate through his body. It was an ordinary journey but, for him, one filled with expectation. The train clanked forward with determination, heads nodding in unison.

She looked up from her phone and caught his eye. He immediately looked down. The train was crowded and, when she rose to leave, he had difficulty pushing through the commuters to reach the door in time. Her blond bob was visible ahead. He walked quickly behind her, up the escalators, his pulse quickening. Out in the sunlight he could see her ahead, making for a large office building. He would wait outside. She'd maybe leave at lunchtime. The pavements were busy with city folk, lots of beautiful people. He pulled his overcoat tight – it would be a long day. The sky darkened and a heavy shower made him look for shelter. A beggar shared the space. How had he sunk so low?

He glanced at his watch, it was already midday. A group of workers was leaving the building and he could see her bob amongst their well-groomed heads. Following at a distance, he watched them enter a pub.

Silently he entered the bar and ordered a whisky. He would need it. He felt slightly sweaty, he always felt this way. With his collar up he hoped she wouldn't see him. The atmosphere was stuffy in the bar, the voices muffled in the gloom. Rays of sunshine gushed in periodically lighting up her hair.

"Anything else," the barman asked.

He shook his head and went outside to wait. He would follow her home, he thought. He would need to know where she lived, with whom she lived. He would need to know more about her.

Laughter startled him as the group left the pub. How was it that laughter always caused him to shrink into himself? He walked away so as not to arouse suspicion. Sitting in a café, clutching his tea, he imagined what she'd be doing. How could he meet her? He could think of nothing else. He tried not to think of returning alone to his flat.

After an hour or so he rose and paid for his tea. Outside a chill was in the air, he would need to walk to keep warm. He found a route around a neighbouring square and walked briskly around. People were scurrying back and forth as if in a Lowry painting. He stopped to buy an evening paper. He must go back to her square and wait, he daren't miss her leaving. Gradually the sky began to darken, and dusk lay its blanket across the city. The streetlights came on, illuminating the hurrying figures. He was freezing. Back in his doorway, the beggar was wrapping himself up for the night. She must be leaving soon. At last, the doors of the building opened, and people began rushing out to begin their long commutes home. He soon saw her running to the Tube station and a rising dread overwhelmed him. What if he lost her in the crowd? He boarded the same compartment as her and found himself sitting opposite her again. Worried that she would recognise him from the morning, he kept his gaze down reading his phone. Only a few people left the train at her station, so he kept well back. He realised he would probably lose her now, like he had lost so many, when she drove home from the station, but, to his relief, she walked away down the hill. The pavements were quiet here, he must be careful. The streetlights seemed too bright, he craved the safety of darkness. Like a lion moving in on his prey he moved up closer. Her footsteps seemed so confident, she was in control. Then before his eyes she reached her home. He held back, noticing the street name.

She was gone, unattainable, he would never know her. His grief was more than he could bear. He rocked back and forth. He could come back here, he thought, now that he knew where she lived. He could watch her again. Maybe even speak to her. He saw a light go on upstairs and the curtains being drawn. This was the end of her day, she was safe in her domesticity, cushioned from his fantasies. He turned to leave. Tomorrow he would see her again.

Autumn 2005

The hall was dark, the clutter from the day everywhere. She poured herself a glass of wine, tears rolling down her face. It would be a long night. Try as she might, she couldn't get the words of the letter out of her mind. Tomorrow she had to take minutes in an important contracts meeting, she would need a clear head. A good night's sleep would be essential. There was also a school concert she had to get to after work. How would she cope? Creeping upstairs and into her bedroom she saw that Mat was fast asleep. Darkness enveloped her. She remembered her journey home and finding the letter from the solicitor on the hall table. Suddenly, the image of a fellow passenger came to her mind. He was a strange man who seemed to stare at her with piercing eyes, as if looking right through her. He had made her feel most uncomfortable, and she was glad when she reached her station and could walk briskly home.

The night stretched long before her. She felt hot then cold, her arms tingled, her breathing was shallow. A mounting feeling of panic rose through her body. She could hear the wind in the trees outside. It began to rain. Sleep wouldn't come. The bedclothes were heavy, the air oppressive, thick. At last, she drifted into a fitful sleep, dreaming of running and escaping from an unknown predator.

He would grab a bite to eat in the local pub before he went home, he planned. He was hungry, cold, and empty. His coat wasn't warm enough. Autumn had come early.

The chatter in the pub deafened him, he couldn't wait to leave. No one ever spoke to him and he spoke to no one. No one would listen, he felt sure of that. He had nothing to say, nothing. But he felt a burning desire for human contact, for someone with whom to share his feelings and aspirations. Realising he was weeping he hurriedly left the pub and started back to his flat. It would be cold and damp, smelling of smoke and fried fish, but he needed to rest, to think. The dark brown walls of the hallway crowded in on him as he mounted the stairs; they seemed to be barring him from climbing. He needed to get into his flat quickly. Fumbling for his key, he heard his neighbour, Mr Foubisher, coming up the stairs.

"Evening Brian," he mumbled, "how are you doing?"

"Not bad, just cold" came the curt reply.

He was glad to be in his flat, away from everyone. It was dark and uninviting, the paint was peeling off in patches and the carpet was threadbare. It was sparsely furnished, the small bedroom had simply a bed and a bedside cabinet and wardrobe. The living/dining room had a small kitchenette, two dark green comfortable chairs by the electric fire with a low coffee table, and a small dining table and chairs. The walls were a coffee colour and the carpet brown. In fact, the overall impression was of a brown room with little natural light. It was more of a burrow than a place to live. Somewhere to hide from the stresses of life. He had never set much store by decorating and furnishing his home, but it was a safe place for him. He didn't have to hear conversations he could never join. He could at least lie down and think. Life seemed to have let him down. He'd tried to overcome his illness but, somehow, it had just taken a hold. He thought back to his childhood, carefree days when life held promise. He could hear his mother calling him in from the yard for supper. Grubby hands and cut knees to attend to. Hot stew and dumplings, comfort food. Steamed pudding and custard. The pleasures of childhood. Then school, where he had struggled, both with his studies and social skills. Friendly yet friendless, cheerful but sad. He'd tried, by God he'd tried.

He put on the electric fire and huddled close, keeping his coat on. He still had a little whisky left he remembered, small comfort for a lonely heart. He lay on his bed and immediately fell into a deep sleep. Dreams tumbled from him so that he woke feeling exhausted. It was 7 a.m. A grey light filtered through the shuttered windows catching the dust. It was time to get ready. He must see her again, if only from a distance.

She woke with a start, it was still dark. She lay motionless waiting for Mat to waken.

"You were late to bed, "Mat said. "How was Liz?"

"Oh, the same as usual, worried about her mother," she lied. When she'd left the house last night, she had told Mat she was popping into a neighbour's house for a drink.

They heard the children stirring and stumbled out of bed. Her suit lay crumpled where she had left it. She would need something smart today, her boss would expect nothing less. An olive-green skirt, white blouse and black jacket, that would do, she thought.

Polly and Ben were already dressed and eating breakfast, excitedly talking about the school concert. She could barely think of what lay ahead, how it would all work out. Mat was stomping about the house grumbling that he always had to get the children ready. He was looking tired these days, she thought. They needed a holiday. He fled out of the house, children in tow. She needed time to collect her thoughts but realised she was late. Running to the station, she felt the panic rising again. Why was she so anxious? Trying to control her breathing, she boarded the train.

Suddenly she gasped. Was that him, the same man who had stared at her yesterday? He was making his way down the aisle. He found a seat diagonally opposite her. She glanced up and he smiled. He looked directly at her with his piercing, weary eyes. His lined, unshaven face wore the pain of his struggles. Averting her gaze, she felt pity for him. What lay behind those troubled features? He could be her uncle Jack, who had suffered so much. But something wasn't right, was he following her? She shifted in her seat, trying to concentrate on the news, feeling the tingling coming back into her arms, the mounting panic. She needed to get off the train, so when the train pulled up at the station before her destination, she pushed her way through the commuters to the door. If he follows me, she thought, I shall call in at the police station and report him, then I can forget him and concentrate on the day. She knew that wouldn't be easy and she was relieved that, when she glanced behind her, he was nowhere to be seen. So, it was all in her imagination. He was a lonely, harmless man, eager to connect with a fellow passenger. Travelling daily to his humdrum job. Maybe he had mental health issues. How could she have been so suspicious?

She shivered in the chilly autumnal wind and pulled her collar up round her neck. A newspaper vendor stamped his feet, his breath visible in the cold air. Kicking the leaves in the park she took another glance behind her. No, there was no one following. Her panic eased, and she began to think about the meeting. An important contract was being negotiated and her boss would be anxious to complete. She had to minute the meeting so she must have her wits about her.

Autumn 2005

He lit a cigarette and warmed some milk for his coffee. It was brightening up outside. Maybe it would be a better day. The atmosphere in his flat was oppressive. He felt trapped like the fly crawling along the window sill and he was glad to step out into the fresh autumnal air. Opposite his flat, the bus stop in front of the boarded up shop already had a queue of people shuffling their feet to keep warm. Clouds blew fast across the sky, the sun peeping through, though giving no warmth. The traffic hummed as he tramped the dirty pavements towards the station. He would have to be quick to catch a train to take him to her stop, to be sure of making the train she caught.

There was no guarantee that he would see her today. That feeling caused him to sweat and tremble. He pushed on. Feeling a gnawing in his stomach, he realised he'd forgotten to eat anything. Jumping onto the train he found a seat and settled in to observe the passengers opposite. An elderly, bespectacled woman with greasy hair and a languid expression, a businessman in a pinstriped suit and an overweight, unkempt youth who was chewing gum. All lives he somehow envied. The resilience of age, the conforming life with regular employment, and the time stretching before the young. Life had passed him by, his dark episodes becoming ever more frequent. He had failed to comply with the doctor's advice, preferring to seek alternative therapy. It gave him a feeling of being more in control. However, maybe things would be better if he resumed his medication. If he'd had family support things might have been easier. He wondered how many other people on this train were struggling quietly behind their calm appearances.

He saw her board and quickly moved to her compartment, managing to get a seat opposite her. Fear of recognition was surpassed by the need to gaze at her constantly. When she looked up, he smiled. An overwhelming warmth suffused him as he noticed her smile. He looked down, almost bashfully. Was it possible that he could get to know her? When he looked again, she was gone. Panicking, he left the train. Throngs of people with a purpose surged forward taking him with them. Emerging into the bright sunlight he walked towards the office building. Like yesterday, he would wait in the doorway and see her leave. He would see her leave and go after her.

The meeting was long and tedious but successful. Calum, her boss, was pleased and announced lunch in the local pub. Helen typed up the minutes quickly. She glanced at her phone. There was no message from Mat, but her father had been trying to reach her. That reminded her, she would have to speak to him about the letter. There again, she thought it might do harm to their relationship, so it was best to leave it for now.

Calum approached her, "Could I have a minute? Could you stay late this afternoon, I have a new client visiting and I want you to minute the meeting."

"Well, it's a little awkward today as there is a school concert I have to get to."

"That's a shame, I had hoped you would be able to stay. If there is any possibility, I would be most grateful." She felt anxiety mounting again." Could you give me a minute to call my husband?" She went into the meeting room and called Mat who was in between lessons.

"Something has cropped up at work and I have to stay late and will miss the concert. Can you make it and apologise to the children?" Feelings of guilt and disappointment welled up.

His curt reply came back, "I guess I'll have to, but things are difficult my end too."

She and Mat were struggling when everything was going well, but since her mother's death things were on a knife edge. It didn't seem possible to make the compromises so essential for a marriage to work. Grief, together with her grandmother's words, came flooding back.

Calum was pacing his office. He was a very impatient, insensitive man who clearly found empathy impossible.

"I will stay late today but it is very inconvenient, and I hope you will give me more notice in future." He nodded apologetically and reminded her of lunch.

"Have you done your sample, Ian?" He was lying on his bed gazing at the ceiling.

"It's there on the cabinet."

The nurse took it, adding as an aside, "Now get off your bed, the doctor will be here any minute." Ian stood up, grunting an unintelligible reply. She marched off perfunctorily.

He began pacing up and down the corridor, silently passing the other bays where patients were rocking, or pacing like him. He was called into the doctor's room. It was spartan, with nothing but three low chairs covered in orange fabric wearing at the corners and a side table. The consultant was dressed in a shabby suit and was reading his large file of notes.

"Well, how are you today, Ian?"

"Much the same."

"Are you getting on well at Occupational Therapy?"

"I find it hard to concentrate."

"That will improve."

They had all said that, but it was taking weeks. This was his sixth month on the ward, and he felt much the same as when he'd been admitted. Further routine questions followed about his sleep, appetite, and bowels. Ian answered, as he always did, saying what he thought they wanted to hear. He was weary of all this. Another day, another basket to make, another portion of mutton stew.

A lifetime of enduring mental illness is a life too long, he thought.

"I think we should be working towards a discharge date in the next couple of weeks. How do you feel about that?"

On the one hand he shuddered at the thought of leaving the safety of the ward, and on the other hand he was longing to be back in his flat, cold and lonely though it was. He would be free to come and go as he pleased.

"I think I'm ready for that, Doctor Prentice, thank you."

"I should like you to attend the Day Hospital for a month or so following your discharge."

"If you think that is necessary."

"You've been here six months now and lots of support is needed when you get home. You live alone, don't you?" These haunting words reverberated in his brain leaving him feeling that sense of emptiness again.

"Yes, I'm afraid I do."

"There is a voluntary service offering a befriender to isolated patients in the community, would you mind if I referred you to it?"

"No, not at all."

"Well, I'll see you again next week."

With that Ian was ushered out of the room into the bleak corridor with peeling green paint.

Visiting time came and went. He never had visitors, apart from the one time his sister had come. She so obviously felt uncomfortable in his presence and didn't want to talk. She had no idea how to deal with mental health problems. He was distraught but over time became reconciled to the situation.

He had tried reading but couldn't concentrate. The TV was always on the wrong channel, and sitting on the plastic-backed chairs next to the other patients with whom he couldn't converse made him feel even more desolate. Escaping to the small outside area to smoke was his one pleasure. The food was unpalatable, but mealtimes were a focus for the day. He swallowed the pills, there was no alternative.

Then one visiting time, he noticed her, an attractive woman accompanied by an older man. They were visiting Jack and he seemed elated to see her. Ian tried not to feel envious, his loneliness made ever more acute. At least envy was better than emptiness. That interminable emptiness. He must make the effort to speak to Jack, he thought, and ask him about his visitors. The opportunity came later that day during supper.

"I see you had a couple of visitors."

"Yes, my brother, George, and my niece Helen, it was lovely to see them."

"Do they live locally?"

"Helen is in South East London and George in Kent. They are very good to me on the whole. I don't see them that often. I'm very close to my niece."

Ian noticed that he looked very downcast as he said this. He had warmed to Jack who had been on the ward longer than him. He found him thoughtful, and friendly yet respectful of his privacy. No one talked much about themselves on the ward. He had found it a difficult, sterile environment in which to climb back up from the pit of his depression.

"I spent a lot of time with my niece when she was growing up. Her mother was very good to me."

"What was your line of work Jack?"

"I worked for BT as an engineer. They were good employers considering how much time I've been off sick."

"Same with the Post Office. We've been lucky that way at least."

"Have you a date for discharge?"

31

"They're talking about a couple more weeks, which is good. It's always hard to get back out there though, isn't it? How about you?"

"I'm going to hear tomorrow, I think it will be quite soon too. I am desperate to get out of here"

"Do you feel better?"

"The trouble is I will never feel well, at least not as well as when I was younger. No one tells you this bugger of an illness gets worse as you get older. There are all the problems of ageing of course to compound things. Living on our own makes it difficult, too. How I'm going to fill my day is a perennial problem."

They went back to their meals continuing in silence. Ian returned to the TV room. A game show was playing – not one he recognised. He sat next to a young woman who was wringing her hands. It was impossible to stay, and he left, returning to his bed to wait for bedtime. He would share the night with his dreams, the escape he craved, only to wake to another day.

Autumn 2005

Lunch was a drawn-out affair. Her boss was convivial and patronising. She overheard him talking about female employees with part-time mentalities. She would begin the search for another job tomorrow, she resolved.

It was hard to keep focussed in the afternoon. There were letters to type, invoices to check, but nothing that would normally tax her. The image of the man on the train kept coming into her mind. His smiling face was eerily familiar. If I see him again, I'll avoid his gaze, she thought. No one acknowledges other passengers even though the same faces crowd the same carriages every day at the same time. Life for many is a mass of same days. Anonymity is what we all crave, that and love and security.

She thought of the loves in her life and sadly reflected that she and Mat had, for some time, exhibited no love for one another. Her mother's death came back with a vengeance, and she realised the huge love she'd lost. She had lost her mother, however, years before her death, due to her cruel illness.

Trying to get back to the task in hand she didn't notice David approaching her from the other end of the office.

"Are you free after work to have a quick drink? I want to discuss some issues regarding Calum."

She was intrigued but had no intention of meeting David outside the office, so was glad she had a good excuse.

"I'm afraid I have to stay late for a meeting."

"Is that in your contract to work out of hours?"

Her eyes gazed upward in lieu of a reply and he sauntered off.

Calum called her into the office just as everyone was leaving. He was looking sheepish, his suit was crumpled. She felt an unexpected pity for him.

"The meeting has been cancelled, so you're off the hook. It seems he has an alternative offer. Anyway, thanks for agreeing to stay on. You have been a loyal employee." She was speechless and left him standing without a backward glance.

Grabbing her coat, she ran from the building, phoning Mat at the same time. She would make the school concert after all. She remembered that she hadn't called her father but that could wait until tomorrow. Tonight she must focus on Mat and the children.

Spring 2000

It was her mother's birthday and her parents were hosting a family lunch in the garden. Helen, Mat and the children were the first to arrive and they found Dorothy making the finishing touches to the table under the apple tree. The sun's rays sparkled on the glassware, the small vase of spring flowers, picked that morning and arranged perfectly, took centre stage. The garden scents were intoxicating. The big rambling house hung back, inviting them to soak up the memories. The stage was set for the players, all tied in blood and love, to perform.

"How lovely to see you all," Dorothy beamed.

"Happy Birthday Granny," the children shouted.

Helen noticed that her mother was having a little difficulty setting the table. She seemed slower than usual. Her hand was a bit shaky, and she looked drawn and preoccupied.

"Can I get drinks for everyone? Dad's in the kitchen."

Helen had made an effort, she wore a new green dress which matched the colour of her eyes. Her hair was tied up and she had remembered to apply eyeliner. Mat, too, was smarter than usual. Over the years he had grown fond of her parents. George's sense of humour was legendary, and Dorothy's good nature and generosity knew no bounds. The children, too, were always welcome here and loved coming to visit. Helen found her father preparing a marinade. He looked rather worn out, Helen thought, but he gave her a welcome hug and fixed their drinks. Coming home was always the same, same pre-lunch drinks, same table décor, same welcome. Sameness was comforting in the context of family. It was an anchor. Yet somehow her parents seemed more vulnerable this time.

"Greg and Julian may be a little late, something to do with Julian's exhibition opening tomorrow. Abigail and James are coming by train. I'm off to pick them up just now. Go back outside and keep your mother company."

"Is she OK Dad?"

"Well, I think she'll talk to you about herself later. She's asked me not to say anything"

He knew she would be worried and put his hand affectionately on her shoulder.

Distracted, she asked, "can I do anything?"

"No, all is under control, as long as I remember to put the lamb in the oven. I can't rely on your mother to prompt me anymore."

He disappeared to get the car, and Helen returned to the garden where Polly and Ben were entertaining their grandmother with all the latest news.

"How's work Helen?" Dorothy asked, as she sat down beside her.

"Oh, much the same. I'm still struggling with my boss, who has absolutely no sympathy with his female employees. If the children are sick there is no way he'd let me go home. It is always Mat who has to leave the school and pick them up."

"You need to look for something else."

"Easier said than done."

"Have you any trips planned, Dorothy?" Mat asked.

"I'm not sure, you'll have to ask George. He organises everything these days."

Helen was surprised, her mother had always loved booking holidays and was very good at it.

Dorothy seemed lost in thought, not really engaging in conversation.

"There's something I've forgotten, and I can't remember what it is."

Mat stifled a chuckle.

"Don't worry, it happens to us all. Why don't you show us your garden?" Dorothy walked with them around the borders while the children played with the dog. The delphiniums were just coming out, a shade of blue echoing the sky. Apple blossom flew through the air landing on them as they walked. They settled into their familiarity, not asking any more questions. The expectant table, the warm sunshine, the view over the hills, it was a perfect setting for a family scene.

Abigail and James had arrived and greeted Dorothy with hugs and birthday wishes. George had disappeared into the house muttering something about a lamb. Dorothy looked so happy.

"How's the practice?" Helen asked Abigail.

"Oh, pretty stressful."

"No new partner then?"

"Not yet, we're having trouble recruiting. No-one wants a partnership these days. They don't want to commit, preferring to do locums, which pay so well."

Helen thought Abigail was looking rather dowdy. She had certainly not taken much care over her outfit, a bright red skirt and orange jumper, and her nails were chipped. She was nervously picking at her fingers. Helen wondered if she suffered from depression like their father. Mat was talking to James about education and the huge disciplinary problems he had to deal with. James was a good listener, and his job as a couple counsellor suited him well. It was a shame they never had children, Helen thought. He and Abigail made a good couple, sharing the same interests in opera and art. It was a pity Abigail was always so stressed about her job as a General Practitioner.

At that moment Greg arrived with a huge bouquet of flowers, Julian following close behind, his usual ebullient self, wearing a loud flowery waistcoat.

"So sorry we're late Mum, Julian had to hang his work for tomorrow, it's a big day for him."

"Where is your exhibition this time, Julian?" Mat asked.

"At a gallery in Hampstead. It's the first time I've exhibited there, and they are especially fussy about the hanging. It's on for two weeks so hopefully I'll get some sales." He looked rather smug, Helen thought. They were an odd couple, Greg and Julian. Greg was so quiet, self-effacing and thoughtful, and gave his voluntary job in the Mental Health Sector every ounce of himself. Julian was a rather self-centred man who loved the limelight. They were devoted to each other, which was all that counted, she reflected.

"Send us the address, we'll try and look in," James said.

"What a glorious day, I'm so happy you could all make it down." George sat back in his chair, a glass of red wine in his hand, his rotund torso bursting through his grubby apron.

Everyone seemed to relax, and Dorothy looked radiant, her silver hair tied back in a bun and her tailored pale blue dress fitting her so well.

Lunch was not quite as delicious as usual, but the wine flowed, and everyone was eager to make it all work out, if only for Dorothy and George. Julian spoke more about his exhibition. "It's important to get a good hanger, that's half the battle. Poorly hung exhibitions are a turn off. You need expansive white walls and loads of light." Helen thought he was stating the obvious. She didn't like Julian's work, it was abstract but very angular and harsh. There was no subtlety in the colour palette. He was successful however and liked everyone to know it. It was difficult to get a word in edgeways, but at last the conversation moved on to George and Dorothys' next trip. George had planned a week in Dorset, an old favourite haunt of theirs. Dorothy became quite animated talking about it, but she seemed to lose the thread of a sentence at one point. She looked anxious. The dishes were cleared for dessert. This was a simple offering of stewed fruit, not the usual impressive concoction.

"No baked Alaska today, I'm afraid," George said.

After dessert Dorothy stood and, clinking her glass, spoke, her voice trembling.

"Thank you all for coming today. It has been a very happy birthday and one which I will remember and treasure. I'm afraid, though, I have some news that might upset you."

Helen looked at Mat with apprehension.

"I've been told by my doctor that I am in the early stages of dementia, Alzheimer's disease. I wanted to tell you today as I need to remember this day as one of happiness, one I must cling on to over the coming months and years. I may not recognise you in the future, so I must remember today and all your faces and smiles. I cannot let go of them."

Her voice faltered. She sat down. No-one spoke. Greg broke the silence.

"My God, Mum, we are all so shocked. We'd never have known. What can we do?"

"Just be," she said, "be here. We need you all."

The blossom fell onto the table blanketing their plates, the sun shone. Lunch had been perfect but was shattered now. Life would change for ever. Helen mopped her eyes. She looked over at her mother and noticed that she, too, was crying. Why did she tell us like this, Helen thought, why spoil her day?

Everyone started talking nervously, trying to blot out the last few minutes and return to the birthday party. Once more the table hummed and George, producing coffee, collapsed in his chair and sighed. They stayed talking until the sun began to dip down and the air chilled a little. Their parents refused to let any of them help clear the table. "We've got all the time in the world," George said, suddenly realising the irony of what he'd said.

As they left, her father whispered to Helen that he'd suspected for a long time that her mother was ill. She had insight and had been very distressed about her memory, but, recently, had come to accept it and was calm.

"It's hard, but we'll be OK."

Helen glanced back at them waving at the gate, it was hard leaving them. How cruel, she thought, but how brave her mother had been.

Dorothy looked at the table and grimaced. "All this work, how will I cope?"

He took her arm and led her to a garden seat at the bottom of the garden.

"We'll cope", he said soothing her. The sun dipped down behind the hills. The air was distinctly chilly now. He put his arm around her, and they wept together.

Summer 2000

It all seemed unreal, the streets, houses, people living their lives outside. The sun was shining on the pedestrians going about their daily chores, all oblivious of each other and especially of those like him who had been incarcerated for so long. He spied a gang of teenagers loafing around a street corner and an elderly woman bent over carrying her shopping basket. Fruit and vegetable stalls splayed out onto the pavement, the colours complementing each other invitingly. There was the library, his favourite haunt. After six months on the ward this was his first time outside the hospital, and he was finding it hard. There seemed a mountain to climb to get back to his old life. The occupational therapist, Kay, was taking him back to his flat for a couple of hours. His social worker had spent some time explaining the benefits he would be entitled to. He couldn't remember the details. He knew he couldn't work. It was possible that he would have to take early retirement. That thought filled him with dread. He would have to attend the day hospital for a few months, until he was well enough to be fully discharged. It was all such an uphill struggle.

"Whereabouts along here do I park?" Kay asked.

"Just here will do," he replied.

They climbed the stairs, his apprehension mounting. There was a pile of junk mail behind the door and a musty smell.

"Shall we open a few windows?" she asked.

She helped him go through the mail. There was a letter about an Insurance Premium Renewal, a bank statement and a couple of bills. He was overwhelmed.

"Do you know your neighbours?" she asked.

"Not really, everyone keeps to themselves round here. I nod to them, that's all."

"How do you plan to spend your day when you get home?"

"On the days I'm not at the day hospital, I'll go along to the public library. You can get coffee there and the staff are very friendly. I'll read a paper or two and take a walk round the block and maybe pop into a café for lunch."

She was clearly concerned about him.

"I know you have no real contact with your sister, but do you think we ought to tell her you are coming home?"

"I don't think there's much point. She's seen me like this on and off for years and is weary of worrying. I don't want to bother her anymore."

Cathy seemed to have cut off all ties with him. They had been close as children, but when their father died she seemed to reject the family. Ian was left soaking up his mother's grief. He didn't know how to cope with her outbursts. Life for him became unbearable. He was behind in his school work and withdrawing into himself. It was soon after his father's death that he had had his first admission.

"There is a be-friending service that operates in the borough. I'll give them a call and see if they can send someone along. They would take you out for coffee or even the cinema if you'd like"

He felt anxious. "Dr Prentice mentioned that, I think he was going to refer me."

They drank black tea and checked the flat. His bed was crumpled as he had left it, his pyjamas on the floor.

There was dirty crockery in the sink. Kay set to and changed the bed while he washed up and tidied the kitchen.

"We'd best be getting back," she said. The traffic was building up outside. Curiously, he wanted to stay, even in this cold, unwelcoming place. He wanted to start to build a sense of himself again. To wake up and do what he wanted to do. It was a glimmer of hope. One that he would cling on to. He closed the door of the flat behind him. He had just two more nights on the ward and then he was on his own. It was a bleak prospect, but he would improve. He had to.

Tears were rolling down their faces, they hadn't laughed so much in ages. The release of their tension was deep and satisfying. Primary one to three had been singing so lustily and there were such characters amongst them. She had managed to get a seat beside Mat, and he was clearly so pleased to see her. It was a great show, all the children enjoying every minute.

"What happened at work then?" he asked while they were waiting for the children outside. She explained about the cancelled meeting and how unreasonable her boss had been earlier. "I've just about had enough, I must look for something else."

"Why don't you just have a break for a while. I'm sure we can manage for a few months, and you've had such a bad time of it recently."

The idea of being at home when the children came home from school gave her great comfort. She sighed.

"We'll talk about it in the morning."

The children were very talkative all the way home and reluctant to go to bed. She and Mat were desperate for time alone together and Mat was getting irritable. At last, all was quiet, and they opened a bottle of wine. They sat side by side on the sofa, her head nestled on his shoulder. She felt the warmth of his love revive her.

"Tomorrow we must ask Ann to come over and we'll go out for dinner," he suggested.

"That would be lovely." How she had missed him. Yes, she would hand in her notice, she thought, tomorrow. She thought of not commuting every day, not having to see the same faces. The lonely man's face came into her mind, she wondered what he did all day. He looked too old to be working. She realised she may never see him again. Strangely, she felt disappointed. It was as if she needed to reach out to him to find out more about him, to help. The embers of the fire were dying as they drained the last of the wine. She felt a lightness, a release of anxiety, as if she were floating above her life, like a leaf on a breeze.

Lying in bed she thought back to the times she had spent with her family during her mother's illness. A huge bond had been formed which sustained them all. A warm glow spread through her as she drifted into a deep sleep.

He walked around the square a few times during the course of the morning, as it was bitterly cold standing in the doorway. At noon he saw her leave in a group of people heading towards the same pub as yesterday. He decided not to go in but to wait in the café opposite. It was warm and steamy inside, and the bowl of hot vegetable soup was comforting. He kept a constant watch for her leaving the pub. He had decided that he would follow her home this one more time, and try and pluck up the courage to speak to her. He could ask her directions or the time, he just wanted to hear her voice. But then he thought again, carrying on like this was futile. He needed to stop and resume his usual routine.

The woman on the table next to him dropped her purse and he bent down to pick it up. She thanked him and went to pay. He couldn't leave the window for fear of missing her. When at last the group appeared, he quickly paid and went out into the square to get one more glimpse of her. She didn't see him standing in the shadow of the doorway, but he could see her face clearly. She looked sad and pensive, he thought, obviously preoccupied about something. Then she was gone. There was just the journey home to see her.

He went for a long walk and found a bookshop where he browsed for a while thumbing through photography books and travel journals. Maybe he could plan a trip. Money was tight but he could manage something, and it would surely be good for him to get away. He bought a small travel guide on Spain and settled back in the café to read. At five he was again standing waiting for her in the doorway. Commuters, their gazes down, were walking briskly across the square. Spotting her, he set off at a distance as she headed for the station. She was quite far ahead and buried in a sea of bodies. He lost sight of her as he left the square. He felt a panic setting in, his breathing quickened. He began to run, weaving in and out of the hunched figures deep in thought. But there was still no sight of her as he reached the top of the escalator.

He must have missed her getting on the train. The platform had been more crowded than yesterday, and she was nowhere to be seen. Crest-fallen he boarded the train. He had to stand all the way to his stop, right next to the businessman in the suit he had seen that morning. So, his hopes of speaking to her were dashed. He would try once more tomorrow and then stop. It was a compulsion and he had to fight it. The image of her kept coming back. Everywhere he looked there were smart city people. His shabby coat made a sharp contrast to their polished attire. He felt hemmed in, an imposter, riding the sea in a life he could never be at home in. He had to keep these dark thoughts at bay, they would attack him when he least expected them.

He picked up a microwave meal from the supermarket at the end of his road and made his way to the flat. Tomorrow, after going into the city first thing, he would return and go to the library to access the computer to plan his trip. He felt suddenly as if the burden could lift. He would find it easier to talk to people when he was out of London. There was something so impersonal about the scale of the capital that made it impossible to reach out and connect with anyone. His community nurse who had been a lifeline, and the young man who had befriended him had both withdrawn their support. He was as well as he was ever going to be. The thought frightened him. He ate his curry and after watching the news stumbled into bed. He would get up early in the morning. He tried to feel positive, tomorrow might be a better day.

Autumn 2005

In the morning Mat phoned Ann and arranged for her to come at seven to babysit. He rushed out of the house with the children, leaving Helen to gather her thoughts. She must see her father this weekend, she thought, as she dialled his number. She had a headache, was it the wine? She acknowledged her anxiety about writing her letter of resignation, could she face it today? Always indecisive, she helped herself to another cup of coffee.

"Hello, Helen," his voice sounded gruff.

"Hi, Dad, I was wondering if I could come over on Sunday and we could go out for lunch."

"That would be wonderful, what time shall I expect you?"

"I'll get to you about twelve thirty, maybe we could try that new pub in the village."

"Great, I'll see you then."

He had no idea about her grandmother's letter. He didn't need to know. He had been a truly wonderful father to her. Let's leave it there, she thought. But at the back of her mind, she couldn't help wondering if he knew. Grabbing her briefcase, she ran out of the house and up the hill to the station. Out of the corner of her eye she thought the figure of a man in a long raincoat looked familiar. He was approaching her on the platform. It was him, the man who had smiled at her yesterday. He came right up to her.

"Excuse me, do you know if the next train goes through to Bank?"

"It says so up there on the screen."

"Oh, sorry I should have looked. Apologies."

He walked away, shoulders hunched. For some reason she felt immense pity for him but turned and walked to the opposite end of the platform. So, he got on at her station. She felt a cold shiver pass down her spine. Why was he always there? What did he want? She decided she would tell Mat about him and ask his advice. Maybe she should take the bus for a week. She needed to think about her letter of resignation. She would hand it in today, then in a month she needn't worry about anyone following or watching her.

The train pulled in, she boarded and was relieved to see that he wasn't in her compartment. She would get off a stop early like yesterday. She drafted her letter and sat back gazing out of the window. She could see the other passengers' reflections. Almost all of them on their mobile phones.

"Excuse me," someone needed to get past her.

She got off the train one stop before Bank and walked briskly along the platform. She felt distinctly uncomfortable, as if someone was behind her. She looked over her shoulder. No, he wasn't there. Up the escalator and along the corridor, up the next escalator, she felt her pace quicken, she couldn't wait to get out into the fresh air. Her pulse was rapid, her breathing shallow, she felt light-headed as if she was going to faint. Then everything went black.

"Are you OK?" He was leaning over her. She could smell his breath. A faint smell of cigarette smoke mixed with coffee. She felt a wave of nausea.

"You collapsed at the top of the escalator. Someone has called the paramedics, but I think you've just fainted."

He needed a shave, and his teeth were yellowing. "I think I'm fine, please leave me, I must get to work."

"I insist on accompanying you once the paramedics have checked you over."

His face looked kind, concerned, his eyes no longer piercing.

She could hear the siren of the ambulance. Two bustling paramedics pushed their way through the gathering crowd and proceeded to take a history and examine her.

"Did you have breakfast this morning? Your blood glucose is very low." One of them remarked.

She realised that in the rush of phoning her dad she had forgotten to eat anything.

They gave her a glucose tablet and said she could make her way to the office, provided someone accompanied her.

"This kind gentleman has offered to do just that," she said.

The paramedics left and she gingerly got to her feet. The crowd of onlookers dispersed as she dusted herself down.

"I'm sure I'm alright to walk on my own," she told him.

"I've been instructed to, so I will accompany you," he replied. They walked out into the open air. She was feeling better now, thank goodness.

"Where do you work and what do you do?" he asked

He was leaning towards her, maybe because he had difficulty hearing her above the traffic.

"I work as a secretary in a law firm, but I'm going to hand in my notice today."

It all felt quite threatening, him asking her these questions, invading her space. Her pace quickened.

"So, you won't be travelling to the city anymore?"

"No, I'm going to take a few months off to decide what I want to do."

"I've noticed you on the train a few times. I've thought you looked very tired and preoccupied."

Without thinking, she said "Well I've just lost my mother, and what with problems at work I haven't been sleeping."

She really wasn't sure why she was telling him all this.

"What about your job? What do you do?"

He went quiet. "I haven't worked for five years. I had to retire on health grounds."

She didn't want to pry any further."Well, here we are," she said, "I must thank you for your kind attention. What did you say your name was?"

"Ian", he replied, "Ian Soames."

Well, goodbye Mr Soames, it was nice talking to you."

She left him standing at the entrance to the building and walked towards the lift. As she entered, she glanced behind her. He was already walking away.

Autumn 2005

On wakening he felt a surge of optimism that was quickly followed by the usual fog. His thoughts were jumbled. He had connected with her. Their lives had crossed. That was enough. He knew he wouldn't see her again. But he had spoken to her and had helped her. That gave him such a good feeling about himself. He jumped out of bed and got dressed immediately. He wanted to get out of the flat as soon as he could. It was a bright sunny day outside, the sort of day when the crisp orange leaves crunch under your feet reminding you of childhood. The smell of autumn was as far from decay as it could be and yet everything was dying back. He loved this time of year. He caught himself smiling in the reflection of the train window. He would stop off early and get a breakfast before heading to the library. He reached for the travel guide in his pocket. The pages seemed to swim in front of his eyes. He couldn't make any sense of the text. Maybe it would be easier after breakfast, he thought. I think I'll make an appointment to see Dr Grove and discuss medication again. I think I should take something if I'm going to travel. He had been told to keep on his medication particularly at times of stress and life change. The first sign of him not being so well was usually difficulty reading something simple. He hoped it wasn't happening to him again.

The first episode, when he was a teenager after his father died, came flooding back to him. He had no idea what was happening to him. His mind was a fog, he felt ugly, dirty, and worthless. No one spoke to him at school. Things got really bad after a school trip when some boys bullied him for not joining in with their antics. One night he tried to harm himself with a kitchen knife. His mother found him and called the GP. Initially, he refused to go to hospital but then he relented and went voluntarily. He was on the ward for six months. Life was never the same after that.

"Are you planning a trip to Spain?" the elderly lady opposite asked him. She had a kind, wrinkly face with a very warm smile. Taken aback, he said that he was thinking of it but couldn't speak the language.

"I don't think you'll have any problem in the main tourist centres. When I went several times with my late husband everyone spoke English. They are lovely, friendly people, the Spaniards," she added. Thanking her, he got up to leave.

His usual café was busy, but he managed to get a table by a radiator and warmed his hands. He watched the other customers intently as he couldn't concentrate on his guide. There was a young mother with a toddler who was throwing every bit of food she was offered to the floor, much to her mother's irritation; a balding man in a great big overcoat reading a copy of the financial times, and a couple of middle-aged ladies deep in conversation over their scones and coffee. His plate of piping hot bacon and eggs arrived, and he tucked in, the yolk dribbling down his chin. Hoping no one had noticed he mopped it away with his napkin. He knew the waitress by name, Sheila, who was very kind and always offered him a free top-up of tea, which he gratefully received. He felt better. He had two jobs to do today. Book a flight to Spain and make an appointment to see Dr Grove. He hated the doctor's waiting room, he always felt the panic mounting before he was called in. Best to get this done as quickly as possible. He reached for his mobile phone. No, he should do this outside. He quickly paid, smiling at the toddler in her highchair as he brushed past her, and left the café. He managed to get a cancellation with Dr Grove for the following morning which was very unusual. He couldn't remember if he had any old pills in his flat. He should look and take them along with him.

He pushed open the heavy doors of the library. He just loved this space. The squeaky wooden floor, the shelves upon shelves of knowledge waiting for him. The smell. Handling the books, filing them away. The only trouble was that for so much of his life he had been unable to read. Concentration had eluded him and all he could manage were short, simple articles in magazines. He hoped he wasn't going to find that now as he decided to search for a crime thriller. Something that would capture his imagination and keep him with it. He flicked through a few thrillers and sure enough the paragraphs just didn't seem to click. He felt tears welling up. He would try the computer and newspaper room.

He settled into a comfortable seat with a copy of the local paper and scanned the headlines. The room was full of retired men and women, all in their old worlds, killing time until lunchtime.

At a computer he managed to look at a few sites for cheap flights to Spain but couldn't decide where and when he wanted to go, so abandoned the search and instead looked at a tourist information site for Spain detailing the different regions. Somewhere near the beach but not too busy, he finally decided. Maybe he could ask someone. He would try a travel agent, there was one in the High Street. Resolved, he went back to the thriller section, grabbing the first book that came to hand and went to the counter.

"Good morning Mr Soames," the friendly mousey librarian said, stamping the book, "How are you today?"

"Very well," he said, wishing he believed it.

"I hope you enjoy the book, it's gripping, one of the best of its kind."

"Thank you, I'm sure I will."

He grabbed his coat and made his way to the door when he heard a voice calling, "Ian?" Turning, he saw Greg, the young befriender who had helped him so much after his last admission. He was wearing a bomber jacket and jeans and carried a canvas shoulder bag. Ian noticed that his hair was receding.

"Do you fancy a coffee?"

"Sure, that would be great."

What luck, he could tell him all about his plans and pick his brains. He could tell him he was going to see the doctor and about how he felt. Maybe he could nip this one in the bud.

"How have you been?" They had last met at least eighteen months ago.

"Oh, not so bad. I go up to the city a few times a week. I like walking around watching the people. I come here the other days and help out in the coffee shop when they're short. The girls are very friendly."

"Have you kept on with the lunch club."

"No, I found it all rather depressing. A bit like an extension of the ward really. The trouble is I don't have any friends. I don't have much conversation, so it's all a vicious circle."

"Some colleagues and I are starting up a club for our clients, playing cards and chess. Nothing too pressured, not bridge, just whist and the like. That might really suit you."

He looked down at his feet.

"The trouble is I don't feel so well at the moment, that's why I'm going to see Dr Grove tomorrow. Otherwise, I would come along."

He drained the last of his coffee.

"Thank you for the coffee, it was so kind of you to take an interest. I was thinking a holiday might help and wondered if you could recommend anywhere in Spain."

"It depends what you want."

"Somewhere relaxing near the beach, not too busy. Maybe an old town."

"We went to Nerja a few years back, that would fit your description. Do you want me to help you book something?"

"That would be wonderful."

"Let's meet up again on Friday in the Library, say ten thirty."

"Perfect, thank you so much Greg."

Greg got up to leave, smiling warmly.

He looked up Nerja in the travel guide. It looked very attractive with sandy beaches and hills in the background and not too big.

Things were looking up for him he felt. Though what he would do in Spain, he had no idea. Pulling his coat up around him he went out into the cold. It was busy along the High Street. People were hurrying with purpose like ants on a branch. He was relieved when he got in to his flat. It had been very good to see Greg.

"It's Mum and Dad.' It was Greg on the end of the phone.

"I've called in this evening, and they were having a terrible argument. Mum even hurled a mug of tea. She is very distressed, I almost called the GP. I managed to calm her down, but she just kept going on about a letter, rambling for ages. Dad didn't know what to do with her." Greg's usual calm manner was stretched, she could tell. He had the patience of a saint and was incredibly fond of his mother. To watch her deteriorate had been heart-breaking for him.

"I'll come down," Helen said, "Maybe I should stay over, it would give me a chance to see how they're coping."

"Ok, I'll wait 'til you arrive."

"I've got to fly down to Mum and Dad's, there's some row going on and Mum is very agitated," she told Mat. "I may stay over."

"Good job it's the weekend. Take care, let me know how they are."

She was relieved that the drive through London and the Sussex countryside was easy and quiet. She felt increasingly apprehensive as she neared the village. Greg came out into the drive to greet her.

"Mum's gone off to bed, she's exhausted. Dad's at his wits end, apparently she's been lashing out at him a lot over the past week."

They found George slumped on the sofa, an empty whisky tumbler in his hand.

"Oh Helen, you needn't have driven down tonight."

"No worries Dad, I'm going to stay over and see how Mum is in the morning. How about a cup of tea?"

He was clearly comforted, his anxious face relaxed.

"I don't know how to manage her, I really don't. Sometimes I think she doesn't know where she is or who I am. She goes on and on about her mother as if she's here in the house. It's been quite an acute change. We were going out to lunch last week and she seemed fine. I'll have to get in touch with the community psychiatric nurse again, I hate bothering her."

They talked for another hour. Her father seemed reluctant to go to bed. Suddenly they heard a crash upstairs. Helen rushed up and found her mother on the floor. She was clearly in agony.

"What happened, Mum?"

"I needed the bathroom and fell down."

She was lying with one leg at an angle. Helen feared that she had fractured her hip. She couldn't move.

"Greg, I think we need an ambulance," she shouted.

Greg and her father appeared at the door.

"Oh Dorothy, what have you done, you poor thing." George knelt down beside her, tears in his eyes.

Greg rushed off to make the call while Helen placed a pillow under Dorothy's head. "Don't move her, Dad."

"I was just trying to make her more comfortable, I think she may have broken her leg. Oh my God, what next?"

Dorothy was wincing with the pain. She asked for a drink, but Helen pointed out that if she needed surgery she had to fast, and that included water.

A storm was brewing outside. The trees swirled in the wind, and rain lashed against the windows. Helen thought how dependent her parents were now on their children and how quickly the tables had turned. She put her arm round George and held her mother's hand. It was a waiting game now. There was not much to look forward to. When this is all over, she thought, I'll try and take them away somewhere for a weekend. I should manage if I plan it well. The thought sustained her whilst they waited. It seemed a long time before they heard the sirens of the ambulance. The paramedics quickly assessed her as a probable fractured femur and soft tissue injury to her shoulder and stretchered her out to the ambulance. Helen followed in her car with her father. Greg said he would visit tomorrow and left.

At the A and E department the X-ray confirmed the diagnosis and Dorothy was admitted to the orthopaedic ward. By this time, she was acutely confused and trying to climb out of her bed. George was distraught. The ward sister took him into the interview room to get the background history while Helen stood next to the bed trying to calm her mother. It was 1.30 in the morning and most of the other patients were asleep.

"Does your mother take any night sedation?" A nurse asked.

"No, I don't think so."

"She may need something tonight at this rate. She'll be going to theatre in the morning."

Howling inside, Helen bent over her mother who was momentarily calmer.

"Mum, I'm going to go now. You will need an operation tomorrow to pin your leg, you have broken your hip. Once you're walking we can get you home and I can come and stay for a while. Don't worry, everything will be OK."

"But what about Granny and the letter?" she whispered.

"What letter?"

"Granny wrote a letter to you, I don't know where it is."

"Don't worry about that tonight, we'll find it. Try and get some sleep."

Just then an exhausted looking junior doctor appeared and proceeded to ask a whole lot of questions, most of which Dorothy couldn't answer and seemed irrelevant to Helen. After examining her, he explained that he had written her up for something to help her sleep.

"I'm off now, but I'll see you tomorrow", Helen kissed her damp forehead and went to find George.

He looked shattered and was ready to leave after saying good-bye.

The clinical smell of the ward was causing waves of nausea as Helen realised she needed to sit down.

"You're as white as a sheet. You must lie down for a bit before you leave." The ward sister brought tea for them both. She had a kindly, unflappable manner.

"Your father has been having a tough time of it lately. I think your mother should have a spell of convalescence somewhere post-op to give him a rest."

Her relief was tangible. She realised she hadn't phoned Mat and it was far too late. Feeling better they thanked the staff and left, Helen supporting her father who seemed all of a sudden to be very shaky on his legs.

Back home George asked if she wanted a whisky.

"No, Dad, and I think you'd better not have another. Sleep is what we both need now.

But sleep didn't come easily to either of them. Helen heard her father up in the bathroom several times. At dawn she dropped into a light sleep waking with a start to the telephone's ring. It was Abigail.

"I've just spoken to Greg. Why didn't you phone me last night? I could have met you at the hospital and given Mum's history." She was clearly very angry. Helen didn't have time for this and told her in no uncertain terms that they had been perfectly capable of managing the situation. If she felt she wanted to give more information she was sure the ward would be grateful. This was typical of her sister. Ever ready to muscle in when there was a crisis but always backing off when things settled down. It was hard not to feel resentful. Helen checked herself, this was no time for a family rift.

"I was going to phone you this morning after phoning the ward."

Abigail rang off amidst the emotional rollercoaster of concern and guilt.

She had to call Greg and Mat, but first the ward.

Dorothy had had a bad night. She'd needed two doses of night sedation and was still ranting.

"Has she been confused at home?" the junior nurse asked.

Don't they read the notes?, Helen thought.

"My mother has Alzheimer's disease and it's getting worse."

"Oh, I'm sorry. I'll let the staff know."

"They already know..." The nurse hung up.

Why do we have to go through all this indignity at the end of life, she asked herself. Nothing in life prepares you for this. How would I cope, she wondered. Fear spread through her veins, she felt her breath trapped in her chest. Pulling herself together she went downstairs. Her father needed her support just now.

George was morose when she found him drinking coffee downstairs. She told him Dorothy had had a good night but that she was still a bit confused.

"I'm not sure I can cope with this anymore."

"Don't worry Dad, you won't have to. We'll get her assessed for a residential home."

"Oh no, I can't let her go. Maybe I can have a nurse here with me."

"We'll see Dad. All this costs a lot so we have some hard thinking to do."

The phone rang, it was Mat.

"You poor things, shall we all come down, it might take George's mind off things a bit."

"I'm not sure that's a good idea, Dad is shattered and having difficulty processing all this. Give me a couple of hours and I'll call back. I'm going to ask for a few days compassionate leave so I can stay on here. Maybe Abigail will take over, although she hung up on me earlier."

Her coffee was cold. There was no bread. The milk was sour. She asked Greg to pick up some groceries, then took a shower and lay on her bed. George was pacing downstairs. He knew she was having surgery and couldn't sit.

The cushioning of the bed was comforting. She was in her old bedroom with the familiar coverlet, wallpaper and furnishings. She felt a little girl again, vulnerable, and scared, hearing her parents raised voices downstairs in one of their interminable arguments. Then there were the times when her father just wouldn't speak. A darkness descended on him, and he'd sit, head in hands at the kitchen table. The doctor visited and sometimes he would go off in an ambulance. It all came flooding back. Then there was Uncle Jack. He too suffered deep depressions. She remembered visiting him a few times with her father on the ward. What a cruel illness. It saps everything, energy, personality, confidence, enjoyment. Then there were the manic episodes, when her father had boundless energy and would set to decorating the house or redesigning the garden. Helen liked these phases. The house would resound with his laughter. Her mother looked drawn though, as if the real George was never quite there.

She went downstairs. Greg had arrived and they made toast and coffee. George was still in his dressing gown, unshaven, his hair greasy and straggled. His gait was heavy and hesitant. His spirit was broken, his usual optimism shattered. With encouragement he went upstairs to shower and dress.

"Things are reaching breaking point here," Helen started to cry.

"I thought so. We need to meet up, all of us, and decide the way forward." Greg, the ever-practical member of the family, tended to see things in black and white.

"It's not a business meeting we need, it's a decision to take one of two options: nursing home or nurse at home. It's as simple as that."

"Let's look at the costs." Greg was looking strained.

"Yes, but we must get over this hurdle first, and as I told you, the sister on the ward was very sympathetic and will arrange convalescence in a nursing home if she can."

"If she can, it may not be possible."

Helen cleared the table then phoned Mat. "Yes, come on down, we need all the help we can get. It's going to be a long day."

She wrote the letter in her lunch break and left it on his desk. She knew she would have to work a month's notice, which would be difficult. She was apprehensive about Calum's reaction. He was a man whose punctiliousness and abrupt manner overshadowed a deep insecurity. He tolerated fools badly. He favoured some members of staff over others who were at the mercy of his bullying. He called her into his office. He was seated at his desk, dressed in a dark navy tailored suit with one of his flashy ties. He looked up from her letter meeting her gaze with a withering look.

"I must say this has come as a complete surprise. Have you not been happy in your position?"

"It's not really about the job, although I feel I need a complete change."

"It is a very inconvenient time for you to leave. Can I ask you to reconsider? I may be able to negotiate a salary increase if you did."

There was nothing that would make her stay a moment longer than she had to.

"I'm afraid I need to spend time with my family. Things have been tough for a while, and I'm not prepared to reconsider. I'm sorry if this has left you with a problem. It's not been an easy decision"

She felt tears welling up and needed to leave.

"Well, I guess that's it then. You will have to work a month's notice."

He showed her to the door. His disdainful look only made her more convinced of her decision.

A huge weight lifted from her shoulders. She could visit her father whenever she wanted, have all the school holidays to do things with the kids. They would be poorer but richer in so many ways. Maybe they should downsize or move to a cheaper area of London. There were so many possibilities. Giddy with all her plans she sailed through the rest of the day. She couldn't wait until the evening with Mat. They would have something to celebrate.

The commute home was slow due to work on the track. She wondered if she would see Ian, but she recognised no-one and was grateful for that. She picked up a bottle of wine from the corner shop and popped it in the fridge. The phone rang.

"Helen, it's me. I'm not sure what's happening to me, but I've had to come off work as I broke down in front of a patient.

Abigail's voice was faltering on the line. It was going to be a long conversation.

"What's been happening?"

"Well, a lot of stuff. I've had a formal complaint sent to NHS England about me. I've done nothing wrong, but the patient thinks they were inappropriately investigated. In the end there was nothing seriously wrong, but they had a lot of unnecessary, at least they thought they were unnecessary, invasive tests and anxiety. It's not really about the case; having a complaint made against you, whatever the circumstances, knocks your confidence for six"

Abigail had perfectionist tendencies and was always so self-deprecating. She'd been like it all her life.

"Then there are the partnership problems. We desperately need a new partner. Oh, and James and I haven't been getting on recently. All on account of how I'm feeling I guess."

"Why don't you pop over on Sunday morning, and we can drive down to Dad's together and see how he is". She was pleased she had thought of this plan. Abigail was the most vulnerable of the three of them. She had been highly strung as a child and nearly had a breakdown during her A-levels. She was clearly nearing burn-out and needed a break from work.

"OK then, I'll be over at nine."

She opened the wine. The kids were on their devices, she would have to get them off.

"Just another twenty minutes, you two," she shouted.

Mat appeared and gave her a kiss.

"Well, my notice is in. It's just a teacher's salary now."

"No worries, we can always move."

"I was thinking that, but what about the children's schools."

"Yes, I know, it's not that simple. Let's see how it goes, you may want to get back to work sooner than you think!"

Ben appeared. "Can Rowan come over this evening to play on the PS4?"

"I guess so. We're out and Ann is coming over. He can stay 'til nine but no sleepover." Grunting, Ben left the kitchen.

Polly appeared next asking what was for supper. "Pizza, OK?"

Mat phoned the restaurant while she got the children's meal ready. She would make an effort this evening and wear a dress. This was their evening. A rare event these days. She decided she wouldn't tell Mat about Abigail and their plans. He thought she did too much for her family as it was, and she wanted this evening to be all about them. He deserved more of her attention. Giving up work, she would be able to give that. She had been spread too thin. There was nothing left for herself. Soaking in the bath she wondered how her father was coping in the big house on his own. He had flatly refused to move when her mother had died.

"I can't leave these memories behind," he'd said.

Her skin was crinkly, she needed to get out. She squeezed herself into an old black dress and put on her grandmother's pearls. She tied her blond hair up and applied makeup and stood in front of the full-length mirror. Perfect, she thought.

"Wow, this is going to be a great evening," Mat said as she came down the stairs. They poured themselves another glass of wine and sat down in the conservatory. Rowan had arrived and the kids were all eating pizza.

"I didn't tell you about the man on the train," she said suddenly.

"What man?"

"I thought he was following me. I saw him two or three times and then he asked me something about the Bank train. He seemed to know where I got off, it was a bit creepy. But then, when I fainted yesterday, it was him who came to help me and walk me to the office."

"Why didn't you mention this before?"

"I didn't think to, I've had so much on my mind lately."

"Well, I think if you thought he was following you, you should report him to the police. Could he have followed you home?"

"No, I'm sure not, don't worry, he's just a lonely old man who was so kind to me yesterday. I shouldn't have mentioned it."

"On the contrary, you should have. Now if you see him again, be sure to let me know."

She promised that she would, and they let the matter drop there. Just then the doorbell rang. Polly let Ann in and went back to the TV.

"Hi there, how are things?". Her bright voice was as loud as her makeup.

"Just fine. Rowan's here 'til nine and they must be in bed by 10. We'll be back around then anyway. Help yourself to pizza, coffee and biscuits, anything you want."

"Thanks Helen. My, you look gorgeous tonight, where's he taking you?"

"Cardinals," she replied.

"Golly, I'd better change," he said as he bounded up the stairs.

The restaurant was busy, but they managed to get a quiet table in an alcove. It was up-market bistro food, pretty reliable, and the wine was good. Mat talked about his colleagues and Helen listened attentively. After they had finished a bottle of wine, Mat suggested they order another.

"No, one is quite enough, I'm tired tonight and we should get back. I wasn't going to tell you, but I've arranged to drive Abigail down to see Dad on Sunday. It's three weeks since I was there and Abigail is off work just now, some sort of breakdown."

"I thought there was something up with her last time we saw her," he retorted.

The evening's atmosphere had changed. She regretted telling him already.

"Well, we'd better pay then," he said with a hint of irritation in his voice.

Walking home they hardly spoke. Neither had the energy to try again. It all seemed futile. They were lost in their own worlds, with their own problems. Joined in matrimony for the children alone. She felt devastated. The whole week's events just crowded in on her and she couldn't breathe. At the end of her road, she cracked.

"I've something else to tell you."

He looked at her with anger in his eyes. His patience wearing as thin as his love for her.

"My grandmother wrote me a letter to be read after Mum's death. The solicitor posted it to me the other day."

She couldn't go any further than that, she knew she would break down. Could he ever understand? Would she want him to?

"Let's talk about this when the children are in bed." He put his arm around her as they walked the last few yards to their home. She was grateful for that gesture, she knew they would survive this.

He spent the rest of the day in his flat. He tried to read the travel guide but again he couldn't make much sense of it. He looked up Nerja again and liked what he saw. There were a few photos, and he gleaned a few facts about the town. There was a section on accommodation. He would like a small two- or three-star hotel, one where he wouldn't feel out of place. He looked in the bottom of his wardrobe. Yes, he still had the small suitcase, unused for years. The buckles had some mildew on them, but a damp cloth would sort that. He felt a wave of fatigue coming over him and lay down on his bed. He tried to sleep but thoughts kept coming into his head. He thought about the woman he'd followed and helped. He could go to her house later and wait outside for her to come home. But then he thought better of it and decided he must stop this obsession. He'd followed other women, sometimes for weeks. It only made his loneliness more acute. He would take up Greg's invitation to the whist sessions. He must try and meet people in a more normal environment.

He looked around the room. The sofa, of muddy brown fabric, had seen better days, there were piles of books on the table, together with plates with remnants of meals. The kitchenette was piled high with pots and pans and dirty mugs. There was no space anywhere. The walls seemed to close in on him. He knew he was sinking. It was so hard to pull himself up when he reached this stage.

He realised he hadn't showered for a while, his clothes were smelling, he was letting himself go. A list, that was what was needed. It all seemed an enormous effort but an hour later he was washed, shaved, and dressed. He decided to take a walk to the local pub for a beer. He might meet someone there. There was a dense fog falling all around him as he made his way to the pub. It rolled along the pavement and up around the hunched figures coming towards him. It gave the High Street an other-worldly appearance so that he was glad when he reached the warm interior of the pub. It was quiet inside with only one small group of young people in the corner. He propped himself up at the bar and asked the barman for a half of pale ale.

"Nasty foggy night out there," he remarked.

"Yes, better off in 'ere," came the curt reply.

He bought some peanuts and another half and took a seat near the door. He could watch everyone coming in from here. A couple of be-suited workers came in on their way back from work. He could just about make out what they were saying. They were in the legal profession he gleaned. Then a group of women crowded up to the bar, giggling and laughing. There were five of them and the only table free was next to his. He felt uncomfortable being so close to them so moved back to the bar to finish his drink.

"I'll be off now," he said to the barman.

"See you later," came the reply.

Leaving the pub, the fog gripped his throat as if trying to throttle him. The penetrating headlights seemed to shine directly at him, in a threatening manner. He needed comfort. Food, that would help.

He bought fish and chips and ate them in the newspaper in his flat, downing another glass of beer. He remembered his GP appointment tomorrow. What was he going to say? He'd try and work that out in the morning. His phone rang, he jumped as it rang so rarely.

"Ian?" A woman's voice, "it's Cathy. How are you? Can we meet up sometime for lunch? I could come and pick you up." He was speechless but managed to say an almost inaudible "Thank you, it will be good to catch up."

"How about next Monday one o'clock?"

"Great, I'll be waiting in the flat, you know the address?"

"Same flat you were in the last time we met up I assume?" He couldn't remember how long ago that was.

"Yes."

"Right, see you Monday." She rang off. He got a piece of paper and wrote:

Wednesday a.m. - GP

Wednesday p.m. – walk

Thursday - walk

Friday am Library - Greg

Friday p.m. - walk

Week-end - walk

Monday - lunch with Cathy.

He would fight this descending gloom. He would master it this time.

All was quiet upstairs. Mat poured them a whisky. "Tell me about this letter then," he said.

"I have destroyed it, but I can remember it word for word."

She spoke the words of her grandmother as if she were reading them. Mat looked shocked.

"Are you going to tell your dad?"

"No, I can't see what good would come out of it. He's grieving and has had such a difficult time over the past few years." An image of her mother during the last weeks of her life came flooding back.

"How are you feeling about it?"

"Numb, I guess. It hasn't really sunk in yet." Somehow speaking the words again had made it feel even more unreal. She would do her best to forget it and carry on with her life. Looking back wouldn't help her now. The momentous nature of the revelation weighed on her like lead. She felt as if she was sinking.

"Maybe all this explains why Mum was so distraught when Uncle Jack died. Mum and Dad seemed to go through a very low period after that, do you remember?"

"Yes."

She felt overwhelmed by sadness and the tears streamed down her cheeks. Her hands were cold and clammy. She clung onto Mat, her arms tight around his neck.

"Let's go up to bed, it's been a long day." Nestling in the warmth of him she tried hard to remember her mother as she had been in her prime, when she was juggling her job as a nurse, their home and the family. Dorothy, forever selfless, had always had time for them and all their worries, big or small.

She fell asleep with the smell of her mother's perfume as she bent over to kiss her goodnight.

Abigail arrived just before nine on Sunday and helped herself to coffee. She had dark rings beneath her eyes and her body drooped. Helen listened whilst she spoke at length about the problems in the practice. The complaint had clearly been the final straw.

"The trouble is, a complaint just wrecks your confidence," she said again, "and you need to be so confident in my job."

In most jobs, Helen thought.

"Are you sleeping?"

"Very badly, James has moved to the spare room. I can't read, so it's a long night. I dread the morning when it all starts again."

Helen busied herself in the kitchen. Mat appeared and gave Abigail a kiss.

"Good to see you, Abigail. I'm so sorry to hear you're off work. Let's hope it won't be for long."

"We'll see. I need to see my GP to discuss it with her. In my experience these things take months not weeks".

Abigail looked down, avoiding their concerned faces. Helen put her arm around her sister.

"You know we're always here for you, don't you?"

"Yes, but you both have such busy lives".

"Family comes first," said Helen genuinely.

They were silent in their own thoughts for most of the journey. Focussing on the passing trees and hedgerows, Abigail tried to empty her mind, to stop the rumination. But thoughts of the practice just wouldn't recede. She thought about her father. How bravely he had borne her mother's final few weeks. She hadn't seen him since the funeral. She felt guilty. Helen had borne most of the burden of caring for their parents, and she never complained. They were out in the Sussex countryside now and nearing the village.

"You'll notice a big change in Dad", Helen said.

"In what way?"

"He's lost a lot of weight and aged ten years. He's grief-stricken."

"We should try and get him away for a week or so. Do you fancy taking him abroad?"

Helen wasn't sure she did. Travelling with someone in their eighties was not easy.

They pulled into the drive. The curtains were drawn in the living room. Pushing the heavy front door, they stepped over a pile of mail. They were greeted by Bobby, who jumped up barking vigorously. The remains of last night's meal were on the draining board and the box of bottles in the pantry was overflowing. Helen called upstairs, "We're here."

There was a muffled sound and then a thump as George stumbled out of bed. They were shocked by his appearance. There were food stains on his dressing gown, he was unshaven, and his hair didn't look as if it had been washed for a while.

"Oh, sorry, I must have overslept. Abigail! You too, what a surprise." Helen thought she could smell alcohol on his breath.

"No worries Dad. We'll just do some tidying up while you get showered."

He disappeared and they started clearing the debris on the surfaces.

"I'm sure he's not eating well", Abigail said, examining the contents of the bin. "Now I'm off work I can prepare some freezer meals for him."

Helen had yet to tell Abigail of her resignation. That could wait but she was glad she had offered to help.

They worked in silence. George appeared washed and dressed.

"Now you're both here I can go through this." He produced a jewellery box inlaid with mother-of-pearl. They sat at the kitchen table. Wiping a tear from his eye he opened the box and proceeded to lay the contents on the table. Most of it was costume jewellery but there were Dorothy's wedding and engagement rings and a gold necklace.

"I don't know what her wishes would have been, so you will have to decide between you who gets what. Helen, as the eldest, you go first."

Tentatively, Helen chose the gold necklace and Abigail the engagement ring. He was weeping now. Helen put her arm round him. They sat in silence.

"Can we walk round the garden?" Abigail asked.

"Good idea, I haven't been out there in a while." The garden had been Dorothy's pride and joy. A lot of clearing was needed in the borders.

"Mat can come down one weekend and build a bonfire. The kids would love that." At the mention of the children George perked up.

"That would be great. I couldn't possibly do it myself."

"Let's walk down to the pub, it will be good exercise for you, Dad".

He was already sounding more like his old self. Abigail was relieved. The pub was busy serving lunches and they grabbed the only free table. George ordered a glass of Merlot.

"I haven't had a glass of wine for weeks."

They both knew that this was far from the truth but said nothing. They ordered their food.

"Well, how are your jobs?"

Abigail looked at her feet. Helen decided to tell the truth.

"I'm afraid I've resigned. I shall be free in four weeks' time."

"Golly, what brought that on?" George asked.

"Oh, I've been thinking about it for some time now, and something my boss said last week tipped me into it. I'm going to have a year or so at home."

"How will you manage?"

"We'll manage, don't worry Dad. We've plenty of savings."

This was a white lie, but she didn't want her father to fret. He always did over money.

"I'd no idea you were unhappy in your job," Abigail said.

Helen didn't want to say what she was thinking; that Abigail could never see past her own problems.

"Hopefully you'll be able to come down more often now."

"Absolutely Dad, we'll go on day trips."

The noise in the pub was becoming rowdier and George was finding it hard to hear. He tucked into his steak as if it was his first square meal for weeks. Abigail and Helen exchanged smiles. Never one to forego dessert, George ate far more than was usual and clearly needed to sleep. They made their way back up the hill to the house. The leaves were falling fast now, time marching relentlessly on.

"We'll go for a walk and let you rest for a bit. Is there any more of Mum's stuff you want us to go through?"

"There's a bundle of letters in the bureau, I haven't had the courage to look at them. I feel like burning them, but wondered if we should go through them together."

Helen froze. She was worried what might be revealed in her mother's correspondence.

"Whatever you want Dad," she said.

They walked up the hill behind the house. At the top there was a pile of rocks.

"I haven't been up here since I was living at home," Abigail reminisced. Helen could see them now, two tomboys in shorts jumping from the rocks, their brother running around with a stick as a gun. Theirs had been a happy childhood despite their parents' trials and father's illness.

The sun was just dipping behind the horizon, leaving an orange hue on the fields. From the top they walked down a path leading to the fields where they would pick up the path behind the church. This was the church they had both been married in and they were lost in memories as they approached it. Memories, too, of Polly and Ben's christening and just recently of their mother's funeral.

"Shall we go in?" Helen asked.

"Yes, let's."

The heavy door creaked on its hinges. There was a musty smell inside and it took a while for them to adjust to the darkness. It was dusty and damp. There were some fading white lilies on the alter. They sat on red cushions in the pews deep in thought. Helen got up to leave but Abigail stayed sitting. Helen could see that she was crying. She waited outside, wondering how her sister would cope with being off work. She needed her job, despite its stresses. It defined her.

It was getting cold, and the light was fading. They should get back. The door creaked open, and Abigail appeared, red-eyed.

"Are you alright?"

"Not really. James and I are struggling and we're going to have a trial separation. He's going to stay with a friend. He'll be gone when I get home."

"Oh no, Abigail. I had no idea."

"It's been going on for some time. I think if we'd had children it would have made all the difference. I look at you and Mat and see the couple we could have been. Anyway, I'll just have to wait and see what happens. At least the rowing will stop for a time."

Helen felt immense pity for her. They walked back to the house in silence. The tall hedgerows, laden with berries, were beginning to turn. Abigail shivered.

"I think I'll come down and stay with Dad for a few days. It will do me good to get out of the house, and I'm sure Dad would benefit from more regular meals."

Helen sighed, "Yes, I think you're right. But it's not a permanent solution."

"No but it's early days yet, Mum only died a month ago. He'll pick up."

Helen was not so sure.

George had lit a fire and was sitting huddled over it. He looked so vulnerable, Helen reached out and put her arm round him.

"Did you go to the church?" he asked gazing into the fire.

"Yes, we sat a while thinking of Mum."

"I go down quite a lot just to sit. It's so peaceful." He was clutching a bundle of letters.

"Look, these are Mum's letters, do you want to take them, Helen, and look through them, I can't face it."

Helen reached out and took them, putting them straight in her bag.

They sat and talked for a while, reminiscing about their childhood.

Abigail was wearing her mother's ring. Helen noticed she wasn't wearing her own wedding ring. She seemed lost, hardly in a robust state to help a grieving parent.

"I haven't seen your brother Greg in a while. He says he's very busy with his voluntary work."

"That and helping Julian with his exhibitions. I'm sure he'll come down soon."

"I guess I'll need some help in the house now, it's been neglected for quite a long time."

Both of them agreed. Helen said she would put an ad in the local paper for four hours cleaning a week.

"Dorothy still managed a bit of dusting if I prompted her."

He suddenly started weeping.

"How will I manage on my own?"

Helen jumped up to comfort him. His tears were rolling down his chin onto his neck. He put his head in his hands.

"Look Dad, I'm going to drive down on Wednesday and stay for a week, now that I'm taking a break from work." His face looked ashen, grief was seeping through every pore.

Abigail got up to make a pot of tea.

"We're going to have to get going in a minute, Dad. Will you be alright? I'll make you a sandwich for later."

"No need my love, I can manage that."

She made it anyway. The fridge was empty, and she realised they should have done a shop.

"Dad, you've no food in"

"I've plenty in the freezer."

"I'll sort that on Wednesday when I'm down."

They gave him a big hug as they left, he looked forlorn, broken.

"It's a big house for one person." Abigail said, as they drove away.

"He'll never move."

It was dark and drizzling outside. The headlights lit up the hedgerows and fields as they turned the sharp bends. Helen was extremely tired. She hoped Abigail would keep talking so that she didn't fall asleep.

"We'd better bring up the possibility of moving at some time in the future. Nearer to us both."

"He'll never leave the countryside, Abigail, you know that. Even if he did, he wouldn't move far from the grave."

Abigail's phone rang.

"Is that you away then? We're on our way back. I'll speak to you in a couple of days. I'll be down here for a few days so you can pop back if you've forgotten anything." Her voice was calm and matter of fact.

Helen tried to imagine being in her situation. She couldn't bear the thought.

"Do you want to come in for a bite to eat?" she asked as they drew up outside the house.

"No thanks, I best be getting back. I need to be on my own just now."

That was the last thing she needed, Helen thought. She watched her drive off and walked into the warm glow of her family congregated around the kitchen table.

Autumn 2005

The GP's waiting room was stark, with plastic covered upright chairs all round the walls. In the centre was a small table with last years gardening and motoring magazines. He was restless and agitated and found it impossible to keep still. He was kept waiting for half an hour. It was agony. Dr Grove eventually called him in. He was wearing an old jumper over a striped shirt and grey trousers. He was clean shaven with a receding hairline.

"Take a seat, Mr Soames," he said warmly. "I haven't seen you in a while, how are you doing?"

He took a deep breath. "I haven't been feeling so well lately and I've come to discuss medication with you." Dr Grove looked up at the computer screen, scratching his head.

"Well, I see you haven't been ordering your pills for some time. That was flagged up some time ago and I contacted the CPN, but I don't think she ever got back to me."

He had slipped through the net. He remembered the CPN getting in touch. He had told her he was wanting to have a trial off medication. Initially she was very reluctant to recommend it and said she'd speak to her consultant. He was surprised when she rang him to say that the consultant had approved his plan, providing Ian kept in touch with the CPN. This he had done for six months or so. She had discharged him from follow up at that point as he was stable.

Dr Grove was reading past letters. There was no eye contact for several minutes. He felt increasingly agitated.

"Oh, there's a letter here from Dr Macintosh stating that, as you were well and the CPN was monitoring you, you were going to have a spell off medication."

"I'm not sure it has been a good idea, my mood has been deteriorating for the past two months."

Dr Grove asked him all the standard questions. Looking over his glasses he struck an austere image.

Ian suddenly felt panicky. Maybe he shouldn't have come.

"I am impressed that you have insight into your current mental state. On previous occasions you have been a lot worse before you have been seen. You are quite right, after several episodes of depression maintenance treatment is recommended. I am surprised at your consultant's decision. I suggest you resume the regime you were on last."

Ian felt a sense of relief, the consultation would soon be over.

Dr Grove issued a prescription and arranged a follow up appointment, and he was soon out on the pavement.

He felt detached from the world, as if he were in a bubble. People walking past him didn't seem real. Waiting at the pharmacy he again felt the panic symptoms. He said he would come back and pick up the drugs, and left, walking briskly round the block. He would have to go in again. Why did he feel such shame and guilt? Everyone else seemed able to cope with life's slings and arrows. It was hard not to think that he'd failed once again. He returned to the pharmacy to find a long queue. He could hear the pharmacist ask the woman in front of him whether she'd had the pills before and whether she knew they could make her sleepy. He hoped he wouldn't be asked questions in public. Again, the shame welled up in him. Fortunately, the pharmacist had a record of his having taken both pills before, so he didn't have to answer any questions. At last, with his pills in his pocket, he made his way back to the safety of his flat.

He looked at the drugs. There were two he had to take, an antidepressant and a mood stabiliser. He realised they were essential, and he fetched a glass of water and immediately took one of each. He remembered how resistant he had been to medication in his teens. How after that first admission he had stopped taking the antidepressant soon after he left hospital. He had felt so much better and had started working well at school. He got through his GCSEs and A levels with little difficulty. His mother was in a better place. Cathy had left home. Why did it all go wrong again?

Sitting back in his chair he felt calmer and more in control. His muscles relaxed, his breathing slowed. He knew it would take several weeks for the medication to take effect. He could wait, he'd waited before. Waiting was part of the price one paid for suffering this horrendous condition.

He remembered the list he had written. This afternoon he would walk and tomorrow he would take the train and walk to her house. He would wait to see her. That was all he needed.

Late summer 2004

Mat arrived with the children just before lunchtime. Helen had spoken to the ward. The operation had gone well. She was advised that two people could visit in the evening.

She gave Mat and the children a quick hug and busied herself preparing lunch.

"Is there anything I can do for you, George?" Mat asked. Helen smiled with relief, so grateful for Mat's practical nature.

"Can you bring some wood in for the fire, and maybe take Bobby for a walk."

Mat disappeared with the children.

George was pacing up and down. The sight of Helen at the sink reminded him of Dorothy. The same frame, the same posture, the same-coloured hair as when she was younger. She even wore Dorothy's apron. It was unnerving. He was finding it too hard to bear. Would she ever get home again? He tried to read the newspaper, but the words just went in and out of focus.

"Sherry, love?" he asked.

"No, I don't think that's a good idea, Dad," she replied.

He poured a large one for himself in defiance.

The phone rang, it was Abigail.

"No, only two people are allowed to see her today. Yes, I know you will be able to assess her better than us. Yes, probably better than the nursing staff. Maybe you could see her tomorrow. I'm taking Dad in this evening. Ok then we'll speak tomorrow."

"She's not happy."

"Well, she should be here."

"There'll be plenty of time for her to be here and help in the future, Dad."

He grunted and went back to his paper.

"Do you think you need someone here to help you look after her now?"

"No, I can manage, providing she doesn't lash out at me. It's been heading that way. Maybe she'll be better when she gets home after this."

Helen knew that it would be far from better. She had a sinking feeling that the worst was yet to come. She and the others would have to brace themselves. She felt the strongest of the three of them. Greg was always too emotional, and Abigail far too caught up with her own problems. She put the plate of sandwiches on the table and went outside to see where Mat and the children had got to. It was a bright morning and after the storm there were a few branches blown across the grass. The garden needed attention, she would ask Mat to mow the lawn and do some clearing. The Michaelmas daisies, roses and hollyhocks filled the border with colour. Butterflies were alighting on the shrubs, their highly painted wings shimmering in the sunlight.

She heard the others coming down the path from the hill with Bobby following behind, the children shrieking with delight.

"Can we see Granny later?" Polly asked.

"No, I'm afraid you can't today but maybe tomorrow."

"But we came here to see her."

"Run along and talk to Granddad. He's a bit fed up because she's in hospital."

Taking Mat's arm, she showed him what needed doing in the garden.

"This place is too big for them now," he said.

They looked at the rambling house, paint peeling from the windows, a few roof tiles missing after the storm. Suddenly she remembered the lunch party when Dorothy had announced her diagnosis. What an emotional roller coaster of a day. She could smell her mother's fragrance, see her radiant smile through the tears. A blackbird sang in the apple tree. Clouds billowed across the sky. She didn't want to go inside, she wanted to stay with the memory, to hold it tight. To watch her mother deteriorate had been so cruel. No-one should have to go through this, she thought.

She hugged Mat, no words were needed. They ambled inside.

"Can we play a game after lunch?"

"We'll go for a walk first while Granddad takes a nap, then we can play knock-out whist with him, OK?"

"Ok," said Ben grumpily.

George was a little tipsy after his sherry and attacked the sandwiches.

"Did you say Abigail was coming down today?" he asked.

"No, tomorrow."

"Good. I think Mum will be very sleepy today. I can't wait to see her. Why did she have to fall?"

Helen thought how precarious their lives were. How one little stumble could result in a major operation. She knew that fractured femurs often caused a person's general health to deteriorate, some never recovered. She wondered if her father realised the seriousness of the situation. He'd hardly uttered a word during lunch, looking so downcast.

The children finished lunch and went out in the garden with Bobby. The afternoon sun was streaming through the kitchen windows showing up all the dust. Helen suddenly felt exhausted.

"I'm going to take a nap before we walk," she told Mat. She went into the living room and collapsed on the couch. The table beside her father's chair was littered with empty whisky glasses and plates with half-eaten snacks of toast and cheese. It was clear her parents weren't coping. Her father was taking comfort in alcohol, and he needed his wits about him to cope with her mother. It wasn't safe.

She felt drowsy but couldn't sleep. She needed to switch off, but her mind was racing. Tomorrow was Sunday, she would have to decide what to do about work. She hated the thought of leaving her father, so she would ask her boss for a few days compassionate leave. In the stuffy stale heat of the room, she drifted off into a fitful sleep.

He woke when it was still dark. Maybe he could see her one more time. He looked at his phone, 7 a.m. If he rushed for the train, he would just be in time to get to her house before anyone left. He quickly dressed, grabbed a glass of milk, and took his pills. It was frosty outside as he stumbled his way to the station. He remembered that he always felt a lot worse before he felt better when he started medication. He pulled his hat over his ears and shivered. It was on the train that he recalled his encounter with her yesterday. How vulnerable she had seemed, and how grateful for his help. He really should stay away. Going to her house would be a huge mistake. He must focus on himself now and his recovery. He got off at the next station and waited for a train back. He would go to the library for a couple of hours and walk home from there. Pleased with his decision he boarded the train. The compartment was empty apart from an elderly woman in a shabby raincoat. She smiled at him as he sat down. Wasn't she the woman who had asked him about his trip to Spain?

"Cold this morning," she remarked.

"Yes, a sharp frost," he replied.

She got off at his stop and shuffled away in front of him. Outside, he noticed her walking towards the library. What would they do without the libraries, the elderly? No-one bothered you, you could sit for hours in the warm. You could lose yourself in a library. All those books and papers to peruse. He wondered about borrowing a Spanish phrasebook. No, best to buy one to take with him, he thought. The girl behind the counter looked up and smiled as he passed. He made his way to the reading room and picked up a paper. It was very difficult to concentrate on anything but the headlines, so he scanned these and took another paper. Out of the corner of his eye he noticed the woman. She had taken off her coat and was settling down in a comfortable chair with a magazine. There were about a dozen people in the room, all retiral age. All waiting for time to pass. There were a few familiar faces but no-one else he had spoken to. Everyone in their own worlds, trying to live in the present and not the past.

He thought he'd try and find an illustrated book on Spain in the over-sized section. It was always good browsing there. He found a couple of books and sat down to study them. Views of restored mediaeval town centres, roman remains and bullrings. Matadors in their finery and little girls in traditional costume vied with spectacular cathedrals and castles.

He was getting excited about booking his trip, although going abroad alone filled him with trepidation. He certainly wasn't ready for it yet. He would be hearing from his CPN, Hazel, soon, so would discuss it with her. He noticed the woman walking towards him.

"Didn't we meet on the train yesterday and today?" she asked.

"Yes, you asked me if I was going to Spain."

"Do you fancy a coffee?"

"Sure, that would be nice. Shall we go to the café on the corner?"

"Perfect," she smiled, showing her yellowed teeth again. He noticed a faint musty smell, was it cats?

"I'm Phyllis. "

"Ian, pleased to meet you."

"I've seen you in here before, Ian. I've only just started coming here since my local library closed down. I don't know what I'd do without it, I really don't."

They sat in the corner of the café and ordered their drinks.

"Do you live far from here?"

"Just on the High Street, thirty minutes' walk. How about you?"

"Oh, Kennington, just a few stops on the Northern line." She stirred her coffee and took a bite of her scone.

"Have you lived in Kennington for a long time?"

"For as long as I can remember", she replied." I've just got a small flat now - it's sheltered - but before I lived in a terraced house. That was when my husband was alive. He died nine years ago," she looked down at her lap, adding "it seems like yesterday."

An awkward silence ensued. He cleared his throat.

"I don't mean to pry, but do you have any family?" she asked.

"Just a sister, but I hardly ever see her. Do you have family in London?"

"Oh no, they're all abroad, New Zealand and Canada, leading the good life. They come home every few years but only out of duty."

She suddenly seemed so alone, he thought. So many people in this city and so many lonely souls. He drained his coffee.

"What do they do, your children?"

"Robert is a surveyor in Christchurch, married with three children, and Elizabeth is married to a Canadian policeman. They have two young children. I went to visit all of them after Bill died. He couldn't travel you see. On account of his health."

She looked down again.

"I don't think I'll go again. They're so busy that when I get there, I hardly see them."

Another silence, he couldn't think of another question to ask.

"What was your line of work, Ian?"

"I worked at the post-office but was retired on health grounds a few years ago."

"Oh, I see. So, you're used to killing time then?" She smiled again, her face a mass of wrinkles. She had a kind face, the sort you could open up to.

"Well, I suppose you could say that. I try to keep myself busy. Did you work, Phyllis?" he asked.

"I used to help out in a children's nursery. I love children you see."

He thought how sad it was she couldn't see her grandchildren.

"I guess we should let those people have our table." He got up to pay at the counter while she put on her coat.

"Are you going back to the library, Phyllis?"

"No, I'd better get home before it gets dark. I have to walk past a rough neighbourhood."

"Well, it's been very nice talking with you. We should do this again soon."

Another smile and she turned briskly and shuffled off. He was sure he could hear her laughing.

Returning to the library, he picked up the book on Spain and sat for another half an hour. There would be time for a quick half pint on his way home.

Tomorrow he was meeting Greg here. Things were looking up.

Late summer 2004

When she and George reached the ward, the ward sister drew them into the office.

"I'm afraid your wife is very confused, she is trying to climb out of the bed. I'm hoping she will recognise you and calm down a bit. We're loath to sedate her as she's just coming out of the anaesthetic."

George looked crestfallen.

"Can we see her now?"

"I'll just check, the nurses are with her at the moment."

She came back a few minutes later, "Yes you can see her now."

Dorothy was lying holding on to the bedsides with frightened eyes. She had a drip in a very bruised forearm. She looked so weak and vulnerable.

"What am I doing here?" she asked, "Can you take me home?"

"Mum, I'm afraid you've broken your hip and you had to have surgery to fix it. You'll need to be in hospital until you can walk."

"I can walk, don't be so silly. Dad knows I can walk, don't you George?"

"My love, your leg has to heal, it will be a few days before you can get up and walk."

A nurse had overheard the conversation.

"Actually, we get them up and mobilising as soon as we can."

"When can I get home?" Dorothy wailed.

George held her hand, but she withdrew it abruptly.

"Where am I and who are all these people?"

Patiently George tried to calm her fears, but to no avail, she was trying to pull herself up the whole time.

Helen was beside herself. They will have to sedate her, she thought. She left the bed and went to find a nurse.

"I think my mother will need some sort of sedation so she can settle for the night," she said.

"We'll get the junior doctor to review her on his ward round."

"Thanks, we'll be in again tomorrow - can my children visit as well? "

"As long as only two people are by her bed at any one time that should be fine," the nurse replied.

Helen found George trying to embrace Dorothy, which was physically difficult over the bed restraints.

"I think we should leave Dad, the doctor is going to see her soon."

"Just a few more minutes."

Dorothy seemed calmer, she was muttering something about having to cook supper. Other visitors were leaving their loved ones. A new patient was wheeled in next to Dorothy, an elderly woman who was very agitated. Why put her next to her mother? Helen wondered. She guessed that their beds were nearest to the nurses' station for observation. She hoped they wouldn't disturb each other.

Walking down the squeaky clean corridors George gave a big sigh. Helen took his arm. That was all that was needed. Neither of them said anything on the drive home. George greeted the children with open arms. They were eager to hear how their grandmother was.

"She's come through the operation fine," Helen told them. "Now she has to have physiotherapy to help her walk again. You can visit tomorrow."

George collapsed in a chair asking for a sherry.

"I think I'll head off home now and we'll drive down in the morning," Mat said, "I forgot to pack overnight things. We'll grab supper on the way. Oh, I've done a shop, so the fridge is full."

Helen hugged him, "Thanks so much."

Mat bundled the children into the car and drove off with Bobby following to the gate barking. Helen turned to go back in the house. The smells of autumn foliage and the warm glow of light illuminating the gravel path brought home how much she loved this house and how sad it would be when her parents left it. A sherry seemed a good idea.

Greg was waiting for him at the entrance. He was wearing a tailored jacket and jeans and his youthful face shone as he welcomed him.

"Hello Ian, good to see you again. I thought we would look at where you fancied going in Spain and then think about dates, flights, and accommodation. How did you get on with your GP?"

"Oh, alright. He's started me back on the same medication, so I have to wait for that to work. I don't think realistically I'll be well enough to travel 'til the spring at the earliest."

"Yes, I think you're right. We could delay booking 'til the New year, but it may be worth looking at availability now if you're up to it?"

"Sure, that would be helpful, thanks."

They made their way to the computer room. Fortunately, there was only one man there so they sat at the other end of the room where, hopefully, they wouldn't disturb him. He was intensely focussed, hunched over the computer. Greg managed to find a small three-star hotel in Nerja which had single rooms and offered half board. It also had a view of the sea. Ian felt anxious at the prospect of making a decision and was relieved that it would be deferred for now. There were frequent flights to Malaga with a budget airline and Greg showed him how to book them.

"Are you happy with Nerja? There's not a lot to do except gentle walks, pavement cafés and the beach. There are the caves of course, which are very spectacular."

"I think that will suit me well," he replied, not at all sure that it would.

"I could always take the bus into Malaga one day."

"It's very popular with Brits, so you may meet people at your hotel. Here, take this note of the search we've done. If you want help booking again let me know, you have my number, don't you?"

He said that he did and pocketed the note.

"How about a coffee, I've just got time before my next client. Shall we just go to the library café? Have you been helping out recently?"

"Yes, last week once."

The café was bright and airy with a warm smell of freshly ground coffee. There were several people sitting alone at tables reading papers or books. It was a comforting place, familiar and safe.

"Now, would you like to come along to the whist evening next Tuesday? It's in the Baptist church hall and starts at 7 p.m."

"I've forgotten how to play and I'm not sure I'm up to mixing with a crowd of people just now," he replied.

"You'll pick it up easily, I'm sure, and they are a very friendly bunch of people who go, all ages and from all walks of life."

The thought of meeting people and making conversation suddenly seemed daunting. But he remembered that he had spoken to the young woman the day before yesterday and the elderly lady yesterday. One to one it was different. His hands felt sweaty. Should he go, or shouldn't he?

"OK, I'll give it a try," he said.

"Great, I can pick you up if you like, ten to seven."

"There were no limits to this young man's kindness," he thought.

"I think I'll keep in close touch with you until you get back on your feet. It's always a tricky time going back on the medication. I guess your CPN will also be seeing you regularly?"

"I expect so." He suddenly felt extremely tired.

Greg got up to leave." See you on Tuesday then, and you can always call me if you change your mind."
He would try and go, he decided, putting it off would only make his anxiety worse.

Walking back to his flat he thought back to his last admission five years previously. He'd lost count of the times he'd been in hospital, the memories all merged into one. His head was reeling, he felt his grasp on reality fading fast. The traffic seemed louder, people's voices harsher. Was that man laughing at him? He quickened his step. The High Street was busy, and he had to jostle for room on the pavement. A man brushed his arm as he passed and he jumped, turning to accost him. Thinking better of it, he resumed his fast walk in the direction of the flat. The sooner he was in the safety of the flat the better. A buzzing started in his ear, he could hear voices everywhere. What was happening? A throng of people had congregated around a man collapsed on the pavement. He looked in a bad way. He stopped for a moment but when he heard the ambulance sirens he moved on.

Climbing to his flat he tried to calm his breathing. He had no idea what he should do next. The rest of the day seemed to stretch out so far before him. He collapsed in his armchair and closed his eyes. Tingling sensations crawled along his skin, his muscles seemed to twitch. Breathe in slowly, he told himself. He had no one to phone. Again the voices he had heard in the street came back to him, they seemed to be telling him something, that he was no good, a failure, alone in this world. Where had he just been? He couldn't think. He felt in his pocket and found a piece of paper. On it were the details of a hotel in Spain and flight times. Of course, Greg. He had his number somewhere. He searched for his address book and phoned him. A recorded message, he wasn't answering.

"Hello, it's Ian here. I'm sorry to call you, but I feel really bad just now and wondered if you were around still to meet up again. If you can call me back when you get this."

He lay back in his chair. Distract yourself, he thought, lunch. He opened the fridge, there was a packet of sliced ham curling at the edges and half a loaf. He made a sandwich and put the TV on. The phone rang.

"Greg here. I'm sorry you don't feel well. I thought you weren't great this morning. Look, I've got an errand to do this afternoon which involves driving to Sussex, you're very welcome to come along for the ride."

"Oh, I think that is an imposition, I couldn't possibly do that."

"No, it's fine, I'd like the company, I'll pick you up around two, OK?"

"Thanks so much."

He ate his dry sandwich watching the news. More strife in the Middle East, failure of agreement at a summit on global warming, unemployment figures rising. Nothing to raise the spirits.

A ride in the countryside would be very good indeed. I wonder what he has to do in Sussex, he thought. He wouldn't ask, he decided.

The ringing in his ears had stopped as had the voices which he was sure were his own thoughts. He knew the tell-tale signs of an impending depressive episode all too well. Many times in the past though, he hadn't seen it coming. The second time he had been travelling in Europe with a friend, Simon. Things seemed to be going well, but they were rather strapped for cash. They were struggling to agree on their itinerary. He remembered how numb he'd suddenly felt and how frightened. His friend didn't know what to do when he broke down. They were in Dubrovnik, staying at a campsite. He became fixated on the other campers, thinking they were laughing at him. He refused to speak to a doctor when Simon suggested it. He wasn't sleeping or eating well. After a couple of days Simon suggested they book flights home. Fortunately, he accepted this plan, and they flew home from Ljubljana. The journey home must have been fraught for Simon. Luckily, he couldn't remember much about it. He was admitted soon after he got home and was in hospital for several months. Thinking back now, he realised just how much of his youth he'd lost.

The doorbell buzzed making him jump. He grabbed a jacket and greeted Greg warmly with a smile.

"Do I need anything? I have my wallet."

"No, nothing at all. I have to visit an estate agent in Tunbridge Wells, it shouldn't take long. We can grab a coffee there and maybe take a walk around the town."

"Sounds good to me. I can't thank you enough, Greg."

He suddenly felt very vulnerable and dependent.

"What did you do after we parted this morning?" Greg asked

"Wandered home and had lunch, nothing else."

"Can you read at the moment?"

"No, not really, but I can concentrate on the TV."

"Where do you walk? I know you've always liked walking."

"Well, sometimes I take a train up to the city and walk around the office buildings and down through Temple Bar. I like watching the city gents and ladies. It's a life I should have liked, I think. Sometimes I even follow someone for a while, I know I shouldn't, but it makes me feel a bit closer to them as I imagine their job and life. I feel so detached from the world but when I focus on just one person it seems to help."

He wasn't sure he should be telling Greg all this.

"You have to be careful following people, Ian. It could land you in deep trouble. How far have you followed them?"

He felt the sweat seeping down his back, his voice was shaky. Should he be honest? Maybe he should, get it out in the open and break a trend that was definitely going in the wrong direction.

"Well, the other day I followed a woman I'd seen on the train home to her house."

Greg pulled the car into a layby and faced him. His forehead was furrowed in a deep frown.

"I don't know what I should do with that information, Ian. I know you are lonely and in need of company, but that behaviour is bordering on the criminal. You do realise the seriousness of your position?"

He bowed his face in shame. "I know. I know. I am going to stop now, I want to reassure you of that."

Greg drew his hands through his hair. He wondered whether they should proceed. It was only half an hour to get back to the flat and he would still make the estate agents before they closed. On the other hand, Ian was opening up to him and needed the company this afternoon.

"OK, I will be asking more questions at some point. For now, just let's enjoy the journey and forget about it.

I will have to discuss this with my supervisor, but rest assured it will remain between us and not noted down."

They drove on in silence passing the interminable suburbs of south London in the grey autumn afternoon.

"I'll definitely come to the whist evening next week."

"That's good."

There was another silence.

"Do you mind me asking about your past, Ian? You've told me some things, but I don't have a clear picture of your upbringing and formative years."

He always dreaded questions like this. How could it help him?

"Well, my early childhood was very happy and secure. My father worked on the railways and my mother in a local grocer's shop. My sister, Cathy, who is five years older than me and was always so good at everything, was the apple of their eye. I had friends, friends in the street, friends at school. Primary school that is."

He faltered here, rubbing his eyes.

"Go on, do, please."

"Things seemed pretty stable 'til my father got into a spot of bother at work. He was caught stealing something, I'm not sure what it was, I was only eight or nine at the time. I remember the rows. Then he was at home all the time and suddenly we had no money. My mother did her very best to feed and clothe us, but we were on a knife edge. Then my father just wasn't there. I never saw him again."

"What happened to him?"

"Our mother took us aside some months later and told us he had died. We knew no more than that. My mother was inconsolable for a while, the atmosphere at home was terrible. Cathy took it bad, she locked herself in her room for hours at a time. It wasn't until I was starting secondary school that my mother admitted that my father had taken his own life. Apparently when he left home, he had started drinking and become seriously depressed. He lived a reclusive life and was neglecting himself. He was found unconscious in his bedsit having taken a bottle of pills and a bottle of whisky. He died later in hospital. My mother had tried to shield me from the truth. Cathy had known. This was difficult for anyone to comprehend but for a young teenager struggling with a new school it was horrendous. I was angry and rebellious."

"Did you attend the funeral?"

"Yes, but it's all a blur. I think there was an inquest."

"Did you talk to your sister or mother about it all?"

"No, hardly at all, my mother just buried herself in her work, looking after the house and us. Cathy, by this time, had a boyfriend and was out all the time."

"So, you were left not knowing why it happened. Did you want to know?"

"I'm not sure I did."

They were out in the countryside now and making good progress. Pretty villages with thatched cottages and pristine gardens flashed past. How do people get to have such perfect lives? he asked himself. Garden fetes, polished cars, holidays in Tuscan villas, children all doing well at school, regular jobs, no illness. That was it, no illness. The lottery of life had dealt him a rum card.

"So how did you get on in Secondary school?"

"Not too bad at first, but I had few friends. I liked science and maths and was quite good at them. I also ran a lot and was picked for cross country races."

"You say 'at first'".

"Yes, well, it was my third year I think, and something seemed to happen to me. I lost interest in running, became more insular and withdrew from my friends. They were all chatting up girls and I just couldn't."

He really didn't want to say any more. They had reached Tunbridge Wells.

"Are you happy to stay in the car while I pop into the estate agent?"

"Sure, no worries, take your time."

Greg disappeared along the street. He put on the radio - Classic FM - and watched the shoppers walking by. The light was failing, they wouldn't have long for a walk. He felt strangely calm. This had been a good idea of Greg's. In a few minutes Greg was back opening his door.

"There's a coffee shop just along the road, shall we walk?"

Over coffee they talked more about Greg's trip to Nerja and his other experiences of Spain.

"Let's take a walk to the Pantiles before we head home," Greg suggested.

As they walked Greg spent some time telling him about the history of the Borough and its time as a Spa town.

"Have you ever been to Sussex?"

"We used to come down to Brighton when I was young. Then when Dad died we stopped having holidays, just maybe a daytrip or two. It was all very difficult. I travelled in Europe a bit after I finished school. I was trying to get into university but didn't make the grades. I had missed so much of school. I became ill again when I was abroad. Anyway, it's a long story."

"One I'd like to hear sometime," Greg smiled. "We'd best be getting back."

The journey home was quicker with heavy traffic leaving London. Ian rather dreaded getting back to his flat and the empty evening.

As they approached the High Street, Greg asked "Have you sorted your evening meal yet? There's a very good takeaway just opened up around the corner - Thai, I think - a friend recommended it. Let's get something for you there."

He was overwhelmed with gratitude and vowed he would repay him somehow.

Later that evening, having enjoyed his curry and watched a drama documentary on the Russian Revolution, he reflected that it had been a very good afternoon indeed after a difficult morning. He tried to put things into perspective. He had started his medication, he had a great companion, he would eventually visit Spain. He was doing well. He needed a role, but then so many seek an illusive role. He would check out the charity shops locally, maybe something would turn up.

Going to bed, the bed covers felt strangely more comforting, he felt safe for the first time in a while. He tried not to think of the past. Now was the time for a new beginning.

He left the ward without a backward glance. He had gained weight and felt physically very unfit, but he would remedy that with regular walks. He was to get the bus home. He felt very shaky as he emerged into the bright sunlight. Everything stood out in sharp relief. Once again that feeling of detachment from his surroundings haunted him. He carried his battered old suitcase onto the bus and took a seat at the back. It was July. He had lost six months of his life, several years if he counted all the admissions. He couldn't get them back. What he must try and do was make the most of the years he had left. He was fragile though, lost in a world of follow up. Day hospital, CPN and now this be-friending service that his social worker had arranged. Apparently, a young man called Paul was going to call and arrange to see him. He wasn't sure he wanted someone new to get to know.

The first job to do on getting in the flat was to make a list to stack his fridge. He'd no idea what to cook. Six months of hospital food had deadened his appetite. His appetite for everything. He reached his stop and he stepped onto the pavement in the drizzle. He searched for his keys and for one dreadful moment thought he had lost them, finding them in the outside compartment of his suitcase.

"Excuse me, but can you tell me the way to Fortingale Avenue?" a young woman in a bright red coat asked.

"I think it's the third turning on the left," he replied nervously. Realising this was the first time he had spoken to anyone outside the hospital in six months he wished he could have more of a conversation. But in a flash she was gone and he was left holding his suitcase looking for all the world as if it was him that was lost. He walked to his flat each footstep feeling heavier than the last. Why did he have this all-pervading feeling of dread? Once in the flat he would be fine, he thought. At last, he was climbing the stairs up to his front door. He felt his heart racing, he needed to sit down fast. Slumping in his armchair he let out a sigh of relief. The first hurdle was over. He lit a cigarette and inhaled deeply. It was eleven o'clock. The day stretched before him. He got a piece of paper and wrote: "Got the bus, gave directions to woman in red coat. To do: Shop, make list for rest of week." He realised he was alone in the world and hadn't a clue where to start to rebuild his life. He sat back in his chair and gazed up at the ceiling. Cigarette smoke floated up.

His phone rang, "Is that Ian?"

"Yes."

"Paul here from the befriending service. I'd like to pop round and see you tomorrow morning if that's OK?"

"That would be fine, thank you."

"Ten o'clock tomorrow then."

"See you then".

He stubbed out his cigarette and drew a deep breath.

Dragging himself around the supermarket was torture. Everywhere he looked the shoppers were efficiently placing objects in their baskets whilst he dithered at every item. Eventually he reached the checkout.

"Do you have a club card?"

"No, I don't think so."

"That will be thirty-two pounds and seven pence."

More words with a stranger, he was outside in the real world.

Back in the flat, once he had unpacked, he looked at his watch, it was 1.30. A spot of lunch and then a walk. Maybe he should take a train up to the Thames and walk along the river. This was something he had loved to do. Feeling invigorated he fixed himself a sandwich and a glass of milk.

It was drizzling when he went outside, that fine drizzle that clings to you and seeps through your clothes. He walked briskly to the station. His Oyster card was out of credit, so he queued up at the machine only to find it wasn't working so he had to start again. The train was warm and comforting and when he got out at London Bridge the drizzle had stopped. It was a warm summer's afternoon and the Thames sparkled in the sunlight. He walked along past the Globe theatre where office workers were meeting up for after work drinks. It was buzzing. He decided to walk along to the Festival Theatre and get a coffee in the foyer. Buskers were playing, the sun's heat was intoxicating. On the one hand he felt liberated, yet on the other trapped by his illness, outside of all this, unable to get in, to connect with the world.

In the Festival Theatre a jazz band was warming up in the foyer, so he got himself a coffee and found a seat. People started to congregate, and the band started playing. This was for real, this is what normal people do, he thought. They don't weave baskets and walk up and down corridors collecting pills. He must connect. He would connect. He thought someone was looking at him strangely, so he got up to go, but thought better of it and sat down again. It was probably his imagination. He looked down at his feet, best not to make eye contact with anyone. The musicians played on.

It was six o'clock when he left, feeling relaxed and optimistic. A good stroll back along the South Bank was ideal to finish off the afternoon.

"Excuse me, but did you drop this?" A middle-aged woman handed him his wallet.

"Oh, thank you so much," he replied as he took it.

Maybe a half pint at the pub near London Bridge would set him up for the journey home, he thought. The pub was heaving with workers, but he managed to jostle himself to the bar. "Steady on, guvnor'," the man on his left shouted," I was next in the queue."

"I'm sorry, go ahead," he replied.

"Don't worry. You here alone?"

"Yes."

"Want to join me for a fag outside?"

"Thank you," though he wasn't sure that he did.

Outside there were no seats but he found the man propped against a wall.

"'ere, have one of mine," he offered him a cigarette.

They puffed away without speaking.

"You from round here?"

"Clapham, and you?"

"I'm just on a contract, I come from Southend me, so this is all new up here."

"What sort of contract?"

"Building, you know, heavy work." He looked at him and noted the steel-tipped boots and dirty trousers. He should have guessed.

"What line of work are you in?"

"Oh, I've got a desk job round the corner," he lied. They continued in silence.

"Well, I best be getting home."

"The Missus will be waiting for you then?"

"Probably."

"Good talking to yah," he grinned as he walked away. Relieved to be on his own yet pleased to have met the guy, he walked to the Tube. This had been a good decision, coming in to the river. The river was always a good place to be, it seemed, for everyone. No-one could walk along it without being uplifted. He smiled to himself as he got on the train.

"How did it go?" Mat gave her a welcoming hug.
"Well, Dad is clearly struggling, and Abigail's marriage
is breaking up, but otherwise pretty well!"

"Oh my God, poor Abigail. They were the last couple
I expected it to happen to."

I agree, thought Helen.

He handed her a glass of red wine.

"I'm going back down on Wednesday. I know I have
to work my notice, but I'll phone in sick or something. I
have to see how he's coping. I'm worried he'll get
depressed again."

"You take on too much. You must make time for
yourself, and us."

"In my position you'd do the same. Oh, Dad gave me
these to look through."

She produced the bundle of letters.

"I suggest you do that in a couple of days when you're
a bit more rested. Here let's collapse, the kids are off to
bed now."

She could hear them upstairs and went up to say good
night. She threw the bundle of letters into the study so
that she wasn't temped to read them.

"How's Granddad?" Polly asked.

"Well, sad as you would expect, but he's OK and
looking forward to seeing you both again."

"When are we going down?"

"Maybe at the weekend, we'll see. Are you going to
read for a while?"

Polly reached for her Harry Potter book and lay back
on the pillows. Helen kissed her and after checking on
Ben went down to join Mat.

She snuggled up to him.

"What must it be like to lose your life-long partner, someone with whom you've shared the highs and lows, the laughter, the tears. I think he's doing pretty well considering. But he's drinking, and I have to get the measure of that."

"Yes, I agree, it's very early days. I'm sure your visits are a great comfort to him."

"It's Abigail I'm more worried about now," she sighed.

She suddenly realised how exhausted she was, and she had to decide how she was going to ask her boss for time off during her month's notice. She was due annual leave but had no idea if taking it now was appropriate.

"I'm off to bed," she rose and headed for the stairs.

"I'll be up in a minute."

Popping her head into the study she saw the bundle of letters. Best hide them, she thought, and she put them at the back of a drawer in her desk. She wasn't sure when she'd have the emotional energy to read them. She climbed into bed and grabbed her novel. It was a family saga and one she was having trouble engaging with. Maybe a gripping crime novel would be a better choice just now, she thought. After a paragraph she put it down and, switching off the light, fell into a deep sleep.

The next morning she woke early, it was still dark outside. She crept out of bed and downstairs. She made herself a mug of tea and opened her laptop. Her inbox was full of unread messages, but the last was from Abigail entitled SOS.

Oh Helen, I feel much worse, he's cleared out all his stuff, he must have hired a van. He's taken the music system and computer and all his books. I can't sleep, what am I going to do? I'm so restless, I keep pacing around. Please ring me when you can, lots of love.

Her head reeled. How can you advise a GP that she should see her own GP? she thought. I'll ring her at coffee time, she may be sleeping now. There were the usual e-mails from charities and leisure activities she subscribed to and one from her father.

Helen, did you take that bundle of letters home? I've been looking everywhere for them. If you have them, can you bring them down on Wednesday when you come? Thanks, Dad X.

She sent a brief reply saying she would bring them down. She had a sudden urge to read them, but she would have to wait until this evening. There was movement upstairs.

"Helen what time did you get up?"

"Only half an hour ago."

"Do you realise the time, it's only six, come back to bed 'til the alarm."

She crept under the warm covers and spooned him.

"I've heard from Abigail. She's in a real state as James has cleared out all his stuff."

"I'm surprised he didn't take a bit of his own medicine," he said with a hint of sarcasm in his voice.

"She's not the easiest person to live with."

"No, but it seems to have come out of the blue."

"Yes, Abigail doesn't seem to have had any warning of this, although she did say that things had been difficult for some time."

"Well, I think you have both been struggling since Dorothy died, now don't deny it."

He was right. She saw her mother's face and wept silently.

Maybe losing her mother and her job so close together would be difficult to cope with. But she knew she couldn't support her father, sister and her family and work in a job which was so unforgiving. She tried to doze but Mat was wide awake.

"I'm going to get up now."

"No stay a while, it's so comforting to hold you."

He relaxed and took her in a warm embrace.

Minutes later she glanced at the clock.

"Hell, I must get going, I need to gather my thoughts about what I'm going to tell my boss. I must get down to Dad on Wednesday."

"He's unlikely to be very sympathetic given the time you had off when your Mum died."

"No, but I have nothing to lose now, I can extend my period of notice if he insists, and anyway I'm due two weeks holiday."

"Well good luck, that's all I can say."

She dived into the bathroom giving the children their first warning. Whatever happened today she mustn't forget to phone Abigail.

He woke thinking there was something he was going to do that day. It was Saturday and it wasn't until Monday that Cathy was picking him up for lunch. Then he remembered: charity shops. There were several in the High Street, he would go along this morning and enquire whether any of them needed any voluntary helpers. Feeling enlivened he got out of bed and opened the blinds. A bright sunny day greeted him. His flat was in desperate need of a coat of paint, but that could wait. It was strange but his mood already felt a little lighter. The coffee was warming. He had no bread or milk but found a packet of biscuits in the cupboard. With purpose he got washed and dressed and putting on his warm overcoat stepped out into the frosty morning.

Traffic was moving slowly along the High Street, pedestrians were jostling for space on the pavement. He felt detached again but by the time he got to the British Heart Foundation shop he had come to and entered with a confident step. A mousey woman in a brown cardigan several sizes too large for her was cowering behind the till.

"Excuse me but I was wondering whether your shop had any need of more volunteer help."

"My boss is in the back, I'll just ask." She shuffled away.

"A younger woman appeared in jeans and a sweatshirt.

"Hello, I believe you're offering to help? I'm afraid we don't have need of anyone just now, but if you give me your name and phone number I'll let you know if we do."

He gave her his details and left the shop. He had the same response in the next two shops, and was about to give up when he came to the Mind shop. Something made him more nervous as he opened the door, he wasn't sure what it was. A young man anxiously smoothing his hair and fiddling with his clothes looked up as he approached the till.

"Good morning, is your manager in, I was wondering whether you needed any volunteers."

"I'm afraid she's not in this morning but will be later on today, if you want to come back around three. I think someone's just left so you may be lucky." There was no eye contact. The young man smoothed his hair again and looked down.

He thanked him and left the shop. He picked up some groceries from the convenience store and headed back to his flat feeling quite optimistic. It only needed one shop to say yes.

At three he was back in the Mind shop waiting for the manager to arrive. He looked around at the novels and chose a couple of thrillers. He knew he couldn't read at the moment, but maybe in a few weeks he would be able to. Rows of worn garments hung from their hangers, giving off a musty smell of old wardrobes of past lives, living history of someone's loved ones. The door opened and a smart older woman entered. The young man had gone, and a grey-haired bespectacled lady was manning the till. He went up and explained that he had come back to see the manager about volunteering.

"Have you had any previous experience?" the smart woman asked.

"I'm afraid not," he replied.

"Well, you would have to shadow someone for a week, and I will need a reference. Please drop that in with your application and a brief account of your previous employment and I'll consider it. We do have a vacancy just now so you could start straight away."

He felt his anxiety increasing as he realised he would have to be honest about his employment history. But this charity, above all, should be sympathetic towards people like him. He left the shop, but just a few steps along the street he realised, to his horror, that he had not paid for the books, so he doubled back.

"I'm terribly sorry but I forgot to pay for these."

"No problem," said the woman and took his money. The young man was emerging from the back of the shop in his coat. He looked familiar, he thought. Could he have been at the day hospital following his last admission? He hoped he would see him again if he was accepted as a volunteer. It would be good to connect with someone who had been through the same experience.

It was Sunday tomorrow, just one more day to kill and he would see his sister. One more day of the pills and the road to recovery. He thought he would text Greg and tell him about the application, asking him if he could possibly write him a reference. Greg replied promptly with an encouraging message. Yes, he would gladly act as his referee. He fried up some bacon and mushrooms and settled in front of the television. It had been a good day. He had achieved something. He would sleep well tonight.

But lying on his bed he once again thought back over his life. After he got out of hospital that second time, he enrolled on an HND course on computing. He was a lot better and taking his medication. That was where he'd met Carole. She was a pretty brunette, slight, with glasses. He was very shy, but she was forward and very friendly. They had coffee together after the class. He plucked up the courage to ask her to go to the cinema with him. It was a great evening. The film was good, a comedy, and they popped into a pub for a drink on the way home. Soon after that they began seeing each other regularly. One evening she asked him back to her house as her parents were away. He was terrified. What if she was expecting him to stay overnight? He wasn't ready for that. Opening the front door, she pulled him towards her. It was a terrible moment. He fumbled and drew back.

"Let's have another drink, my father's got some whisky."

"I'm afraid I have to go. This is all wrong, I'm not ready."

She sighed and fastened her blouse.

"Oh well, if you must, Ian. Let me know if you want another drink sometime. See you."

Was that it, he thought. Confused and tearful he had made his way home. They did, however, continue seeing each other and gradually he relaxed. He lost his virginity a few weeks later.

He lay back on the pillow remembering that night. The sweetness of it. How did things turn so sour? He tossed and turned, sleep wouldn't come. He was haunted by his thoughts, swamped by his fears. The noise of the traffic eventually soothed him into a shallow slumber.

She bathed in the glow of the embers holding her sherry. George was dozing in his chair. The light was fading outside. The doorbell rang, making her jump.

"Who on earth can that be? We're not expecting anyone are we?" George said.

Abigail was on the doorstep.

"I couldn't wait 'til tomorrow to come down, I'm sorry. How did you find her on the ward?"

Helen filled her in with the details, quietly resenting the intrusion into the cosy evening she had planned with her father.

"I can't say I'm surprised, she was bound to be acutely confused post-op. Anyway, I'm glad the surgery was a success. Rehab is going to be a challenge, though."

Helen agreed. "Would you like a drink? Dad and I have just had a sherry."

"No, I'll just have tea. Would you like me to go and get something for supper? Or maybe we could go out?"

"I don't think I want to leave the house just now in case the ward phones," George said.

"Well, maybe you could go and get a curry or something from the supermarket, there are a few other things Mat has forgotten." She wrote a list.

Abigail was looking harassed and tired. She fiddled with her wedding ring and seemed very distracted.

"Have you come straight from work?" Helen asked.

"Yes, and I've taken the rest of the week off as annual leave. I need a break."

Abigail was always stressed with her work. Helen was sure the demands of practice were enormous, but somehow Abigail could never get the work-life balance right.

"I'm sure you do. Listen I'll head off and get these things, you stay with Dad."

"Thanks Helen, you're a brick. That fire looks so inviting."

It was a half-hour drive to the supermarket and Helen was exhausted. She grabbed things quickly in the aisles and was out again in no time. Reversing the car, she didn't notice someone reversing opposite. She heard the crunch and screamed. "God, what else."

"You idiot," an irate man shouted.

"I'm so sorry. Let's exchange details and I'll sort it with my insurance company."

"This couldn't have happened at a worse time. My wife is in hospital and I'm on my way to visit her."
Helen couldn't bear it any more.

"Here, these are my details, I'm afraid I don't have my insurance company's address, but I can e-mail you with that when I get home in a few days. I'm staying with my father whilst my mother is in hospital."

"OK, here you are, my e-mail address and phone number. We'd best get going then."

Helen surveyed the damage, a dent to the bumper that would no doubt cost a lot to repair. His car had much less damage but still had a visible dent.

Why do things always happen in runs? Anyway, I'm glad it didn't happen to Abigail. She's not in a good place at the moment, she thought. She put the music on high - Beethoven's Eroica symphony - at least that was uplifting.

It was dark when she got back. Abigail was clutching a large sherry and George was on his second.

"I rang the ward. Apparently, she's much more settled after a sedative, thank goodness."

"What time is visiting?"

"Three 'til eight with only two allowed at the bedside at any one time."

"Can I do anything?"

"No, I must phone Mat, I had a collision in the car park."

"Oh God, no, was it your fault?"

"Definitely, unfortunately. A lot on my mind."

"I'll pay," George added," you can't be worrying about that just now."

Helen gave him a hug and went off to phone.

"That's all she needed after last night," Abigail said.

Mat was very understanding. "Don't worry, it's a minor problem, I'll sort it when you get home."

She heaved a sigh of relief, dealing with insurance companies was something she didn't feel up to at the moment.

"Abigail's here, she looks in a bad way, stressed at work as usual. I'd better go."

She found her in the kitchen unpacking the shopping.

"Can I leave you to prepare the meal? I need to collapse."

Abigail nodded.

"How are you feeling?" she asked George.

"Pretty shattered. I'm ready for my bed."

His well-worn face bore the weight of worry. He had had to watch his wife slowly deteriorate over the past three years, from irritating forgetfulness to constant confusion. It broke his heart when she had insight at first and would leave post-its everywhere, reminding herself what to do, what day it was and what was happening. She would look up "dementia" on the internet and try and understand the pathology. Her job as a nurse in a geriatric ward made this particularly difficult for her. This was a terrible stage. He couldn't imagine how harrowing it must have been for her to realise her mind was slipping away. To not know the day or month or even season. To find simple tasks like organising the shopping or the washing impossible. Even dressing was getting difficult. One day he lost her in the supermarket and found her walking up and down an aisle in floods of tears. They argued and he felt guilty. He sometimes tested her memory. He couldn't believe what was happening to them. There had been no family history and no risk factors. Gradually, as she lost insight, she became less distressed but somehow this increased his distress. That she had lost the ability to reason, a part of her character, seemed such a cruel pointer of things to come. The GP had been blunt and peripheral, not seeming to want to be involved. If it hadn't been for the Alzheimer's Society lunch club, where he could chat to other carers, he wouldn't have coped over the past year. His children were always there if he needed them, but he didn't like to call, to admit he was struggling. Things had come to a head just a few weeks ago when she had started shouting one evening, asking for her mother. It had taken him a couple of hours to calm her down for bed. Then one night she had looked at him with horror as he got into bed with her, clearly not recognising him. Her frightened eyes, like a rabbit's in the headlamps. He knew it was only a matter of time before he would have to ask for help, but the options for her future care were too awful to contemplate.

"Dinner's up," Abigail called. "Heating up a curry has hardly been preparing a meal Helen, please let me manage the food for the rest of the week." Helen was mildly irritated.

George opened a bottle of white wine. "White goes better with curry don't you think?"

Helen thought he'd had quite enough alcohol but kept quiet.

"There's a Foyle's War on at nine I'd like to watch," he muttered, helping himself to a large glass.

"Good, that will be ideal tonight."

The phone rang.

"Damn, why does it always ring at mealtimes?" Helen got up to take it.

It was Greg.

"Can I call you back in thirty?"

She took a large slug of wine. "I hope this isn't too hot for you."

"The hotter the better." George replied.

They ate in silence. Dorothy's chair was painfully empty. George kept looking at it.

"I wonder if she ate anything this evening," he said.

"It won't matter if not," Abigail replied, "as long as they keep her hydrated. I'll check on things when we're in tomorrow, don't worry Dad."

"Easier said than done." He went back to his curry. "I'm not hungry, I'm afraid."

He pushed his plate away. It was hard to see him like this.

"Take a seat by the fire and I'll bring you some dessert," Helen said.

He shuffled off and they heard the TV being switched on.

"It's hit him hard," Helen remarked.

"Bound to. It's been such a long haul."

"Do you think she'll come home?"

"She'll probably have to, in the short-term anyway."

"I think he's at breaking point."

"Yes, but with a good package of care and regular respite, he should cope for a while longer."

"How do you know? You haven't seen them for ages." She was getting heated.

Abigail was taken aback.

"Well, I've had a lot on my plate."

"We all have Abigail. I'm afraid you're always the same, you think you're the only one who has problems at work." She was raising her voice now.

"I'm sorry." She looked genuinely repentant.

Helen too felt sorry, they didn't need an argument tonight of all nights.

She cleared the table and got a bowl of ice cream and raspberries for George.

"Thank you love." He was watching the news. "What were you talking about in there? I heard your voices. It sounded as if you were arguing."

"Oh, nothing Dad, we'll be in soon, I must phone Greg, do you want to talk to him?"

"No, tell him I'll ring tomorrow, there'll be more news then."

Greg was very concerned on the phone "I should come down but there's a client I mustn't disappoint tomorrow. He's been doing so well."

"Don't worry, she can't have many visitors at the moment, next week would be better and I'm sure Dad would value your support then."

"Ok, I'll phone tomorrow." He hung up.

She poured the rest of the wine into her glass and went to join the others. Foyle's War was just starting. She collapsed on the sofa.

"That's me for the rest of the evening," she sighed putting her feet up.

"Monday - Day hospital
Tuesday - Walk
Weds – Day Hospital
Thurs - Library
Fri - Day Hospital."

He put his pen down. The walk on the South Bank had exhilarated him, but when he looked at his week he felt the weight of his illness bearing down on him again. He added,

"Tomorrow - Paul is calling
Sat - Southbank
Sun - Southbank."

He felt better. London was calling and he would respond. There were galleries and museums. He would cope.

He needed to eat. Maybe he'd collect fish and chips this evening. Tomorrow, after Paul's visit he would take a walk. He thought about taking a Tube into the city and walking around. Yes, a good plan. He went into the bathroom. Looking at himself in the mirror he hardly recognised himself. He had more lines and bags under his eyes, his mouth was downturned. His hair was straggly. His jumper was fraying at the sleeves. He needed a shave. He smiled to himself and shaved and combed his hair. He found a clean and newer jumper and a light-weight anorak that looked reasonably smart. That was better, he thought. He must make the effort, every day. Women apply make-up, it's a mask they hide behind. Men don't have that opportunity so have to try doubly hard to conceal their anguish. It was anguish he felt, it tore him apart.

On the way out of the flat he bumped into his elderly neighbour.

"Good evening, I haven't seen you for ages, have you been away?"

"Yes, I have been visiting my sister in New Zealand."

"Lovely country, I would love to visit, where does she live?"

He racked his brains to think of a city suddenly remembering, "Wellington, the capital."

He hoped there wouldn't be more questions. He found it difficult, lying.

"Oh well, welcome back to sunny London." He disappeared into his flat.

They are probably the only words I'll exchange with him for months, he thought.

The queue at the fish and chip shop extended around the corner and he waited patiently behind a young mother and her toddler.

"Lovely evening," he remarked.

"Yeh."

"Great fish and chips here, aren't they?"

"Brilliant."

"How old is he?"

"Two and a half."

He gave up, it was better to be silent. The queue moved slowly, painfully slowly. At last, he was served, and he made his way quickly back to the flat. He was ravenous. He was apprehensive about Paul's visit, what would happen, would they go out? Best not to think about it this evening. He remembered his medication and went to take it. Two capsules and three pills. Down in one. Don't think about it, just swallow them, he told himself. Other people have to take tablets for diabetes and thyroid disorders. This is just another chemical imbalance. One that hopefully will be fixed in time. How long would he have to wait? He'd been waiting years and still it came back to haunt him. Darkness seemed to cloud his mind. He needed light, something to lift him. A walk? It was still sunny. Yes, he would go out again, there was nothing to lose, maybe the charity shops would still be open, and he could browse. He must get out of the flat. He rushed to get his jacket, stuffed the newspaper from his fish supper in the bin and tore down the stairs. He took a deep breath as he emerged on the pavement and set off down the High Street.

She kept looking behind her just in case he was there. But a sea of unrecognisable faces followed her, all weary and worn from their travelling. All intent on their daily business. All in worlds of their own. All impervious to their fellow commuters. All unable to connect with each other. She was so relieved that her days of this were numbered. On the one hand she was relieved not to see him, but on the other she felt curiously disappointed. He had connected with her after all, and he'd seemed very concerned. He was old enough to be her father, she told herself again. She reached her building and went up in the lift with David. He was wearing his shiny suit and had an unnerving habit of getting up really close to speak. The smell of aftershave was stifling.

"Did you work late the other day?"

"No, I didn't have to," she replied.

"You shouldn't, you know, it's not in our contracts, you could see HR about it. They'll call him in. I've just about had enough of his bullying."

The smell was making her feel faint.

They got out of the lift. "I'm leaving in a month anyway, so you'll have to fight this battle without me."

She reached her desk and sat down.

Calum was in his office, she would have to get this over with quickly.

"I'm sorry to have to ask this of you again, but I need time off to spend with my father. He's seriously depressed after my mother's death. I'm owed some annual leave, can I take a week of that from Wednesday?"

"Yes, I guess so. I'm sorry your father isn't well. Can you take this down?" He proceeded to dictate a couple of letters. He was such an old-fashioned man, so set in his ways, refusing to use a dictaphone. She certainly wouldn't miss working for him.

David was hovering when she got back to her desk. He leaned over her, his tie dropping onto her shoulder.

"Are you planning a leaving do?"

"Not if I can help it."

"But you've been here six years, we must do something, if only the usual pub lunch."

"Oh, OK, I suppose I will, let me think about it, will you?"

At coffee break she went outside to phone Abigail.

"Sorry to get your message last night. Do you want to come and stay? You're very welcome."

She had clearly been weeping, her nose was blocked, and her voice was croaky.

"No, I'll be best here on my own. I have to get used to it and anyway I'm seeing my GP tomorrow. He started me on some antidepressants two weeks ago and I guess he's expecting me to say I feel a bit better." Her voice sounded very shaky.

"I don't suppose you do, dealing with all this," Helen added.

"Can I come over this evening, I can bring a takeaway."

"Of course, see you then"

That evening it was raining and windy as she walked to the Tube station. She slipped on some wet leaves and nearly fell. A stranger brushed past her, uncaring. The gloomy light was only made bearable by the shop windows. It was almost the pre-Christmas season - oh no, how she hated the build-up. The dreadful commercialisation of what was effectively a long family weekend. She wouldn't miss this journey, no she wouldn't. Clutching her briefcase, she pushed herself onto the crowded train and managed to grasp an overhead handle to keep herself from bumping into a city gent. Everyone smelt damp and tired, and it was only Monday.

Autumn 2005

He leant over the blank sheet. Name, date of birth, address. Place of birth. All this was easy. Qualifications. He didn't know how far back to go. To O-levels? He couldn't even remember all the grades he'd got. Three A-levels, Geography, Art and English, D, C and D, respectively. His first job was in the local newsagent. He'd applied to University but hadn't got in so went backpacking in Europe. That was when things started to go wrong again. Jobs, jobs, get back to jobs. Evening classes in computing. His teacher thought he should do an HND. Then he applied for a job as a postman and got it. It was a foot in the door of the Post Office, maybe there would be promotion. But things went wrong again, and he was admitted to hospital for the third time. Carole had not known how to cope with his illness, and he was pushing her away. He didn't feel worthy of her. The final straw came when she found him with his tablets and a bottle of whisky. She called an ambulance. When he got out of the ward three months later, she was gone from his life. As if she'd never been there. Sadly, he'd never met anyone else. Carole was, for him, the only one. He had three or four more admissions over the years, and it always took so long for him to recover. Fortunately, his job at the Post Office was held for him and over the course of a few years he was promoted to manager of the sorting office. This was his job until his illness forced him to retire five years ago. He often wished he had looked for something else but, as change was such a potent stressor for him, he never did. It was a sparse CV, so he thought his chances of being accepted were very low. He would hand it in as soon as he got his reference. Hopefully a character reference will be good enough, he thought.

He put on the radio, but for some reason the noise jarred. He needed complete silence. The sounds from the street below permeated up into his flat. He could not escape the bustle of London. He began to long for a break from the city and from his existence in it. The dirt, the grime, the crowds. Maybe a train to the coast tomorrow would be a good idea. He picked up one of the crime novels. It was well thumbed. To his surprise he managed to read thirty pages without a break, it gripped him from the start. A serial killer who stalked his victims made him shudder. Why had he followed these women, what compelled him to do it, and had he managed to successfully stop? He thought back to the first time. He had been on the Southbank watching all the office workers having their early evening drinks. One smart, pretty woman had caught his eye. He felt he had to follow her, keep her within his sight. Somehow that made him feel more alive, in the real world, as if he could join her world and leave his and imagine what it was like to be her. He wanted that sense of purpose, that feeling of belonging. He followed her, when she left the table, to the Tube station. Getting on the same train made him feel he was entering her life, it would give meaning to his. How disconnected and distanced he felt, how immaterial. He managed to get in the same carriage as her and leave the train when she did. He followed her to the car park but then he lost her as she drove away. It created an emptiness in him which had to be met by someone else. And so it had gone on. Travelling by Tube spotting young women, usually city workers. It was an obsession he could do nothing about. He felt powerless to overcome it. Yet he knew it was wrong, he knew he had to curb the impulse. There was nothing sexual about it. He craved the feeling of acceptance, the feeling of belonging. At no time did he feel he had been exposed. He felt completely invisible. He was invisible to himself just as he was to the world. He had come a long way since then, now he was applying for a job where he would interact with the public. He would have no need of solitary fixations. He could greet people, help people, have a role.

He decided to text Greg again.

Can you let me have my reference sometime next week? I'm eager to complete my application as soon as possible.

Minutes later the reply came.

Let's meet for coffee next Tuesday at the library, 10 a.m.

Great.

That afternoon he spent a couple of hours reading his book, then walked to the local pub for a pint. It was damp and misty outside, and people were hurrying home in the dark. The warmth of the bar gave him little comfort. Groups of workers, again, gave him that feeling of exclusion. Their shrill voices grated, their laughter mocked him. He couldn't wait to leave. He had another takeaway, this time Chinese, in front of his electric bar fire, his scarf still on as he felt the damp had permeated his bones. The noise from the kitchen tap dripping irritated him, he felt his anxiety mounting again. This flat was grim, he had to do something to brighten it up. Gradually he relaxed in front of the television, he felt exhausted, weary of life, of his struggles. He watched the news. The forecast tomorrow was good. He suddenly thought that tomorrow he would take the train to Brighton and sit on the beach.

She woke to bright sunlight streaming through the windows. It was nine already and she could hear Abigail downstairs. Today would be difficult, she knew. Abigail would muscle in on the ward, interfering with her mother's care. She would have to be diplomatic.

She pulled on her dressing gown and went downstairs. Abigail was eating cereal looking at her phone.

"Did you sleep well?" she asked.

"No, did you?"

"Like a log, I was shattered," Helen replied.

"Lucky you."

George appeared looking very dishevelled and morose.

"Morning girls, it's great to have you here I must say. Shall we go for a walk this morning, I'm going to be very restless until we can visit her."

"Good idea."

"Where do you suggest?"

"We can walk along the river and pick up a coffee at that nice coffee shop in the village."

"Perfect."

They ate in silence, each deep in their thoughts.

"I'll have a look at your damaged car," George said.

"Oh, don't remind me!"

"Sorry, of course, sore point. It's so easy to do, especially when one is distracted."

He went out of the back door, letting Bobby out into the garden.

"Dad's coping well," Abigail said.

"Yes, I guess he is."

"Golly you did give it a knock, didn't you?"

"His car wasn't badly damaged though, thank goodness."

"Yes, small mercy."

"More coffee?"

"No, I'll go and get showered."

The walk along the river was fresh, green, and fragrant. The brambles looked tempting and the red berries heartening. They all felt uplifted. The warm aroma of coffee greeted them at the end of their walk. It was a perfect morning. They sat outside the café opposite the river, flowing fast, twinkling in the sunlight. There was warmth in the sun, and the warmth suffused them.

"We'd best be getting back," George said.

"I guess so. I wonder what sort of night she's had."

They were all thinking of her.

Back along the path George led the way, striding ahead. The path was overgrown in places, and they had to hold back brambles to pass through. All the time the melodic sound of the river soothed them. A robin perched on a branch and kept flying ahead.

When they got home they found Greg waiting in the garden.

"Hi there, good to see you all. I've brought lunch from our Deli."

"Great, thanks."

"Are we all going in together?" he said.

"I guess so, but only two at a time at the bedside," Helen reminded them.

Over cold meats and delicious salads they talked about old times. It was rare for them all to be together. George was loving it, all the differences of the past melted away as they spoke. A crisis can bring out the best in families, he thought.

Greg was clearly anxious about visiting the hospital. He hated anything to do with acute illness.

At three they were waiting outside the ward. The bell rang and a nurse ushered George and Abigail in. Dorothy was sleeping and the nurse by her side told them she had had to have a strong sedative as she was very confused in the night, trying to get out of bed again. Abigail went to ask a nurse what drug they had given her. She was clearly not pleased with the answer.

"Do you realise the treatment of demented patients with this class of drug has been shown to shorten their lives?"

"It is only short term."

"She seems a bit chesty. Is she getting physio?"

"I don't think so, I'll check."

Abigail was angry now and said she thought she should speak to the consultant. When she mentioned this to George he became agitated.

"Oh, don't make a fuss, I'm sure they're looking after her very well."

He went outside to have a word with Greg and Helen.

"I'm afraid your sister isn't happy with the drug Mum has been given, she's making a complaint."

"Oh dear, how is she?"

"Asleep, rather, sedated."

"I must admit I'd hoped to see her up in her chair," Helen said. "Shall I go in and have a word with Abigail?"

George nodded, letting her pass. Helen went to the bedside. She tried to fight back the tears, looking at her mother. She looked so weak and vulnerable. Abigail returned.

"The consultant is in clinic, but the junior doctor is coming to have a word with us." At that moment a young girl appeared at the foot of the bed. She looked shattered, Helen thought, with unbrushed hair and smudged mascara.

"Hello, I'm Doctor Winslow, the Junior House Officer, how can I help you?"

Abigail answered, "Well, we're not at all happy that our mother has been heavily sedated when she should be up in a chair and looking to mobilise. She also sounds quite chesty. Are you doing anything about that?"

"In brief, she was so confused and restless all night, struggling with the bed-sides and calling out. The nurses phoned my colleague and he decided to give her something at eight this morning as she was clearly exhausted. We are hoping that she'll be more settled tonight and we can start physio tomorrow."

"Well, I certainly hope so," came Abigail's shirty reply.

Just then Dorothy opened her eyes and looked at them. She smiled and said," How lovely to see you, my darlings. I'll get up in a minute. I must have overslept."

"Mum, you're in hospital, you have to rest today and tomorrow you'll get out of bed, and someone will come and help you walk."

"I don't need anyone to help me walk!"

"You've had a major operation on your leg which was broken. You will need help to walk. It will be painful at first."

Amazingly, she seemed to take this in.

"Are there any more questions or issues?" the doctor asked.

"No, I shall be in tomorrow and will keep an eye on her breathing. I don't want her to have a post-operative chest infection," Abigail said.

"Of course, I shall see her first thing tomorrow. I shall also speak to the doctor on-call tonight and ask him to avoid medication if at all possible."

"I should hope that is a high priority."

"What are you talking about?"

"Nothing that you need to worry about Mum. The doctor gave you something to make you sleep, but it was very strong, and you've slept nearly all day."

"I'm very thirsty, can I have a drink?"

Helen sat her up and gave her a feeder beaker of water.

"This is basic nursing, ensuring adequate hydration. Before we know it she'll have a urinary tract infection too," Abigail said.

"Come on, we must let Greg and Dad come in, especially as she's awake.

Helen found her Father pacing around the visitors' room, looking very anxious and worn.

"She's woken up, Dad, and they are going to hold off from giving her any more of that strong sedation. She's very thirsty, so if you can give her some more water."Giving him something to do to directly help her seemed a good idea.

George's face relaxed. "Thank goodness, thanks for speaking to the staff, Abigail. I don't know what we'd do without you." He brushed a tear from his eye and went into the ward with Greg in tow.

"How do you think she'll be tonight?" Helen asked.
"Goodness knows, but it may become a vicious circle. At night, with dim lighting, she may get more confused, and of course she's more rested now. The staff will be under a lot of pressure to keep her quiet, so as not to disturb the other patients."

"So, it may happen again?"

"I sincerely hope not. I think I'll have one more word with the nurse in charge before we leave."

"Don't you think you've said enough?"

"Helen, this message must be rammed home. We cannot sit tight and watch her deteriorate."

Abigail went into the ward, leaving Helen alone. "The staff must hate having medical families to deal with," Helen thought. Other visitors were leaving the ward now. Helen hoped she could have one last word with her mother before they left. She also wanted to give her more water. The nurses seemed so busy, and Dorothy couldn't reach the beaker herself. She wondered if she'd eat anything this evening.

"I think I've got the message across now. The nurse said she'd pass it on to the night staff. There's no more I can do."

"No, you've been great. Let's hope all goes well tonight."

George and Greg reappeared, George looked quite euphoric.

"She seems to be fine now, she took a good drink and is saying she's hungry. The nurse is going to get her some toast."

"We'll just pop in to say good-bye." Abigail said.

They found Dorothy sitting up in bed eating some toast.

"Oh, this is good, breakfast in bed." She coughed. Helen smiled at Abigail who took a chart from the foot of the bed and studied it.

"Her temperature is normal, thank goodness."

"Mum, we're going to go now, and we'll see you tomorrow. I hope you sleep well."

"I'm going to get up now," Dorothy retorted, "where are my clothes?"

"It's best you stay in bed until the nurses come."

"But I need the toilet, oh dear."

"Helen rushed to the office to get a nurse.

"I'm afraid I've had an accident."

"Don't worry Mum, a nurse is coming."

The indignity of it all was overwhelming. The nurse pulled the curtains around the bed and asked them to leave.

"We'll say good-bye now, Mum," Abigail said, giving her a kiss. Helen embraced her, tears dripping from her chin.

"God, it's hard to leave her like this, isn't it?"

"I'm going to phone later to check on things," Abigail replied.

They decided to get a cup of tea in the hospital canteen before the drive home. Greg had lots of questions and Abigail answered them reassuringly. They were all worried, but Abigail, with her medical background, managed an emotional distance that was enviable. It was easier to hide behind medical facts, Helen thought. Seeing her mother so vulnerable had been a huge shock, which she was reeling from.

George was tucking into his shortbread and very matter of fact. "I'm glad she had that toast, she looked starving!"

"Talking of food, shall we go down to the pub this evening?" Greg asked.

"Good idea, it's not often I have all my three children together."

Sitting beside a glowing log fire in the oak beamed room you could be forgiven for thinking that all was well with this household. They laughed and joked and drank, forgetting the scenes on the ward. Meanwhile, Dorothy was beginning to call out, first for George, then for her mother, then for Helen. There was nothing the nurses could do to soothe her troubled mind. Her illness was taking over. It would defeat her and all the others.

Summer 2000

He browsed in the Oxfam shop and found a jumper that he thought would do. He would have to wash it first, to remove the traces of its previous owner. It was a muddy shade of brown. He checked the DVDs and found a couple of old black and white films he thought he would enjoy. He was doing well. Next up was the British Heart Foundation shop and he decided to peruse the bookshelves. Nothing jumped out at him so again he checked the clothes rails. There was a leather jacket, it was in good condition but a bit tight. He left and made his way back up the High Street. All the shops were closing now, it was time to head home and watch one of those films.

It seemed like the morning dawned early and he woke with a start. There had been no dawns in the hospital, just blazing lights and people shouting. He lay in bed relishing the quiet. Gradually he became aware of the noises of the flat: the quiet hum of the fridge, the steady drone of the traffic, the odd bird song. Life. Something he had missed when in hospital. Putting his feet on the lino floor he stretched and stood up. Maybe he should go for an early morning stroll to the park, to get an appetite for breakfast. Then he was expecting Paul, this young man who was going to help him, he knew not how. He pulled on his clothes. It felt so good to be free, free to do what he wanted, whenever he wanted. He took a shower and shaved. Pulling on some clean clothes he couldn't help thinking of the routine in hospital. Collecting the medication was the worst part of the day. Having to queue up and then, when it was your turn, being watched taking the pills to make sure you swallowed them. Forget it all, he told himself. You will get into a routine here, but it will not be humiliating. You will be in control.

He boiled the kettle for tea and took his medication. He had to collect more pills from the pharmacy, something else he hated doing. But that could wait, he had enough pills for a week. I mustn't run out, he told himself. Unfortunately, I need these bloody tablets. He saw the brown jumper thrown onto a chair. He wondered who had been the owner, why had he given it away? He realised that he may have died. Sometimes he felt dead, dead to the world, to himself. He needed fresh air. He opened the window onto the street. The traffic was building up. He would like to walk to the common to get away from it. He would pick up some food for breakfast on his way back to the flat. A plan, good, all was going well so far. It was a short walk to the common. He passed the odd jogger and dog walker, but the park was quiet and peaceful. He sat on a bench opposite the tennis courts and next to some well-kept flowerbeds. Salvias and marigolds vied for attention. The odd crisp packet fluttered in the gutter. He was outside. This was progress. He remembered past admissions and how strange it felt to be released. It was hard to believe that everyone was going about their lives oblivious of his experiences. So few people are aware of how depersonalizing the experience of being on a psychiatric ward can be, he thought. How long it takes to get one's sense of self back again. A young Mother walked past with her toddler in tow. The child stopped and stared at him. He looked away. Seeing young children always saddened him. Aspects of life that he had missed out on, somehow innumerable, bore down on him.

Breakfast, that was the next thing. He walked briskly to the local supermarket and picked up some eggs, bread, and milk. 'Practicalities, I must focus on the day to day,' he told himself.

The doorbell rang as he was washing his breakfast things. A casually dressed young man stood on the doorstep. He had a large shaggy beard and glasses, he looked the studious type, he thought.

"Hello, you must be Ian. I'm Paul from the befriending service, may I come in?"

He nodded, standing back, and ushering him into the flat.

"How have you been getting on since you left the ward?"

"Well, I only left yesterday so it's a bit early to comment. I took a train up to the South Bank yesterday and walked along the river which was good, and I've just come back from a walk in the park."

"Excellent." There was an awkward silence.

"Why are you here exactly?"

"Our service offers a structured approach to rehabilitation after admission and on-going support to prevent readmission. We plan activities and trips, usually weekly, to begin with, falling to monthly after three months or so."

A well-rehearsed patter, he thought. But he was grateful nonetheless.

"That sounds good, I'm at the day hospital three days a week, so that only leaves Tuesday and Thursday and the week-end."

"No problem, let's see, next Tuesday we could maybe go to Chinatown for a Chinese lunch. Do you fancy a coffee just now?"

"Sure."

"First I need to get some details from you for our records."

More questions, he felt exhausted at the thought.

"When was your first admission to hospital?"

"When I was fifteen."

The memories came flooding back. The school trip, becoming suddenly agitated, thinking everyone was talking about him.

"Golly, so young. How many times have you been in hospital?"

"I've lost count, but it seems to be every four or five years or so. It depends on what's happening, what stresses I'm under."

He really did not want to look back or tell this stranger any more.

"Shall we try the coffee shop just down from the station," he said, to change the subject.

Paul put his notebook away. "I guess this can wait 'til another time. Yes, let's get out of the flat."

He hadn't taken to this young man. He seemed too methodical, and there was a coldness about him. Something he couldn't quite put a finger on nagged him. He grabbed his jacket as they left the flat. Outside the traffic was building up. It was hot in the sun, and he felt the sweat on his brow.

"How long have you lived in the High Street?"

"Oh, about thirty years."

"Where were you before?"

"In a small flat in Tottenham. I moved to be nearer my sister, but I hardly see her now."

"Do you have any other family?"

"No, it's only the two of us. I had friends from work, but you probably know that I haven't worked for six months, and I've lost touch with them. I lead a quiet life with my own company."

Arriving at the coffee shop Paul said, "Let's sit outside, I'll go and order, what do you want?"

"Just a black coffee please," he replied.

Over coffee, Paul continued to ask questions about his life, questions he found difficult to answer. Paul's piercing eyes behind his spectacles unnerved him.

"Do you mind talking about something else? I'm finding it difficult thinking of the past. I prefer to try and be in the present and plan tomorrow. I was thinking of going back to the South Bank."

"Good idea. I'm sorry, I wanted to build up a picture of you so I can get to know you. It helps to cement our relationship."

He was not sure he wanted a relationship, especially not with this young man. Still, he was only doing his job.

This was a very nice pavement café, he thought. You overlooked the park and there was plenty of space between the tables. He didn't like to be too close to people. The passers-by wore their colours with pride, everyone looked cheerful in the summer sunshine. He felt that sense of detachment again.

"So, are you happy if I collect you on Tuesday at twelve and we take a train up to Leicester Square?"

"Yes, that sounds good. I can see myself home." He got up to leave but suddenly thought he had sounded a bit perfunctory and added, "Thanks for your visit, see you on Tuesday."

With that he turned and walked away, leaving Paul looking rather perplexed.

He still had the rest of the day. It was a long time until the welcome oblivion of sleep. More walking was in order, he thought. He would take his map and just wander. It would clear his head, push the memories to the back again. He hadn't thought of Carole for ages until these questions of Paul's had started to unravel his past. He would avoid answering them next week. He had to keep things under wraps. It was too painful to unwrap them. Pain was to be avoided. He needed to recover fully and look for work, if there was any work he could possibly do. He knew this was unrealistic but to be optimistic was to progress. Pessimism meant regression. Having to give up his job recently had been devastating. But he knew he couldn't do it. It was too much responsibility. Perhaps this and the stress of some personnel crises at work had been a factor in his last breakdown.

He looked at the adverts in the Post Office window. There were a few for cleaning jobs, one for a janitor of a primary school and one for a gardener for a private house. He took the numbers for the janitor and gardening jobs and decided he would think about applying next week. Cleaning was something he had tried in the past and it hadn't lasted long. He'd hated it and his work had been shoddy as a consequence. The school janitor post would likely be outwith his capability and he had minimal knowledge of gardening so both looked highly unlikely, but he felt as if he was doing something to move forward. He would apply for the janitor's post. He could scrabble together a CV. He would do it.

There was almost a bounce in his step as, defiantly, he made his way back to the flat to collect his map. Something made him think things were going to be different this time.

Mat was in the kitchen supervising the children's homework when she opened the door.

"Abigail's coming over tonight and bringing a takeaway."

She tossed her briefcase on the hall floor.

"How's your day been, did you see that man again?" Mat asked.

"No, thank goodness. Although I'm sure he's quite harmless and probably very lonely."

"Did you get your leave this week?"

"Yes, so I'll be off down to Dad's on Wednesday. I must read those letters before I go."

She thought she should read them alone and not with Abigail, though she was apprehensive that Abigail might ask to see them this evening.

The domestic scene was complete and comforting in the kitchen. Her nuclear family was secure. She felt tired but content. She didn't want to upset the applecart, but her father had given her the letters to read so she had to read them.

The doorbell rang.

"Auntie Abigail!" Ben exclaimed.

"Pizzas for supper, OK you two?"

She looked haggard as if she hadn't slept. Polly and Ben jumped up to greet her and Mat opened a bottle of red wine.

"A drink, Abigail?"

"Yes, thanks, I need one this evening, I can tell you!"

Suddenly the dynamics had changed, Helen felt aggrieved that her needy sister had barged in on her family, even though she had been forewarned. Just when she wanted a quiet evening.

"I think we all do."

"Are you going down to Dad's as planned?" Abigail asked.

"Yes, do you want to come?" She didn't want her to, but couldn't see a way out of asking her in the current circumstances.

"Well, if it's not an imposition, I'd love to. I need to keep myself occupied."

"Exactly, and I could do with your help and advice. We need to plan a few breaks with Dad and organise meals etc. He's just not coping, as you know."

"Yes, before we know it he'll be falling and getting admitted too."

"Why? He's quite stable on his legs."

"Nutrition in the elderly is often forgotten. Poor diet and inactivity are common precedents for falls."

The pizzas were duly consumed despite being rather cool and soggy. The wine bottle was drained and coffee made.

"Did you read those letters?"

"Not yet, but I will do."

"Maybe we should read them now."

"No, I haven't the energy for that tonight, Abigail, I'll look at them tomorrow and we'll discuss on the way down on Wednesday."

Abigail was clearly not pleased. Mat had lit the fire, and everyone collapsed in front of it.

"So how did your boss respond when you asked for leave in your notice period?"

"I sensed he wasn't pleased, but he agreed. I'm so looking forward to leaving!

Helen gazed into the fire, the warm glow relaxing her. The children were doing their music practice so Mat got up to supervise.

"Do you remember that Greg got Dad's house valued a few years ago and researched sheltered accommodation for them. Do you think we should revisit that?" Abigail asked.

"Ideally that would be a good idea, but I think Dad is far from ready to discuss it, and as we said last night, it's hard to imagine him agreeing to leave the house."

Helen knew that a move was a good idea, it would relieve a lot of her anxiety about leaving him, so she fully intended to bring up the question of more supported living for her father, when the time was right. Mistiming it could put the whole discussion in jeopardy.

"How is Greg anyway? Does he ever talk to you about his work? Does he get paid or is it all voluntary?"

"Voluntary, I think," replied Helen, "he has four or five clients that he sees, some weekly, some less often. He gets quite attached to some of them, I think."

"Maybe that's not a good thing."

"But it is a befriending service and it's very well supervised. He has someone whom he sees monthly to discuss how things are going."

"It must be quite a strain sometimes, especially when clients are just out of hospital."

"Yes, he says these are the toughest times for most of them. Occasionally he feels a bit out of his depth, but he can always get advice, and his remit is just to do things with them outside of their homes to get them out and interacting with the world."

"Do you think we should give him a call this evening to say we've been down to see Dad and are going down again, if he wants to join us?"

"Why not, I'll get the phone."

She handed it to Abigail, "you ring, I'm just going to check on the kids."

Greg answered promptly. "Hi there Abigail, how are you?"

"Well. I've been better but I'm at Helen's and we're going down to see Dad again on Wednesday (we were down at the weekend) and wondered if you wanted to meet us there? He's struggling quite a bit."

"Wednesday is a bit busy for me, but I could get down on Friday, any good?"

"I'll ask Helen if she's planning on staying 'til the weekend, I think she is."

"That would be good, just let me know and I'll see you then. I'll go down anyway, I haven't seen him for weeks, as you know, I've been busy with clients."

"Of course, well hope to see you." She rang off. Abigail lay back in the chair. She suddenly felt an overwhelming affection for her siblings who had held together so well during the past difficult years. So often at times like these family rifts can occur, but they all knew each other's strengths and weaknesses and knew how to accommodate them. She got up to go, she mustn't outstay her welcome, she thought. Popping her head into the dining room where Ben was playing the piano, she told Helen about Greg's plans.

"That's good, are you off then?"

"Yes, I'd best get back, I have to get used to being on my own." The thought filled her with dread.

"See you here on Wednesday around ten then?"

"Perfect, see you all, lots of love," and with that she went out into the cold, unwelcoming night to be alone with her thoughts and fears.

Abigail never thought it could happen to them. James was such a patient man and a couple counsellor of all things. Maybe she was at fault, maybe she'd been too wrapped up with problems at work. It was true that they hadn't been physically close for a long time, but sex had never been a big part of their marriage. Years of infertility treatment had seen to that. Maybe there was someone else. But if there is, I can do nothing about it, she thought, but wait it out. The trouble was she still loved him dearly, love that felt unrequited and forlorn. Tears started streaming down her face, making it difficult to focus on the traffic. She pulled in and wiped her eyes. It was hard not to feel sorry for herself when she compared her cold empty flat to Helen's warm household with its buzz of activity. After a few minutes she regained her composure and set off again. She mustn't forget that she had a GP's appointment in the morning to review her treatment. Whilst in her situation she found it hard to believe that medication was going to help her, she knew she had had the symptoms of clinical depression for some months, and if the roles had been reversed she would have prescribed anti-depressants just as her GP had done. It began to rain. She shivered. Winter was approaching with its interminable dark nights. She would have to develop a strategy for coping with all those long evenings. She could try evening classes organised by the local university once her concentration improved. Then there was her monthly book club. She could go swimming. The possibilities were endless, but it all seemed so pointless. Get a grip, she told herself, feeling the tears welling up again.

The journey was slow and tedious, but she eventually drew up outside her flat and dragged herself in, getting soaked in the process. A hot bath seemed like a good idea, but she had to wait for the water to heat up. A glass of wine? No that would be a mistake, opening a bottle. She put the TV on and watched a comedy news quiz, one of her favourites. Thank goodness it would be bedtime soon. Only another day and she would have Helen's company again for a few days. She went to get her pill. At least they help me sleep, she thought. It was hard to believe she needed these after so many years of coping with her down periods without. But she knew she did, so she swallowed the bitter pill with resignation.

Helen, meanwhile, had tucked the kids up in bed and had watched the same news quiz. Some light relief for life in which worries all too often pile up on each other and wear you down. Tomorrow she would read those letters.

Autumn 2005

It was a crisp bright sunny day for his trip to the coast, and he felt lighter on his feet as he made his way to the station. He hadn't been to Brighton for many years, but had spent a lot of time on the beach there as a boy. The train rattled through the Sussex countryside. He gazed at beautiful houses and manicured gardens with polished cars in the driveways, all redolent of success and good health. He thought of his sister and how she had always seemed disappointed in him. He had long ago stopped feeling guilty for being ill. It was hardly his fault. Life just dealt the cards, and you were stuck with them. His Father's untimely death undoubtedly hadn't helped either. He looked around him. The compartment was empty except for a young woman in jeans and a sweatshirt listening to her phone. He wondered if she knew anything about mental health problems. So many people are ignorant of them, he thought. He so desperately wanted to talk to her. She looked up and he averted his gaze. Just one more stop to go. As he left the station he was surprised to see a couple of beggars sitting on the pavement. No doubt they know, he thought. How near he felt to them, alone, jobless, with a future he didn't dare contemplate.

Pushing these thoughts to the back of his mind he went into the first coffee shop he found and ordered a strong black coffee. Revived, he walked down through the lanes and on to the sea front. It was busy with day trippers like himself. A rollerblader shot past him on the promenade nearly knocking him off his feet. He found a bench overlooking the sea and sat for an hour watching people walk past. The sun still had some heat in it. He closed his eyes and basked in it. The warmth cheered him.

He would walk to the Pavilion and the Museum. All was going well. A pavement artist caught his eye - a stunning landscape of a sunset in chalk. He left a pound coin and moved on. He lingered in the impressive gardens of the Pavilion where the flower beds were a riot of colour. A busker was playing the guitar and singing. He dropped another pound coin in his guitar case. The museum was quiet, and he spent some time downstairs looking at the Art Nouveau furniture and china. Then he went upstairs to the art gallery. There was an exhibition of wildlife photography. This absorbed him so that he hardly noticed the time passing, and it was two o'clock when he left the building, blinking in the bright sunlight. Lunch, he thought, heading back to the seafront. Fish, he would have some fish. Wasn't there a good fish restaurant just along from the pier? He found what looked like a reasonable place which was quite busy and sat at a table near the window. The waiter brought the menu and a jug of water. He ordered the fish of the day - a whole plaice in butter with capers. It was delicious. He vowed he would buy the beggars at the station a hot drink and a sandwich on his way home and give them some money.

"Anything else, Sir," the waiter asked.

"No, just the bill, thank you."

"Just here for the day, are you?" a man at the next table asked.

"Yes, down from London, and you?"

"No, I live here, and my late wife and I used to come to this restaurant every week for the fish of the day - good choice."

"Yes, it was very good. Have you lived here long?"

"I retired here from Birmingham ten years ago, the best thing we ever did. The climate is second to none on this coast and the sun cheers the heart."

"Yes, I second that," he replied.

He got up to go.

"Do you fancy a walk along the prom, we could get a cup of tea before you head home?"

He was a bit overwhelmed but didn't like to refuse.

"Yes, why not," he said, a little uncertainly.

They left the restaurant and headed west. The sky was brooding now keeping the sun at bay The waves were bigger with an onshore wind and there were a few body surfers out. "Where do you live in London?"

"Clapham High Street. It's a far cry from this. I rather envy you down here."

"I'm Alan by the way."

"Ian, very good to talk to you Alan," he offered his hand which Alan took with a warm handshake. He was wearing a faded suit and a grey overcoat and had a red scarf tied around his neck. He was wearing hearing aids and had trouble hearing Ian above the noise of the waves.

"Shall we take a seat here?" Alan said, pointing to a pavement café.

They ordered tea and sat in silence. Neither seemed bothered that they didn't speak. Both were pleased to be with someone, to have met someone.

"Well, I guess I'd best be getting back to the station, there are a couple of chores I need to do on the way."

"Well, goodbye then, nice meeting you." Alan offered his hand, which he shook warmly.

He picked up a couple of sandwiches and two cups of tea on the way back to the station and handed them to the two beggars, placing a five-pound note in each of their pots. They both thanked him, immediately opening the sandwiches, and taking huge bites.

He'd had a good day and tomorrow Cathy was calling to take him for lunch. His week was filling up. It was dark when he got home. The enveloping damp of his flat made him shiver, but he was sustained by the warmth of his encounter with Alan. He would sleep well tonight.

Autumn 2005

My darling Dorothy,

I know that our love binds us together, but the problems ahead seem insurmountable.
The only course of action is for us to put the past behind us and focus on the present. Your family needs you, above all George. I love my brother dearly and I could not hurt him.
This is hard to write, I'm trembling now, but I don't know what tomorrow will bring. Forgive me for writing this, you will be forever in my heart.

Jack

She checked the date, 13th August 2000. The next day he was dead.

She could read no more. Why had her mother kept the letter? Was it guilt? No one should see this, least of all her father. What must Jack have been going through. The anguish of buried love. He who was always so cheerful when he was well, falling into the abyss of time that is death. And by his own hand. An unnatural end for a tortured soul.

She put the bundle of letters back in the draw. She would conveniently forget them tomorrow. Then something made her look again.

There was a bundle of notes in childish writing, and she realised that her mother had kept sheets from their school jotters. She could take these down and say she hadn't had time to go through the rest. That should keep Abigail happy.

Then one letter caught her eye. It was in an envelope addressed to George in the same handwriting.

Dear George,

This is very difficult to write. I have struggled for too long with this illness. I need relief. I know you will understand what I'm going through. You have been there often enough.

My action could be construed as cowardice, but it has taken a lot of thought. I don't want to be remembered as I am but as I was when I was well. Your wedding day. The children's christening services. I don't crave pity but forgiveness. I have not taken this decision lightly. It has been long in the making. Forgive me, dear brother, you have been so good to me.

Jack

She felt faint, tears flowed. Did her father show her mother this, was it posted at the same time as Jack's letter to her? Once again she pictured her uncle, her real father, head in hands, a river of tears falling down his cheeks, sitting alone in his room with a bottle of pills. It was as if it was yesterday. Nothing good will come out of reading these with her father, she thought. Yet she couldn't bring herself to destroy them. Maybe her father wanted her to see them. What sadness lay in his heart? Once again, she went to put the letters back, but somehow felt compelled to take one more look. There was a bundle marked 'For Helen', her pulse quickened.

Dear Helen,

You will be surprised to get this letter. I'm afraid, by the time you read it, it will be too late to ask me any questions. This is by design, I'm sorry to say.

I will be blunt. The year of your birth was a tumultuous one for the family. Your father was very ill and in hospital. Your mother and I visited him regularly. Consequently, we spent a lot of time together and became very close. We fell in love. We broke convention and began an affair which, your mother is certain, resulted in your conception. Therefore, I speak as your father and uncle as one. I cannot bear the burden of guilt any longer. What this knowledge would do to your father I dread to think, so please keep it from him. If he finds out there is nothing we can do but hope it doesn't make him ill or desperate again. You are a loving family, so he has all your support, I know.

Love knows no bounds, as they say, and you are the product of our love. Please do not hate me or my memory. It gives me comfort to write these words, I wanted to tell you in person but never had the courage.

Good-bye, my love, I am sorry for everything.

Uncle Jack

She broke down and sobbed. The next letter was in her mother's hand. Like the others it had already been opened.

Dear Helen,

By the time you read this you will probably already know what I am going to tell you. But I feel I must explain in my own words. I owe it to you.

Your father and Jack suffer from bipolar disorder, as you know. The low episodes can be very severe and prolonged in this condition. When your father was in hospital in 1969, the year before you were born, Uncle Jack and I had a relationship. You will have guessed what I am going to say. Your father knows. It was terrible at first. He wanted nothing to do with me or Jack. But as his mental health improved, gradually he came round to accepting the pregnancy, and we decided to proceed as if Dad was your father. Rightly or wrongly, that is what we did.

Jack and I are both cowards. We couldn't face telling you in person. Your grandmother has written, and you will probably have read her letter.

Darling, we are not proud of what happened, but you must know that you were conceived in love.

Yours forever,

Mum

"Your father knows." These words reverberated in her head. Jack and her Grandmother implied that he didn't know. What was the truth? How should she approach her father not knowing what he knew? Should she share it with Abigail?

"Helen, supper's ready," Mat called.

She quickly bundled the letters together taking the school pages out and ran downstairs.

"What have you been doing? Mat asked.

"Oh, just going through some of Mum's things," she replied.

The children appeared and Mat served up the cottage pie.

"I'm going back down to stay with Granddad tomorrow with Abigail," she explained.

"How long will you be there?" Ben asked.

"Just 'til the weekend."

"Can we go down again and see him and Bobby?"

"Maybe on Sunday, we'll see," said Mat. Later that evening Helen told Mat about the letters.

"Goodness, that's awkward. I see your dilemma. I wonder if you shouldn't just let your father read them all. I don't know legally who they belong to now. If Jack didn't know that your mum had told your dad, that would explain your dad's rather strained relationship with his brother and Jack's oblivious reactions."

"But he always visited him in hospital. I went with him several times, especially during his last admission."

"Yes, but whenever they were with your mum you could feel the tension."

"I guess so."

"I think you'd better sleep on it. One thing's for certain, I think it's best not to tell Abigail about all this, try and catch him on his own."

Easier said than done, she thought.

Summer 2000

He managed to find his old CV. Having not worked for the past six months wouldn't look good, but he would just have to be honest. He was sweating, it was warm, and he felt claustrophobic in the flat, but he must try and persevere with this application. Then again, realistically what chance did he have? None. He'd been retired from the Post Office on health grounds, and he was just out of hospital. He tore the sheet of paper up. He thought about his trip to the river, he would do it again tomorrow and the next day. Walking through all that history, it was good for the soul and spirit. Forget jobs, just walk. Time will heal.

He lit a cigarette, resting back in his chair. Deep breathing, that's what he had to do when he felt like this. Slow deep breaths. In and out. He felt the energy drain from him. He had to escape the flat, but he also had to stay in it. What to do? The cigarette hadn't calmed his restlessness, what else could he do? He remembered he had a picture puzzle. That might do the trick. He found it and emptied all the pieces onto a tray. This would keep him occupied now 'til supper time. He put on the radio, a Chopin nocturne was playing. Gradually he felt calmer, less sweaty, the crisis had passed. He made some coffee and lit another cigarette.

His phone rang.

"Hello, is that Ian?"

"Yes, who's calling?"

"It's Jack here, do you remember me? I was on the ward with you."

Yes, he remembered, he'd liked Jack.

"Oh hello, good to hear from you, are you home now too?"

"No, but I am getting discharged on Monday and will be at the Day Hospital on Wednesday. I wondered if you would be there too?"

"Yes, I'm supposed to be going. I must say I'm not that keen, but I guess I have to go."

"Well, that's great. It will be good to see a familiar face. See you then"

"Yes, good-bye." He hung up.

It really was good news. He had spent some time talking to Jack on the ward. Finding out about his family. He would like to get to know him better, maybe they could meet up for lunch some days.

He went back to his puzzle but didn't have the concentration, so fixed his meal instead. Maybe another walk to the common before bed would be a good idea.

The Southbank was buzzing again. He walked through the Borough Market with all its lively stalls and vendors and out to the magnificent Southwark Cathedral. The mixture of Gothic, Norman and mediaeval elements had created an architectural masterpiece. He stepped inside. The glorious sound of a choir rehearsing soared up to the vaulted ceiling, the harmonies calming him. He sat, closing his eyes, letting the music soak into his soul. After a while the choir stopped, and he wandered around gazing up at the stained glass. One window depicted scenes from Shakespeare's plays. Rays of sunlight streamed in illuminating a statue of the playwright. Feeling the need for fresh air, he left the cathedral and walked past the Globe Theatre. Pavement cafés were full of people taking coffee and chatting. He stopped at one overlooking St Pauls. London really is a beautiful city, he thought. The sun was shining, with just a few fluffy white clouds in the sky. He sipped his coffee and looked at the tables around him. Next to him sat a young woman in jeans and a denim jacket. She was speaking into her phone in an agitated manner, flicking her hair back and gesticulating with her left arm. It wasn't easy to make out what she was saying, but he got the odd phrase.

"Well, you can take it or leave it then."

"I'm going to hang up now, and don't bother phoning me back."

She put the phone in her bag and called the waiter for her bill. A strange feeling came over him. He wanted to see what would happen, where she would go. So he quickly paid and just managed to see her disappear off towards the Festival Theatre. Walking quickly after her he noticed her climbing the steps to the bridge. He had to quicken his pace to keep up with her and nearly lost her in the crowds of tourists making their way down to the Tube platform.

Something made him follow her onto the train. It gave him a sense of power, of ownership. He alone could decide how far this would go. They were on a north-bound train to High Barnet, and she got off at Highgate walking down towards Crouch End. He kept a distance now. Maybe he could follow her to her house, then he would return to the South Bank. She turned into a cul-de-sac overlooking a park and stopped at a house halfway along. He kept back, fearing that she would notice him. She entered and was gone. He felt deflated but strangely excited. He felt this was wrong, but it gave him a good feeling. He turned and walked back up the hill to the station.

The Tube was crowded with people going into the centre for the day, and he couldn't get a seat. There were a lot of different languages spoken. That was something he loved about London: the multi-ethnic vibrancy. He was sure he could live nowhere else. But how easy it was to feel alone in this city. Soon he was back out in the sunshine walking towards the Festival Theatre. He would get lunch in the café there. It was busy and he had to queue for a long time, but he found a seat opposite a young family that he could watch. He browsed in the shop after lunch and then decided he would walk up to Leicester Square to catch the train home. Crossing the river, he paused to look at the view, the new and the old spires vying for attention. The greys and whites, all blended in harmony. It was a perfect vista.

He walked quickly across the bridge and up towards Covent Garden. Buskers were out in plenty there and he spent a full hour watching them all, giving money to each one. This was a great afternoon, he thought. He browsed the stalls and sat in a café for a coffee, watching the passers-by. He'd almost forgotten the woman from this morning, but a young girl in similar attire walked by jogging his memory. He got up to follow her but stopped just in time.

"Your bill Sir." The waiter was prompt.

"Thank you," he said, handing him a note.

The journey home was relatively quiet, and he felt tired when he got into his flat. He got himself a beer and collapsed in his chair. Tomorrow he would do the same, and next week. There were always new crowds, new people to follow, new feelings to experience. There was a world out there. One he couldn't touch but that was almost within reach.

They climbed the hill back from the pub. A full moon lit up the path. The alcohol had given each of them a warm glow, some respite from the worry of the day. But as they approached the house George clearly became more agitated. The air was damp and clingy and the house felt chilly when they opened the door.

"Let's have tea," Abigail said.

"Good idea," George said, making his way into the sitting room.

"I need to get off to bed, I'm exhausted," Helen said.

It was too late to light a fire, so they huddled together in their worry, holding mugs of tea. Reality surfaced, each of them in their own contemplation.

"Well, I'm off to bed." George got up to go.

The others stayed, the silence only interrupted by Bobby's snores.

Helen slept fitfully and dreamt of being trapped in a room, faces peering down at her. She was struggling to get out of a bed. She woke with a start and for a moment was disorientated. She could hear movement downstairs, so dragged herself out of bed and quickly showered.

"Morning," she greeted Greg.

"Hi there," he replied going back to his phone.

They ate in silence. A silence that was familiar and comforting. The sun was just coming up and, low in the sky, illuminated the table.

"We should take Dad into Tunbridge Wells for a change this morning. It's best to keep him occupied."

"I agree," Greg replied.

"I'm just going to phone the ward."

"I'll just get the nurse who's looking after her." The voice on the other line was sharp and officious.

"Hello, Nurse Morgan here. Dorothy had a comfortable night but she's very drowsy this morning and quite chesty. We've called the duty doctor to come and assess her."

"Oh dear, I hope she didn't need any more sedation," Helen said anxiously.

"I'm afraid she got some at 2 a.m., she was so distressed."

"My sister, Abigail, who is a GP, won't be happy about that. We'll be in later."

Helen returned to the kitchen.

"Well?"

"Not great, she's chesty and the doctor is going to examine her. I suggest we don't say anything to the others, they'll find out when we get there."

"Do you think that's a good idea? Abigail would be mad if you didn't tell her everything the nurse said."

"I guess you're right."

Abigail appeared, and Helen told her what the nurse had reported, whereupon she immediately phoned the ward again for a further update. The doctor was arranging a chest Xray straight away.

"If she's developed a pneumonia that's not good news. We won't tell Dad. The ward will need to discuss resuscitation wishes with us, they haven't done that yet, have they?" she asked Helen.

"No, not with me anyway."

"Dad, who has Power of Attorney, will need to lead this discussion. I don't look forward to it."

"Morning, Dad," Abigail said, as George walked in fully dressed and shaved. "Tea? We thought we should take a trip into Tunbridge Wells this morning for coffee. We need to get some bread and milk."

George nodded in agreement, he looked weary and sad.

"Have you phoned the ward yet?" he asked.

"Yes, she had a good night after some more sedation and she's having a chest Xray as we speak."

"Oh dear, is there a problem?"

"They just want to check on her chest post-op," Abigail explained.

After breakfast Helen took Bobby for a walk up the hill. The view from the top was up-lifting. The autumn colours shone in the sunlight. The golden bracken brushed against her legs, the mossy grass was wet with dew. She was dreading going into the ward. Pushing the thought to the back of her mind she made her way down to the house. Abigail was running towards her.

"The ward has just phoned, Mum has taken a turn for the worse and has been put on oxygen and intravenous antibiotics. We can go in any time. Oh, and Dad has just had a dizzy turn. He's OK now."

They rushed in and Abigail checked her father's pulse, he was lying on the sofa.

"Nice and steady, Dad, I'm sure it was all the stress."

He grunted. "I think we should go in and speak with the doctor."

"Yes, we'll go now."

The ward was busy, there was a big ward-round in progress with junior doctors and medical students in tow. Abigail asked if she could speak with the consultant. The nurse said she would enquire but it would likely be at the end of the ward-round. They sat in the visitors' room, all on the edge of their seats. George looked ashen.

"Let's go into the centre and get lunch after we've seen Mum," Helen suggested.

"Good idea," George replied.

There were a few old magazines on a table in the centre of the room. Greg picked one up and flicked through it. There were no windows, the air was oppressive. The anxiety they all felt rose as the nurse entered.

"Mr Smith will see you now."

A grey-haired man with half-moon glasses in a white coat came in.

"Good morning, I'm Mr Smith, the Consultant looking after Dorothy. You must be her husband?"

"Yes, and this is her son and two daughters. Thank you for taking the time to talk to us."

"How is she?" Abigail took the lead.

"I'm afraid she's got a basal pneumonia and we're treating her with high doses of penicillin. One of you is in the medical profession, is that right?"

"Yes, I'm a GP."

"She should respond in 36 hours. There are, of course, more broad spectrum antibiotics we can use if need be. I wanted to ask you about her resuscitation status. Have you Power of Attorney, as I understand she has dementia?"

"Yes, I have. And I want her resuscitated," George said firmly.

"Dad, do you think that is best, the chances of a successful outcome, should she have a cardiac arrest, are very slim."

"But she has nothing wrong with her heart," he retorted."

"Maybe we could discuss this as a family and let you know," Helen said sensibly.

"Certainly, just have a word with the nursing staff and they will write it in her notes. I should say that the surgery went very well, and her wound is healing nicely. It may be that she had the beginnings of a chest infection before she fell."

"I think that's very unlikely. She was very well the day before the accident," George said. "Can we see her now?"

"I'll just check with the nursing staff, and someone will be back to let you know."

With that he left as quickly as he had arrived.

George was in tears. "There's no way we can let them put a DNR on her records," Abigail said.

"DNR?"

"Do not resuscitate."

"No, I agree," said Greg. Helen nodded in agreement.

"That's settled then, we'll let them know."

George and Abigail went into the ward.

"Dad's just not ready to let her go," Helen said.

"No, I know. I can't blame him. It's hard to hear this being raised in such a matter-of-fact manner. This is our mother's life, for goodness sake."

"But it's a daily routine in hospital. It should have been discussed with us on admission, Abigail says."

"But that would have been a dreadful time to discuss it, so late at night."

Helen agreed. Greg was feeling very claustrophobic in the room.

"I think I'll go for a walk down the corridor. I'm not feeling so great."

"Don't be long, we must go in soon and then we can get out into the fresh air."

When Abigail and George came back Greg was outside the ward anxious to hear their news.

"She's peaceful but breathing quite rapidly," Abigail informed them. "I've let them know our decision."

Helen and Greg found Dorothy lying on her side sleeping. Helen held her hand and she stirred briefly. "Hello Mum, it's me Helen. Greg is here too. It's good that you're resting, you need to sleep. You have a chest infection that the doctors are treating with antibiotics through the drip in your arm. You will be better soon."

She thought it very unlikely that her mother would hear this, let alone take it in, but it felt the right thing to say. She wanted to stay, holding her but the nurses came to sit her up and give her a wash so they left saying they would be back later.

George didn't say a word driving into the centre of town.

"Do you fancy a Chinese, Dad?"

"No, I couldn't eat that, just a bowl of soup, I think."

They found a small coffee shop that did lunches, and waited on a table.

None of them had much appetite.

"There's not much point in us sitting for long with her is there?" Greg asked.

"Probably not," Abigail replied. "It's impossible to know if she's aware of our presence. Tomorrow will be more important, as I'm sure as she improves they will want her to mobilise."

"I'd like to stay with her a while, maybe you could leave me and come back later," George said.

"If you want Dad, but wouldn't you like to go home first for a rest?"

"No, I need to be with her just now."

They were in no doubt that he did.

"We'll pick up those groceries we need and go for a walk then and come back around three, OK?"

"Fine, yes."

Driving back to the hospital, Helen thought how unreal this all seemed. Back and forth to the ward. It was as if time had stopped for them. She felt completely detached from the world and her day-to-day life.

They dropped George at the entrance and watched him walk in, his shoulders stooped, he looked a shadow of his former self.

"We should have a discussion about future care for Mum now," Greg said, "I think you put it succinctly the other day when you said the choice was between a nursing home or employing a nurse at home, and we have to take Dad's wishes into account."

"Indeed, he should have the final say, and I bet he'll say he can cope. But it's early days and we don't know how she'll be when they want to discharge her," Helen said.

"Well, I've done some investigations. St Mary's nursing home would be £950 a week, and a local nursing agency in the town here, Special Care, would cost £1100 for a live-in nurse, again per week."

"I'm not sure Dad would want a stranger in the house, but I don't think he's ready to let her go into care. It's so difficult."

Abigail had been silent until now. "It's impractical for any of us to take a role in her care but I feel Dad is close to breaking point, as you know. So we must discuss this with him sooner rather then later."

They agreed. Helen knew that financially her Father could cope with either option. She herself would prefer the live-in nurse providing they got the right person. There would have to be a team of them to provide night shifts, weekly relief, and holiday cover. It would be a huge adjustment for her father, but she was sure he would cope. To have someone there at night would surely reassure him, so he could get a good night's sleep.

They were back in town now and found a parking spot near the Pantiles.

"Let's walk and get some coffee," Helen said. "Where is St Mary's Nursing Home? Do you think we could visit?"

"It's up near Camden Park. Shall we give them a ring?"

"Good idea."

Greg was on his phone, he had clearly looked up the site before. He was soon speaking to someone. "Right, we'll come up in half an hour then, thank you."

"Great, it will give us an idea anyway, and we could put her name down on the waiting list. There's no harm in that, people must come off the list all the time."

They grabbed a coffee to go and the groceries they needed and walked back to the car.

"Look, it's right there on the left. You drive in here."

The smell hit them as soon as they walked in the door. They signed in at the office and waited for the person in charge. A smart, rather brusque middle-aged woman approached.

"Hello, my name is Mrs Wyllie, welcome to St Mary's. Is this for your mother or father?"

"Mother. She is in hospital at the moment with a fractured femur and chest infection. She also has dementia."

"I see. We have a dementia wing here which is secure and staffed with highly trained nurses. Would you like to see it?"

"Yes, that would be good, thank you."

She led the way down a yellow painted corridor with black and white photographs of 40's film stars. There was a battered old piano in a small sitting area. Two residents were fast asleep.

"A lot of our residents sleep at this time of day, after lunch. We have activities from 10 a.m. to 12 noon and again from 3 p.m. to 5p.m. Visiting is any time for family. Here we are."

They had reached locked doors. Mrs Wyllie used her pass to get in and the door clanged behind them. The corridor was no longer carpeted. There was a woman approaching them, thin and gaunt looking with frightened eyes, mumbling to herself.

"Hello, Grace," she touched her arm gently. They walked to the day area. Nothing could have prepared them for what they saw there, and the smell was overpowering. Residents were seated around the room on plastic covered chairs, some asleep, one or two rocking back and forth, one shouting out constantly. Two carers were lifting one woman from her chair into a wheelchair. Helen found it impossible to imagine her mother amongst these poor souls.

"As you can see, most of these residents have quite advanced dementia. Some of them would have been in the other wing for a while before they came here. That would probably be more appropriate for your mother."

Abigail was interested in the staff to patient ratio and how many nurses were on duty at any one time. She was invited into the office to speak with the nurse in charge.

"Is this the first nursing home you've looked at?" Mrs Wyllie asked.

"Yes, and of course our father will need to visit. We think he'll be very reluctant to let her go."

"Yes, that is a common problem with spouses. But sometimes they struggle on for too long and their health suffers."

"Can we see the dining room and one of the bedrooms?"

"Of course, come this way. We only have a couple of en-suite bedrooms, but as most of our residents need help with toileting that doesn't seem to be a problem."

The dining room was bleak. Formica-topped tables and a window overlooking a small courtyard and then a brick wall. The bedroom was simple and sparse, a soft toy on the bed, a family photo on the chest of drawers. Again, that smell and yellow painted walls. Greg took his pocket handkerchief and blew his nose loudly.

Abigail reappeared.

"Well, thank you for showing us round Mrs Wyllie. Could we put our mother's name on the waiting list?" Abigail said. Helen gave her a glare.

"Don't you think we should wait until Dad has visited?"

"There's no harm in putting your mother's name on the list. You can always phone if you want it removed. There are quite a few names on the list already, however."

They walked back to the main part of the home. It seemed immediately more homely and comfortable. There were a few residents walking in the corridors now and two having a conversation. Helen felt more relaxed. Mrs Wyllie took their details and saw them out.

"Goodness, we must get back to the ward, it's nearly 3 o'clock. I do think you were a bit premature putting her name on the list. It feels as though we've sealed her fate."

"Nonsense, it's realistic. She is only going to deteriorate, we need to be pragmatic."

Greg had been silent during the whole visit, he was shell-shocked.

"I can't help thinking that having her stay in her own home is a kinder way to go," he said.

Helen drove fast to get to the hospital. Abigail went in to join her father.

"That was a difficult experience," Greg said.

"Yes, we're not used to seeing so many frail elderly together. It's frightening to think we are all going there."

"What do you mean?"

"We all have to go through that stage of life when our faculties fail, it's inevitable, unless illness takes us earlier."

"Of course, I just don't need to think about it just now."

Their father appeared looking very drawn.

"The nurses say she's a little better this afternoon, but she's hardly opened her eyes and has taken very few sips of water."

"Don't worry, Dad, she's on a drip so will be getting fluids. I'll go in."

"Don't be long, I'm ready to go home now."

Dorothy was lying more propped up and had a high colour in her cheeks. Her breathing still seemed rapid, her lips were dry. Abigail came back from the office.

"They need to start mouth care as she's not taking anything by mouth," she said. "I've just told the nurse. It's basic nursing care. They are so busy filling out forms in there."

New patients kept arriving, it was hardly surprising there was a lot of paperwork to do, Helen thought.

"We'd better let Greg come in and see her, Dad is desperate to get home, he's shattered."

"Of course."

Abigail left, and shortly afterwards Greg appeared.

Hello, Mum, it's Greg and Helen here," she said, "can you open your eyes and see us?"

She opened her eyes and smiled, it was a heart-warming moment. She gave a fruity cough. "That's good, Mum, you have a good cough. We need to get your chest better."

"Where am I?" Her voice was feeble.

Again, Helen explained patiently: Dorothy was too weak to struggle, too exhausted to shout out.

"Would you like to see Dad, he's outside?"

"Yes."

Greg went to get him. The joy on his face when he saw her smile was heart-warming. Helen brushed back a tear.

"We have to go now, my love, but we'll see you in the morning. I'm sure you'll be feeling better then. Just have a little drink before we go." She took a sip.

They left, glancing back to see that she had drifted off to sleep again.

"Well, I think she's on the mend, I can't wait to get her home."

She looked older. There were bags under her eyes. Her grey hair was neatly tied back, and her posture looked more stooped. She wore a smart pair of trousers and a navy tailored jacket and carried a tan handbag. He wouldn't have recognised her in the street, but her smile was the same and her eyes were kind.

"I'm so sorry I haven't been in touch for so long. David has been ill, and we've been going through a very rough patch."

There was always an excuse, though this seemed a genuine one.

"I'm so sorry to hear that. What's been the problem?"

"Oh, he's been having tests for back pain and weight loss. A scan has shown cancer in the bones, but they don't know the site of the primary so don't know what to treat him with."

Cathy was a radiographer at St Thomas's hospital.

"My goodness, how is he in himself?"

"Remarkably, he's keeping his spirits up, I think he's actually doing better than me."

They were sitting in an Italian restaurant just off the Common.

"But how are you doing?"

"Not too bad. I'm trying to get voluntary work in the Mind charity shop in the High Street. My befriender, Greg, is doing a reference for me."

"Excellent. Are you getting out much?"

"Every day, walking at least, occasionally going into the centre. I go to the local library regularly, too. The other day Greg took me down to Kent as he had to visit an estate agent, so we had a very good chat in the car. Oh, and yesterday I went to Brighton and met a very nice man in the restaurant who walked along the front with me."

"You seem to be a lot better than when I last saw you."

"I've been off medication for a while but have restarted it this week as I thought I was slipping again. It's so difficult to judge. I want to plan a holiday to Spain."

"Do you think that's wise?"

"It wouldn't be 'til next year."

Cathy looked down. Who knew what next year would bring for her?

"David and I are thinking of going to the Festival Hall to an orchestral concert, would you like me to get you a ticket?"

"I'd like that very much."

"Good, there are concerts on Tuesday and Thursday next week."

"Thursdays is a better evening for me, I'm going to start going to a club on Tuesdays to play cards and the like."

"OK, then I'll let you know. We'd better get the bill."

They emerged from the restaurant into bright sunshine.

"Let's walk on the Common. I don't have to get back to work for an hour, I've taken an extended lunch break."

The leaves were falling fast now, gently floating down in the breeze. The air was crisp and fresh. The dappled sunlight through the trees danced on the path. He felt relieved to have met her after all this time. How could he support her through the months ahead?

"It will be good to see David again, it's been a very long time."

"You'll see a huge change in him."

"We've all changed, but we're still the same, with the same needs and fears."

"He doesn't fear death, he told me. The process of dying, yes, but not being dead. He's read a lot about it since his diagnosis. I don't know how he can. It's as if it makes him feel more in control, as if understanding death helps you to cope with life."

Feeling in control is critical to coping with all life events, he thought. That's one thing that was so hard about his illness. He became so incapacitated that feeling in control was impossible.

"I can understand that," he said, though he wasn't sure that he really did.

"I've forgotten to ask how Juliet is." Juliet was married to a South African lawyer and lived in Cape Town.

"She's very well, but dreadfully worried about her Dad, of course. She hopes to come home soon. I don't know how she can live in South Africa."

"It would be really great to see her again."

"Yes, we must have you over when she's here."

Cathy was basically a very generous woman. She was frightened of mental illness, that was the problem. Frightened it would hit her one day as it had her father and brother. She had run away from them both when they were suffering. David, on the other hand, had always been a difficult man, quick tempered and intolerant. Ian wondered what his mental state was like facing death. Cathy had painted a positive picture of it, but he was still apprehensive about meeting him.

They were reaching the other end of the Common now. Joggers and dog walkers were crossing their path. A child was crying. He suddenly turned to her.

"Thank you so much for coming over today, you don't know how much this has meant to me."

She gave him a hug. "I'd best get the Tube now. I'll give you a ring about the concert."

She turned and walked briskly away.

What had brought about this change in her affections? Was it David's prognosis? Was it guilt? Unlikely after all these years. In any event it didn't matter, he was looking forward to the concert.

It was a glorious afternoon now, almost warm. He walked to the library. He would look up the Festival Hall concerts coming up. He wondered if he'd see Phyllis. He walked leisurely, could the pills already be having an effect? The change in him was quite remarkable. Back in the library he discovered that Sir Simon Rattle was performing next week, he hoped Cathy would get tickets for one of his concerts. On the Thursday it was Mahler and Shostakovich. Not an easy programme, but he knew Mahler was one of Simon Rattle's favourite composers so it would be good. He thought he would check out what was on at the Globe and the National Theatre and discuss that with Cathy, she may be up for some regular theatre visits.

He felt a tap on his shoulder. It was Phyllis.

"Do you fancy a cup of tea?"

"How are you doing?" she asked, as they settled into a corner of the museum café.

"Well, thank you, and you?"

"I'm very excited, my daughter is coming home in November for a month."

"Oh, that's wonderful, will she be staying with you all the time?"

"Probably not but most of the time, apparently her husband is taking unpaid leave to look after the children. I hope things are alright between them. It's all rather strange."

He looked down and took another sip of his tea. It was getting darker outside.

"I do hope so. Have they been together long?"

"About ten years. It took a while for them to conceive, which was a strain."

He wanted to change the subject, but she obviously needed to talk.

"Of course I haven't been able to help them with the children and they have no other grandparents. That's been another strain, but one that lots of couples have to live with, of course."

"Of course," he muttered.

He was out of his comfort zone and needed to get away.

"I'm afraid I must go, hope to see you again soon." He rather hoped he wouldn't.

She looked disappointed. "Yes, I'm sure we'll bump into each other here."

He took a printout of the concert programme and left. It was cooler outside now, a definite chill in the air. He decided to text Cathy.

Thanks again for lunch. I was so sorry to hear of David's illness, but look forward to seeing you both next week. Incidentally, there is a very good concert on next Thursday with Sir Simon Rattle if you can get tickets.

Her reply came immediately.

Agree, good to catch up. Will try for tickets, sounds good. X

Their conversation came back to him. Facing certain death in the near future must be a terrifying experience, he thought. He recalled times when he had looked death in the face and turned back from the brink. He always thought of the effect it would have on his loved ones. He'd saved his pills as a teenager and drunk half a bottle of vodka one night planning on taking the lot. Something stopped him, something his mother said. He came out of that dark tunnel and climbed slowly back to health. Again in his twenties it happened. He'd no idea what the trigger was but not getting on with Carole must have contributed. He was sinking then, unable to help himself. Carole had no idea how to deal with it and walked away. It was the last straw. He remembered that bleak evening, alone in his flat, again taking alcohol to give him courage. He had his belt, it would be an easy thing to secure it to the top of a door. Then he stopped. Was this the ultimate in cowardice? No one would miss him, or so he thought. He'd had a choice in the matter, David had none. He felt ashamed and weak. Each time it had happened he'd been admitted. His longest spell in hospital had been twelve months. So much of his life wasted. He'd tried, really tried to stop going down but it always hit him with a sledgehammer, out of the blue usually, and he rapidly lost insight. He stopped washing, had difficulty feeding himself, became a recluse.

These were dark thoughts and were lowering his mood. He remembered them from time to time but let them pass by. This time felt different, he was able to get out, the sunshine was helping. His encounters with strangers too. His contact with Greg and Cathy. It was good to keep numbering the positives. Tomorrow he was getting his reference from Greg, he would then take his CV down to the shop. These were the tasks for the day.

They were driving through the Sussex countryside. It was misty and cold. They could barely make out the cars ahead. Abigail hadn't said a word. Helen decided she must break the ice.

"I looked at the letters late last night. Mum kept some pages from our school jotters that are priceless, I've brought them down to give Dad a laugh."

"What about the other letters?"

"Oh, some are addressed to me and wouldn't interest you. There are several I haven't read yet. I'll let you see them in due course, don't worry."

"Let's stop here for a coffee and pick up something for lunch." She pulled into a farm shop.

The smell of home baking was warm and comforting. They got home-made quiche, salad and cheese scones and a bottle of apple juice. The coffee was strong.

"I know when you're hiding something," Abigail said.

"What do you mean?"

"I can tell by the way you talk about the letters. There's something you don't want Dad or me to see."

She couldn't lie.

"I'll tell you when I'm ready. It's about me and no-one else. Certainly not you and Greg. It's difficult for me. You must be patient."

This seemed to placate her.

"OK, but I'll keep asking."

They paid and left. Helen felt relieved they had discussed the letters. She could look forward to the day now.

"How are you coping, Abigail?" she asked.

"With difficulty I'm afraid. The evenings are the worst part of the day. Somehow loneliness seems worse on going to bed. I'm going to start some evening classes."

"Shall we suggest we take Dad away for a few days? I wondered about Scotland."

"Good idea, let's sound him out." They slipped back into a reticent silence.

As they neared the house the mist cleared and the sun broke through the clouds.

George greeted them at the door, his portly figure standing proud. He was clean-shaven and looking smart. His face looked thinner, and he had a high colour, probably due to the alcohol, Abigail thought.

"Lovely to see you both," he beamed.

"We've brought food for lunch but thought we'd go out this evening."

"Splendid." He seemed on good form.

There was an old shoebox on the coffee table.

"I thought we'd go through some old photographs."

Memories, Helen thought, he's hanging on to memories, that's a good thing. Sharing memories, even better. She wondered how he'd react, though, seeing photographs of Dorothy. She knew he couldn't cope with memories when she was alive, but now he wanted to remember her as she had been in her prime.

"Oh look, there we all are in France, do you remember that camping holiday?"

Helen and Abigail certainly did, the long drives across Europe, packing up the enormous tent every three days. Her parents arguing and the three of them squabbling in the back of the car. They'd had fun, though, and the photograph showed them all smiling by a lakeside. Dorothy looked tanned and healthy.

There were more photos of their holidays, bringing back evocative smells and sounds and even tastes.

Breakfast outside, bacon cooking, the French bread, the smell of the canvas, the noise of water lapping on the shore of a lake. They were transported back into their pasts. The circuitry in their brains firing to release these sensations all stimulated by visual images.

After the holiday photographs there were several of them as babies and toddlers. Their parents looked so young and vigorous.

"Here's Helen as a baby," George said. Helen was shocked, her father was holding her and looking directly at the camera, but his face looked drawn, not content but stressed. He was not himself, she could tell. She quickly picked up another photo of her mother with them as three young children.

"There are more boxes in the attic," George said, "and all the albums of course. Too much to do in one sitting. Oh, here's one of Jack. How well he looks."

He was holding Helen, again as a small baby.

"I think that was your christening, Helen."

Helen took a deep breath. Her father looked long and hard at this photo. Was he trying to communicate something?

"There is an album of all your christenings and confirmations somewhere," he said. Her father had for years been a member of the local congregation, but over recent years had stopped going. Had he lost his faith? She had no idea.

Abigail was absorbed in the photographs. "Maybe we could look at some more this evening, let's go for a walk now."

Emerging into the sunshine they were hit with the present. Smells of falling leaves, the sounds of the birds, the breeze in the trees. But each of them was back in the past, deep in thought. They walked up the hill, Bobby foraging on ahead.

"What a beautiful day." George was breathless but exhilarated.

The remnants of the mist hung low on the plain behind them. The air was crisp and clear.

They took the path down towards the church, the hedgerows becoming taller and full of brambles.

Helen wondered if her father would visit the grave.

"I walk here every day," he said, "and put fresh flowers on her grave every few days. It's good to talk to her."

Helen was pleased he lived so close and could do this. I'm sure it helps the grieving process, she thought. He was doing well, working his way through it, making a big effort, probably for their sakes. They were approaching her grave, George held out his hands to them both.

"Help me over this ground, it's difficult getting close to her. I sometimes want to run away. Each day it seems as if I'm seeing her name on the gravestone for the first time. That it's becoming real and not one long horrendous nightmare." He was crying now.

"Oh Dad," she said, giving him a hug, "it's good to cry." She was weeping too.

Abigail bent down and picked a couple of dead roses out of the bunch. "We'll go and get some flowers after lunch, I'd like to come back with them tomorrow."

George seemed reluctant to leave. "Come on, Dad, let's get home now."

They made their way out of the graveyard and back up to the house.

"I think this house is too big for me really, but I can't imagine moving away from her. How would I get here every day, especially when I won't be able to drive?"

They didn't know how to reply to this.

"I think you're right about the house, Dad. You know Greg looked into flats that are supported? Well, he went to see an estate agent the other day in Tunbridge Wells and there is one available we could go and see. It would give you an idea of what is available. Greg is coming down on Friday, shall I give him a call and he can see if he could arrange it?"

"Don't move too fast, I don't think I'm ready yet."

"There's no harm in looking."

"I suppose not, but I'm not promising I'll agree."

"Absolutely, Dad." Abigail was delighted.

After lunch, while George was sleeping, Helen phoned Greg. A viewing on Friday was arranged easily. They spent the afternoon sorting out Dorothy's wardrobe. It was hard to immerse themselves in all her scents and fragrances, looking at outfits that brought important family events to mind. There was the pale blue dress she had worn at the birthday lunch party on the lawn, the pink two-piece she had worn at Abigail's wedding. It was a huge wardrobe, she had loved her clothes. There were drawers to sort, too.

"Which charity shop do you want us to take them to, Dad?"

"There is one for The Alzheimer's Society in Southborough in the north of Tunbridge Wells I think - check it out. I don't want to see you loading the car up, I'll go and read in the sitting room."

Once they'd put all the black sacs in the car and had a coffee they set off to Tunbridge Wells, leaving George looking through more photographs. He had put an

Opera CD on, Puccini's Tosca. It had been one of Dorothy's favourites. They had both loved Opera. Playing it was bound to be painful for him, but he clearly felt a need to connect with his grief for her through the music.

"This is the hard bit, getting rid of the belongings," Abigail said.

The charity shop was busy. The elderly woman behind the counter was grateful. Helen wondered if she'd had personal experience of dementia.

"It's hard to think of all those rails of dead people's clothes," Abigail said as they left the shop. "All that personal history displayed, made public. Part of me wanted to take Mum's stuff and burn it. The thought of someone walking around in her clothes makes me feel very uncomfortable."

"Better to raise money for the charity. That's what Mum would have wanted."

They picked up some roses at a nearby florist and headed back home.

Helen was rather dreading looking at more photographs that evening. She also wanted desperately to speak to her father on her own, but couldn't see a way how she could do this. Maybe Abigail could be persuaded to take Bobby for his afternoon walk.

George was still fast asleep when they got back.

"We'd better wake him up or he'll not sleep tonight. Do you fancy taking Bobby out and I'll make Dad some tea?"

Abigail, rather reluctantly, called Bobby and headed out. "I'll go to the grave with the roses on the way back."

"Dad here's a cuppa," she said, gently touching his shoulder.

When he had come to she sat directly in front of him, her heart pounding.

"Dad, I read some of those letters from Jack and Mum. Have you read them?"

"Yes, Helen, I have, some of them anyway. Your mother told me before you were born. I have always known. We decided not to tell Jack that I knew. Maybe that was a mistake in the light of what happened. I think it was a burden he bore all his life. But for me your birth was a healing process. I had been very depressed the whole year before, and the joy you brought was indescribable. We were a very happy family."

Helen knew that he was only remembering the good parts. She had always known there was a lot of tension between her parents.

She was puzzled, her grandmother had said in her letter that her father knew nothing of her mother's intention to tell her upon her death. How long had he known about these other letters?

"I don't know what to say." She started to weep.

" There's no need to say anything." He got up and put his arms around her. "You are and will always be my daughter. I had to watch Jack worship you without saying anything. He showered you with gifts and held you at every possibility. I did it for your mother, for our marriage. When Abigail and Greg were born we were both too busy to think about it. Then there were the times when I was ill again. Those were the most stressful for your mother. As far as I know their relationship ended soon after you were born, but I know Jack loved your mother dearly. During his last admission I took her in to visit him. He could not take his eyes off her. He was the same with you when I visited with you. I felt as if I was sharing you both with him. It was very hard. Then when he took his own life, we all felt so guilty. Could we have done more, should we have talked about it?"

"But Dad, you know it was his illness that made him do it. You couldn't have prevented it."

"No, I guess you're right, I've nearly been there myself on more than one occasion."

This shocked and worried her.

They heard the back door.

"Now, not a word about this to Abigail or Greg, this is just between us? OK."

"Of course," she replied.

"I'm afraid Bobby is awfully muddy, we went up a farm track. Have you got a towel I can clean him with, Dad?"

"Yes, in the utility room behind the door."

"Remember, not a word. Will you destroy those letters?" He whispered.

"If you want me to."

"Yes, I think it's for the best, I don't want anyone else seeing them."

Helen was emotionally exhausted. Right now, she needed Mat more than ever. He knew about the letters, and she could trust him. At least she didn't have to bear this burden alone.

"Any idea where we're eating tonight?" Abigail breezed in.

"What about the Black Bull, it's only a thirty-minute drive from here."

"Fine, let's go early before it gets too busy."

Helen phoned Mat, "I've just spoken to Dad. He knew about the letters. He's very composed and we're going to look at old photographs tonight. I could do with you being here."

"I wish I could be with you, but I think you have to spend the next few days with your family. Just try and relax. I'm sure you'll be OK."

The Black Bull was another cosy old pub with oak beams and roaring fires. They took a table opposite one of them and ordered drinks.

"So, we'll look at albums when we get home shall we?" Abigail asked.

George shot Helen a glance before replying, "Yes, I'd like that."

"Greg will be here on Friday and we're going to take a look at that flat. What would you like to do tomorrow, Dad?"

"Go to the coast, I think, Deal maybe, there's a good pub there with delicious fish."

"Good idea, Deal it is."

Pouring over the albums later Helen was amazed how unemotional her Father was. Even looking at the christening photographs when her Uncle was holding her. How was he so controlled when she wanted to scream? There were so many of her and Jack and so few of her and George. Abigail didn't remark on this but to Helen it seemed so obvious.

"Did Mum make the albums, Dad?" she asked.

"Oh yes, she always loved that job. She did it very well too, I think, don't you?"

He shot her another glance and smiled.

Suddenly he got animated and rushed out of the room. He returned a few moments later with some small pocket albums.

"These are the ones I made to take into St Mary's. She loved pouring over them, but of course latterly she couldn't recognise you all. I tried to concentrate on the ones when you were primary school age, one of the happiest times."

He was speaking quickly now. Helen thought he had slept too long that afternoon. He seemed a little high. She remembered one doctor telling her that hypomania or mania could occur after stressful life events such as bereavement. She hoped it wasn't happening now, she didn't think she could cope with her father being ill at the moment.

"This is my favourite one of you all, look, on Eastbourne beach. Oh, and this one."

He was lost in his memories.

"Oh, do you remember this birthday when we had the water chute in the garden?" He laughed. "How much fun we had. I must show Greg these."

Suddenly she remembered the jotter sheets she'd brought down and went to get them.

"Look, Dad, Mum kept these, have a read, they're hilarious."

There was one of Helen's, written when she was six, referring to Greg as 'her bibby'. They roared with laughter. It was a good note to end on.

"I think I'm off to bed now," she said, getting up.

"Don't you want a nightcap?"

"No, I'll take a cup of tea up with me and read, that usually does the trick. Now don't be late, we must be up early tomorrow to make the most of the day. Good night." She gave him a kiss as she left.

When she was on the landing later, she heard him chuckling to himself. She'd no idea when he came to bed as she was out like a light.

Summer 2000

On the Sunday he took the Tube to St Pauls. He wanted to go to a service. There was a board outside, mattins was at 10.15, he had half an hour to wait. It was years since he had been to church. He had been in the church choir as a youth and hated it, but he always liked to hear the choir in St Pauls with its amazing acoustic. There were throngs of people walking up the steps, hurrying to get the best seats. He got lost in them, carried along by their fervour. He managed to get a seat near the front where he could see the choir boys. For an hour he was wrapped up in the service, listening to the chanting, not concentrating on the words, hearing the boy soprano voices drift up to the dome above. He was transported. It was hard to leave when it was over, he lingered in the side aisle until most people had left.

He decided to walk to Tower bridge and back along the Southbank. It was a glorious morning, clear blue sky and not a breath of wind. He would take lunch near the Borough Market, the noise, smells and bright colours of the market always uplifted his senses and mood. Unfortunately, the market was closed, so he took a seat outside Southwark Cathedral. The gulls were circling overhead and one swooped close to him. Children were running around the garden chasing pigeons. He felt alive. He was too hot, so he removed his jacket. His old tattered shirt embarrassed him, but no-one was looking at him. He was the one who was watching. The children were rounded up by their parents and he was left watching the birds. An empty feeling welled up inside him. Southwark Cathedral coffee shop was open, he would take lunch there. Warm baking smells drifted past him as he collected his soup and scone and sat outside at the back of the cathedral. The bells were tolling. Sunday lunchtime, a time for families to gather round roast dinners. Gatherings that were alien to him. He needed to walk again, and decided to take the Southbank all the way to Westminster and the Tate beyond. Looking at some of Turner's paintings would be a good thing to do. He set off with a brisk step, finding himself behind the family with the small children. One of them dropped a soft toy. He bent to retrieve it and handed it to the mother.

"Thanks so much."

"My pleasure," he replied smiling. She smiled back showing perfect teeth. They moved on and he sped up, so as to keep them in sight. As the bank opened up the family stopped by a street entertainer juggling, so he stopped to watch too. He could hear the children's squeals of delight. Further on they stopped again at one of the frozen statues sitting apparently on thin air.

"How does he do that, Mummy?" The little girl asked.

"Oh, it's magic," she replied.

"I want some of that magic."

He smiled silently. It was wonderful to hear the voices of children, their innocence and fun. He felt a huge draw to this family, but soon let them disappear into the crowds as he did himself. Once again, he had connected with someone if only for a minute. Now he was an anonymous Londoner. One who had to go to a Psychiatric day hospital and take lots of medication. Not one of the successful healthy ones with fancy kitchens, perfect children, and pristine teeth but one of life's drifters, unconnected, at sea on the world.

Art, he would take solace in art, and where better to start than Turner. Turner was, above all, the artist who had had fantastic visions of nature with all its grandeur.

He would transport him from the present into a world of light, beauty and colour. The Tate was very quiet, so he could sit and gaze at the canvases for several minutes at a time. He felt calm, although the paintings often had a sense of urgency and movement. He felt the rush of the wind and the crashing of the waves particularly in The Shipwreck. He couldn't help feeling he was one of those men clinging to the boat in the storm. He gazed at the skies and the swell of the sea. How they merged into one. The tumult reflected his mental state when he was ill. He needed a calmer canvas to finish with. He found some of Turner's paintings of Venice. He had been to Venice when he backpacked around Europe. He remembered it as a city of light and reflection. Once you escaped to the back canals you could lose yourself in its watery atmosphere with churches containing Titian's and Tintoretto's paintings. He sat looking at Turner's views, transported back to the vistas he had seen all those years ago. There was something calming about a gallery, it was a great leveller. Everyone was in awe of the power of art. The power to surprise, the power to shock, the power to still the soul, the power to arouse, the power to distil life's wonders into a single image. Sustained by the beauty he had just seen he walked quickly through some of the other rooms, but nothing moved him as Turner's paintings had done. He browsed in the bookshop. He was tempted by a book with illustrations of the Turner collection, but decided coming back to see them regularly was the better option.

Heading outside he blinked in the bright sunlight. It was even warmer, and he needed a drink. He found a pavement café and ordered a mineral water. The passers-by walked languidly. Maybe it was the heat, or maybe they were sluggish after their lunch. His eyes closed and he found himself drifting off to sleep. In that short moment he felt himself drowning, falling through the waves deep into the ocean.

"Excuse me, Sir, your bill." The waiter startled him.

"Thank you, keep the change."

He needed to walk again, walking was his lifeline, it would rescue him from the deep.

The walk along the embankment again lifted his spirits. The sunlight was twinkling on the river, the buildings opposite were in soft focus as if in haze from the heat. A group of people walked towards him gesticulating and talking loudly. He caught a sentence, "You have to see the Manet exhibition in the National, it's exceptional." Manet was not one of his favourite artists but maybe this was something for another day. He would ask Jack if he fancied a trip to the National with him.

He was suddenly transported back to the present. Tomorrow he would have to be up early to make his way to the day hospital. He was apprehensive about going. Surely walking like this through galleries was better for recovery and integration back into normal life? What was normal for him though? He had come so far from normality; it seemed impossible to get back. He was better walking the streets of London, with the dust of the city in the soles of his shoes, than sitting talking to someone about how he felt. The sun beat down on his back, the warmth giving him sustenance.

He walked back over Westminster bridge dodging the tourists with their cameras. Open-topped buses clattered past. He stopped halfway across to take in the view. Suddenly his phone rang.

"Is that Ian? Paul here, you're remembering our outing on Tuesday, I hope."

"Yes, twelve noon, is it?"

"Yes, that will be fine, see you then at the flat."

He rang off.

Perfect, another trip into the city, and with someone this time. Looking forward to it would sustain him during the difficult day ahead. He moved on, a light breeze had picked up which was a great relief, everyone was looking hot and flustered. It was time to head back to the flat and his solitude.

Late summer 2004

Over the course of the next few days Dorothy gradually improved until she was sitting out of bed and tentatively taking a few steps. Her chest infection was clearing with the penicillin and her appetite was returning. George was delighted, but he had completely unrealistic expectations of his ability to cope with her at home. Reluctantly he was coming round to a spell of convalescence and rehabilitation at a nursing home.

The ward sister spoke with Abigail about the options, one of which was St Mary's.

"We have been to see St Mary's and liked it." Abigail said, forgetting the scenes in the dementia unit.

The problem was they all had their lives to lead, jobs to do. They had to leave George to manage this transition, and he was shattered.

"We'll come down at weekends until she's settled, Dad," Helen reassured him.

"I really want to take her home, and she keeps asking when she's coming home. What am I going to tell her? She'll never forgive me for this."

"You have to say that she needs more rehabilitation with nurses who have the skills that we don't have," Abigail said.

George wasn't convinced Dorothy would even understand let alone accept this, nonetheless he nodded, looking defeated.

By the time the ward was ready to discharge her a bed at St Mary's became available and she was duly moved there. Helen, Abigail and Greg were back in London but planned to come down on the Friday.

George was delighted to see them all.

"She seems to have settled in OK. I don't like the place, but I guess it's alright as these places go. She's so confused now, she has no idea where she is or what's happened to her."

"She's in the best place just now, Dad," Greg said.

It was pouring with rain when they arrived at the home the next day. Mrs Wyllie greeted them, "Good to see you again. You do realise that your mother is only with us temporarily as convalescence after her admission."

George was puzzled, he would challenge them later. "How is she?"

"Doing well. Her walking is coming on, though she does have a habit of taking off without her Zimmer."

"That would be Mum," Greg said, smiling.

"We have to watch her carefully so that she doesn't fall again."

"Of course. How do you manage at night?"

"We have to use the bed sides to prevent her getting out of bed unfortunately. She calls out as she's not able to master the buzzer."

Oh, the indignity of it all, Helen thought.

Mrs Wyllie led them into the day room. Dorothy was sitting, her eyes closed, with a few other ladies in the corner of the room.

"You have visitors, Dorothy," Mrs Wyllie announced. Dorothy looked up and a huge beam spread across her face.

"Oh, have you come to take me home? How wonderful."

Helen felt her eyes watering.

"I'm afraid not, Mum, you still need these wonderful nurses to help you walk. Dad couldn't manage that and the bathing at the moment."

"Well, I hope I get home soon, this place is dreadful, where is it? Am I in hospital?"

"No, you're in a nursing home for convalescence," George said, clearly upset.

"Why did Mrs Wyllie say it was good to see you again? Have you been here before? What's going on?"

"We did look round here when she was in hospital, thinking it would be a good place for so-called step-down care Dad."

"Why didn't you discuss it with me?"

"You were so worried about Mum at the time we thought it would just add to your distress," Abigail said.

"Well, I would have thought you would have told me before our visit here today," George retorted.

Dorothy was listening, "what are you talking about, why are you cross?"

"Nothing, my love. I think Helen has some photos to show you."

Helen dug in her bag and produced an envelope containing photos of Polly and Ben, some recent, a few when they were younger.

"Who are these children?"

"Polly and Ben, my children. Polly's nine and Ben's seven. You saw them on your birthday. They will be down to visit next weekend."

"What, will I be here next weekend? I want go home, please take me home, George, please."

This was too much for George. Fortunately, the tea trolley appeared, and they were all offered a cup. They declined saying they would leave and visit her again the next day. She was distracted by her tea as they slipped away. Abigail couldn't resist going back to glance at her. Dorothy was, once again, sitting with her eyes closed, quite still and calm as if the visit hadn't happened.

"The sooner I get her home the better."

"With your permission, Dad, I'd like to speak to Mum's GP to see if he will have an input into managing her discharge home and maybe setting up some support for you."

"Yes, that seems like a good idea, Abigail, thank you."

"There are loads of things to think of, for example Mum couldn't manage the stairs at the moment so she'll either have to sleep downstairs or stay upstairs. A stairlift is another possibility, but will take weeks to get sorted."

It seemed such a mountain to climb.

They were sitting in a tea shop near the Pantiles.

"I'll phone the GP straight away. He should have been notified of her transfer to St Mary's."

"Can we get a full-time nurse in for when she gets home, and move her bed downstairs. I'm sure the nurse could wash her, and we might be able to arrange private physio for stair practice," Greg said. A nurse at home had always been his preferred option. "If you like I'll look into it."

Helen needed a role. "I can sort out the freezer and make sure there are a lot of meals ready prepared."

"What would I do without you all," George sighed.

Abigail came back from phoning the GP. "I've made an appointment for tomorrow, I thought I'd take Dad in to explain the caring situation."

"Good idea."

"I don't believe this is all happening," he was wringing his hands, "Oh Dorothy, Dorothy."

They quickly left and holding onto him Abigail walked him back to the car.

"We'll get home now and relax in front of the fire. Don't worry Dad, we'll sort this."

Helen felt a huge burden weighing down on her shoulders. She wanted to scream, how could this be happening, what had her mother done to deserve this? How were they going to get through the next few months, the next year? Tears blurred her vision and coursed down her cheeks, a river of apprehension. She had to hide her weeping from her father. Quickly she brushed away the tears and pulled away from the car park. She made a mental note to herself that she would write a living will. It was just too painful to think of her children having to face this in the future. Who knows what the future will bring, what sorrows and cares we will have to bear, she thought. Being there for each other was helping them get through this. They would get through it.

Greg was waiting for him in the library coffee shop.
"Here you are, Ian. I hope that it's OK." He handed him
an envelope. He took out the sheet of paper.

Character reference for Ian Soames. 25/03/44

To whom it may concern
I have known Ian Soames for the past three years in a
professional capacity. I have befriended him following
his episode of depression.
He has proven himself to be an honest, diligent, polite,
and relatively cheerful gentleman who has become more
a friend than a client. In his job as manager of a Post
Office sorting room he had ten people he was
responsible for. He enjoyed his work, and it was only a
bout of illness that forced him to retire five years ago.
I continue to see him regularly, more as a friend. If he
were to be successful in his application, I could see him
becoming an asset to your team. He is most keen to meet
the public and converse with them. He is sensitive and
concerned and completely trustworthy.
I have no hesitation in recommending him for the
position of shop assistant in the Mind Charity Shop.

Yours etc.

He put it back in the envelope.
"Thank you, Greg, that is most kind."
"Of course I have been a bit concerned about what
you told me on our way down to Kent the other day."
"Oh, rest assured that won't happen again. It was just
a passing phase, born out of my acute loneliness."

"Yes, I know that loneliness is your main problem. It's such a difficult one to solve, but it would be great if you got this little job."

They finished their coffee.

"I'll see you at seven tomorrow evening, then?"

"Oh yes, I almost forgot, the whist evening."

He popped back to the flat to collect his CV and put it together with the reference in an envelope marked FAO The Manager and headed off down the High Street. The same young man was behind the counter. He looked up, recognising him. "The manager will be back in ten minutes, if you want to wait."

He browsed the books and DVDs. Soon the manager appeared and took the envelope. "Wait here," she said, going into the back of the shop. She soon reappeared asking him to follow her. The back of the shop was littered with piles of clothes, books and bric-a-brac. She removed some piles of clothes from two seats and indicated he should sit down.

"You'll understand that Mind charity supports those with enduring mental health problems. Your reference clearly states that you are one of those people. We do have a policy of trying to include past patients in our workforce. Therefore, I shall be pleased to let you start here with one of our long-standing employees, Mrs Hardcastle, shadowing you for the first week or so until you get the hang of things."

He was delighted, "Thank you so much. I'm sorry, I don't know your name. "

"Sarah. Sarah Jones."

He thought he'd detected a Welsh accent.

"Can you start tomorrow?"

"Yes, that would be fine."

"I'll give Mrs Hardcastle, Jean, a ring and ask her to

come in. Nine o'clock sharp then?"

"Perfect, I'll be here."

He walked home with a spring in his step and texted Greg.

Got the job, thanks so much. Start in the morning. See you at 7 tomorrow.

He would go back to the library after lunch and then for a walk on the common. This was a good day.

He thought he should brush up on his mental arithmetic. He picked out a basic school textbook from the children's section. It wasn't really what he was looking for but had some sums in the back he could do. Aren't the tills designed to add up for you? he thought. No point in getting nervous about this, he would have help, it would be very straight forward, he was sure.

He was up bright and early the next morning. He washed and shaved and made sure he had a good breakfast of eggs and toast. It was a drizzly day but for him the day was about opportunity, a new beginning. The bell rang as he opened the door of the shop. "Ah, you must be Ian? I'm Jean."

Her handshake was warm and firm.

"Now, have you operated a till before?"

He told her he hadn't.

"Well, it's very simple, why don't you choose a couple of items you might want to purchase, and we'll go through it together."

He chose a couple of DVDs, films he hadn't seen and had always wanted to see.

"Right, I'll ring them up and total the price and the first customer that comes in is yours, OK?"

He nodded.

Just then the door opened and Greg walked in.

"Hello Ian, I've just popped in for some novels."

He went to the shelves and five minutes later appeared with four paperbacks.

He had no difficulty totalling the purchase.

"Do you want a bag?"

"No need. I'll see you tonight then?"

He nodded. He didn't know how long his shift was, he'd forgotten to ask Sarah yesterday, but assumed it was just the morning.

Next in was a smart young woman carrying two black sacs full of garments.

"I hope you can take all these, my mother passed away recently and I've been clearing out her wardrobe."

"We get a lot like her," Jean said when she'd left. "I'll go in the back and start pricing. I'll have to show you how we do that in due course, but you stay right here and man the till." The next time the bell rang it was Sarah.

"How are you getting on, Ian?"

"Just fine, thanks."

"Great. Phil is coming in at lunch time. I've been working out a rota, you'll be able to work some afternoons I hope?"

"Of course, just let me know."

"I'll let you have the completed rota later this morning."

The morning passed quickly. He served about ten customers, mainly elderly, but some in their twenties browsing for clothes. He felt elated.

Sarah came in from the back with the rota. "You're on tomorrow afternoon with Phil."

He glanced at the rota, he was working two mornings and two afternoons this week and three mornings and two afternoons next. That meant every day he had a focus to the day. The afternoon passed quickly and at seven he was waiting for Greg outside his door.

"How did you get on this morning?" Greg asked.

"Very well, thank you. I'm working every day for the next two weeks."

"Excellent. Now you may recognise some of the people here tonight, they may have been on the ward or at the day hospital. We try to encourage folk not to talk about their illness but concentrate on what they're doing now. You'll see, just relax and enjoy the evening."

"It's years since I played whist, I hope I remember!"

"Don't worry, no-one takes it too seriously."

They were drawing up outside the church hall. A few people were going into the bright lights inside. The hall had tables and chairs arranged with four people to each table. Greg introduced him to three other players. His partner was a middle-aged woman, Amanda, with greying hair. She looked very nervous, and her hands were shaking. The other couple were two young men in their twenties. Both had nicotine-stained fingers. One, Skip, had tattoos covering his arms and piercings in his nose and eyebrow. The other, John, had a shaved head and was smartly dressed. Amanda didn't say a word, but the lads were chatting together.

"Did you see the Southampton match yesterday? Great play by Arsenal," Skip said.

Knowing nothing about football he couldn't contribute.

"Yes, great win for us. Puts us in a very strong position."

Greg was talking to another man who looked as if he was the organiser. The man suddenly announced that play should begin.

The cards were shuffled, and trumps called.

It was clear that Amanda couldn't concentrate. She made several mistakes and couldn't remember what had been played. He didn't hold out much hope for his score this evening.

Greg came by.

"We're going to do it slightly differently this evening. To encourage mixing we're going to change partners every three games. That way you get to know how others play and get a chance to move on if you're in the winning pair."

Ian thought he could follow this, it would become clear in due course, he felt sure. He and Amanda lost the first three games, and Skip and John moved on to another table. Two elderly ladies joined them. Both were very serious and non-communicative. One had a huge spot on the end of her nose. It was impossible not to stare at it. For some reason Ian found the whole event hugely entertaining. It was surreal, the contrast between the players. What bound them, why did they come along? All of them had suffered, in their own way, with mental health problems. All sympathised with each other. All knew the importance of regular activity. He was enjoying himself. The elderly women beat them hands down and moved on.

"It's not our night Amanda," he said.

"Oh, I'm so sorry, I'm hopeless at this game, no one ever wants to partner me, you've drawn the short straw tonight."

The next couple joining them were an elderly man, Arthur, with some awkward involuntary movements. It made holding the cards difficult for him. Partnering him was a younger woman, Sandra, with dyed blond hair and heavy make-up. They too made an odd couple. We're all odd, he thought, misfits in an imperfect world.

To try and be normal, that was the aim. It felt far from normal, this whist drive.

Once again, he and Amanda were trounced. He was beginning to look forward to a new partner. Greg appeared.

"Now Ian, you play with Sandra and Amanda can play with Arthur. I'll toss a coin to see who moves on, heads you move, tails you stay. Right, tails for you Ian, you stay put and Phil and Brian will join you."

"Hello, Phil." He recognised him from the Mind shop.

"Hi, Ian, good to see you. How's it going? "

"Well, I haven't won a game yet."

"Were you partnering Amanda? That explains it!"

How difficult for the poor woman, he thought.

"Have you been coming to this for long?" he asked.

"Since it started, probably about two months. Paul, my befriender, and Greg set it up for their clients. I find it's good for my memory which hasn't been so hot lately."

He was too young to have memory problems, he thought, but was aware that poor memory and poor concentration went hand in hand and were symptoms of depression. This gave him a strong connection with young Phil. Brian was a middle-aged man of heavy build and worn hands. A joiner or plasterer, he figured, someone used to manual labour.

Mental health issues can hit anyone at any time, he thought. He wondered how Brian had suffered. He thought he looked a bit suspiciously at him at times. Was he a bit paranoid?

This game was much more evenly matched, and he and Sandra won by one trick. They moved on to join a painfully thin young woman called Alice, who was partnering a middle-aged woman, Connie, who seemed to find the whole evening hugely amusing. She talked incessantly about nothing in particular. She asked him lots of questions: "Where do you live? Who introduced you to this? How did you meet him? Have you had a befriender before? Whoops, I shouldn't have played that, sorry Alice." She also fidgeted constantly, straightening her blouse, and fiddling with her rings. Sandra and he won again. It was time for a tea break. He queued behind Alice who, he noticed, didn't take a biscuit. She seemed to want to talk.

"You're new here, aren't you? How do you find it? Is it a bit like being on the ward, all of us here together, undiluted?"

"Well, it did remind me a bit of day hospital, although it's several years since I was a patient there. How do you find it?"

"I'm afraid this is one of the conditions of my discharge plan, that I engage with all the activities that my CPN sets up for me. My Mother brings me every week. I have to come."

"You sound as if you don't enjoy it."

"Like you I want to mix with the public. I need to be out there looking for a job. But every time I get work I get sick and eat even less. I need to lose weight now, but my mother makes me eat."

He was out of his depth. "I wouldn't have thought you needed to lose weight."

"Yes I do, I'm too fat I need to lose half a stone and then I'll be my target weight. If I go below that I get admitted. But I feel good at my target weight of six stones. I feel energised and in control."

One thing he had read was that people with anorexia, which he suspected Alice suffered from, don't like to talk about their weight. This was unusual, Alice talking to a complete stranger. Yet, maybe he didn't pose a threat to her, he thought.

Sandra joined them. "I'm not sure if we'll be partners for the second half but I enjoyed playing with you, Ian, thank you."

She was looking distracted.

"What normally happens after tea?"

"Well, sometimes we play whist again and sometimes we play other card games, just for another half hour or so. I think we're playing whist again this evening."

The rest of the evening passed quickly, and he found himself laughing and joking with Sandra. It was hard to remember when he had last laughed.

"I'll drop you home," Greg said, as they were putting the tables away.

Most folk had left. Paul remembered him from after his last admission.

"How are you doing, Ian?" he asked.

"Oh, quite well thanks. I enjoyed this evening, thank you so much for suggesting it, Greg."

"Great, we'll see you next week, then?"

"Sure, I can make my own way."

"It's really no bother picking you up as I drive past your door anyway."

They locked up the hall and said good-bye to Paul.

"It's nice to see Paul is still working in the service, I thought he'd left."

"No, he had a spell off work for a few months, that's when I took you on." Greg explained.

"One thing we don't encourage is talking about clients outwith the evenings. Of course you're at liberty to meet up with any of them, but you will appreciate that you have all had difficulties of one kind or another, and you are all making a real effort to get back out there."

Ian thought before he replied, "Well, I will see Phil as he's helping me on my shift tomorrow at the shop. I will bear what you say in mind. Thanks for telling me."

He arrived back in the flat in an uplifted mood. He'd only been on his medication for a few days, it can't have been that that was causing the improvement. However, he must continue the pills, he knew he needed them in the long-term to prevent relapse. Even the damp of the flat and the dark furnishings didn't dampen his mood, even the loneliness. Tomorrow he would think how he could change the flat. He hadn't felt as well as this in years.

Their drive down to Deal was in glorious sunshine. George was on great form. It was hard to believe the change in him. Again, he was talking in an animated fashion.

"Do you know, I think I'll look into going away for a few days."

"I think it best if one of us goes with you. It's early days yet and you're a bit up and down," Helen said, glancing at Abigail in the rear-view mirror.

"I'm perfectly alright."

"Yes, but we can do all the organising and it will be much more relaxing for you."

They were driving through Ashford.

"Shall we stop for a coffee?"

"Yes, please."

Over coffee George brought up the topic of travelling again.

"You know your mother wasn't that fond of travelling, although she always liked organising the trips."

"That surprises me, she always came across as having enjoyed your holidays."

"Yes, but she was always so glad to get home."

Suddenly he became morose and withdrawn.

"What's up, Dad," Abigail asked.

"I feel one of my dizzy spells coming on. I need to lie down."

This was difficult in the middle of a busy coffee shop, but Abigail immediately placed his coat on the floor and helped him down. The waitress came over. "Can I help, do you need a doctor or the paramedics?"

"No, I'm a GP and he's just feeling a bit faint, he should be feeling better in a couple of minutes"

She felt his pulse, it was weak but regular, his colour was coming back.

"It is very hot and stuffy in here," he said.

"Should we go home?" Helen asked.

"No, let's see how he goes, we'll get him out into the fresh air soon."

"I must get up, it's very embarrassing lying here."

"Take your time, Dad," Abigail said but he was already struggling to get up. Slowly they walked him to the car, Abigail reclined the passenger seat and he got in.

"Dad, do you want to go home, or carry on?"

"Oh, let's push on, I feel fine now. Sometimes when we talk about her I feel kind of faint. That combined with the heat did it, I'm sure"

Abigail took his pulse again." What a shame I've not got my medical bag, I could do with knowing your blood pressure."

"Let's get on and forget about this for goodness' sake." He was getting irate now.

"OK, we'll carry on, but you must say if it comes back, and we'll turn straight round and go home.

The sisters were worried, their Father could be very pig-headed. His irritability and animation were worrying. He was also very restless. It was still some way to Deal.

The traffic became heavy, there were road works up ahead. It was nearly one o'clock.

"I think we should stop at Hythe," Abigail said. After lunch we can have a walk along the beach and then head home."

The others agreed, George reluctantly.

They found a nice-looking pub on the outskirts of the town and Helen pulled in.

"This will do, I don't want to be looking around for the next hour."

Abigail checked George's pulse once again." Nice and steady Dad, are you hungry?"

"Not really, but I'm sure I'll manage something."

"Come on then, let's make the most of it."

Taking her father away on holiday seemed a bit daunting, but she would try and do it. Maybe they should both go with him. Maybe they should try Scotland, and if that worked that nice seaside resort in the South of Spain that Greg and Julian went to. That was a plan, anyway.

They had a good pub lunch, and George seemed to have fully recovered, tucking into his mussels mariniere.

"I'm not sure mussels were a very good choice, Dad, make sure you don't prise open a closed one, we don't want more problems!"

"Don't worry, I'm well used to them," he retorted.

They drove down to the sea front. There was a cold brisk breeze, but the sun was shining, catching the surf of the big waves crashing onto the shingle. The roar of the sea drowned out their thoughts. They wrapped up warm and set off along the prom.

"What time are we expecting Greg tomorrow?" Abigail asked.

"Around ten, I think, and our appointment to view the flat is eleven thirty."

George was out of breath, walking into the wind, but was clearly enjoying the bracing sea air. "Shall we pop in here for a coffee?" Helen asked as they passed an ice-cream parlour. It was good to get out of the wind. George had an ice-cream sundae with lashings of cream and chocolate. Abigail secretly hoped he wouldn't throw up on the journey home. He had been known to overindulge on many occasions. Still, he was having a good day, and that was what they wanted.

"I'm glad we didn't get to Deal, I think it's a bit early."

"What do you mean, Dad?"

"The restaurant I wanted to take you to, the last time I was there it was with your mother. I would probably have found it very difficult. I would have spoiled it for you both." "No, Dad, you mustn't think this way. Grief will surface when you least expect it, and you must let it out. Suppressing it will only prolong the agony." They walked back to the car and set off for home.

"I don't think I ever properly got over Jack's death."

Helen suddenly shifted in her seat, sitting bolt upright behind the wheel, gripping it tight.

"It was such a shock, him going like that. He seemed so well just before he was discharged. He was planning trips and had got to know a fellow patient, by the name of Ian, I think. Something must have triggered it." Helen tensed again. "Of course your Mother was devastated, she had been especially fond of Jack. And as for Grandma Rose... How she kept going I'll never know." "How did he do it?" asked Abigail. Helen wished she hadn't.

"He took a whole lot of pills and alcohol. It's a peaceful way to go but horridly traumatic for the family as suicide always is. I was angry at first. I remember lots of rows with your mother. It wasn't long after his death that your mother started having memory problems. Then Grandma Rose died. It really has been a terrible few years."

Helen was finding this all very difficult but knew it was good for her father to talk. She felt a mounting pressure to tell Abigail about the letters but knew she should resist it. There was an awkward silence. Then Helen was aware that her father was sobbing.

"Oh Dad, don't worry, it will get easier." She wished she believed it would. Losing a spouse after fifty-two years was probably more than anyone could bear.

"I just miss her as she was three years ago. We were best friends. Nothing can replace that."

"Look Dad, how do you feel about a few days up in Scotland? The autumn colours will be beautiful, and we can take some trips to the West coast. We could stay in the Trossachs."

"That sounds very good, a hotel with a roaring fire, bracing weather, lovely views, great whisky!"

"We could fly up to Edinburgh and spend a night there first, don't you have a friend who lives there?"

"Yes, Roger, an old university mate, but we've not been in touch for years, he may not even be still alive."

"There's no harm in finding out I guess."

Abigail was typing something furiously into her phone. She was distracted and agitated.

"What are we planning this evening?" George asked.

"Nothing planned, I thought we could watch a film, or one of David Attenborough's programmes."

"I vote for the latter."

"That's settled then."

The rest of the journey home was quiet, no one said a word. The traffic was heavy and a light drizzle in the dusk made driving tedious. Helen was tired, she was looking forward to a large glass of wine.

Summer 2000

He woke before the alarm in a cold sweat. He remembered that he had to get to the day hospital for nine. He had to catch two buses, it was a tedious journey, one he'd made many times after previous admissions. This morning the coffee barely revived him. He found it hard to get dressed. He cut himself shaving. It was a bad start to the day. To cap it all it was pouring with rain outside, one of those heavy downpours that were becoming ever more frequent as the planet warmed. He got soaked waiting for the bus and dripped onto it with the other passengers, no one feeling like greeting the driver. The grey streets of London were barely visible through the steamed-up windows. Everyone smelt damp. The bus was silent, no-one spoke. At the stop where he had to change buses he managed to shelter from the rain. The bus was running late, and it was 9.15 by the time he reached the day hospital.

"Hello, you must be Ian?" a woman greeted him, "I'm Hazel, your CPN. How was your journey?" She was a bulky woman wearing a tight-fitting suit, and gave him a beaming smile, immediately putting him at his ease.

"A bit miserable in this weather," he admitted.

"Well, get yourself a hot cup of tea and we'll have a chat."

This was the last thing he wanted to do, to tell yet another stranger about himself, his illness, his problems. He wanted to be on the Southbank, anywhere but here. There were groups of people doing activities at tables, it looked like some were playing games, some cutting and pasting shapes on big sheets of paper, some painting. Altogether there must have been fifteen or so patients, a couple of whom he recognised from the ward. Of course Jack would be there on Wednesday, which would be good. Until then he would make the best of it. He took his tea over to join Hazel.

"How are you doing since you left the ward?"

"Well, pretty well, I think. I've been up to the Southbank a couple of times, to a service at St Pauls and the Turners at the Tate."

"Excellent, that's more than most people achieve over the course of several weeks, well done. You may not need to be here for long if you keep up that activity. This is all about consolidating recovery, simple activities that empty the mind of all those troublesome thoughts. The aim is to try and be in the present and avoid dwelling on your admission or the future. Do you fancy doing some painting or playing a game?"

He fancied neither really but said he would play a game. Knock-out whist was in progress, so he was able to join the group. There were two woman and two men. The younger woman, Isabel, had been on the ward with him. She had been very disturbed, shouting out as if talking to someone, but was clearly much improved, although he noticed a coarse tremor in one of her hands. The other woman introduced herself as Clare. She had greying hair and glasses and was very overweight. One of the men he recognised as Robert, a slight man in his thirties who had also been on the ward. He, too, looked a lot better, but was still rather withdrawn and tired looking. The final man, Andrew, was also overweight with nicotine-stained fingers. They all looked at him, freshly shaved but with a piece of tissue on his chin where he had cut himself. He wore a tattered shirt and grubby jeans and he, too, had nicotine stains. He was balding.

We are a motley crew, he thought, all sharing similar histories, all needing the same distraction, all having to take time out of our lives through no fault of our own.

Play continued. It appeared that if you were knocked out you were able to play the next hand having just one card to play at random. In any event he was unlucky and was knocked out many times. After they had finished the cards Andrew suggested a game of Monopoly. He thought he would scream, this is doing me no good at all, he thought. Still, he stayed and played, winning hands down. Then it was time for a break. He wondered if he could make an excuse and leave, but he had to stay, it was part of his discharge plan.

He found himself next to Andrew.

"When did you get out of hospital?" Andrew asked.

"Just last week, and you?"

"About a month ago, I'm coming here every day. But my CPN is hoping to get me on a back to work scheme through the job centre."

"What was your line of work?"

"I worked for the council painting and decorating council properties, but I got made redundant because of my illness and I haven't worked for eleven years."

He counted himself lucky that he had worked for as long as he had.

"Do you know what the back to work plan will entail?"

"Well I think some form of voluntary work in the first instance. There's a church hall that Hazel knows of that needs painting and they're looking for volunteers."

"That sounds promising."

"Hopefully something will turn up for you, too."

"Yes, I don't think I'll get back to the Post Office, but some admin job for a charity or basic office work. I do have some computing skills."

Hazel came up. "Good, I see you're getting to know each other. We're going to have our group discussion now."

This was a very stressful session. All the patients sitting round in a circle taking it in turns to say how they were feeling and how they were coping. He wanted to be anywhere but there. His palms were sweaty, and he felt himself taking rapid shallow breaths.

"Are you OK, Ian?" His vision was black, and her voice echoed.

"Put your head between your knees and breathe deeply and slowly.' Gradually he began to feel better, his vision returned, and he sat up straight.

"I think I'd better go outside for some fresh air."

Hazel accompanied him. "Don't worry, everyone finds these sessions hard at first, but it helps to hear how others are overcoming their difficulties."

"I'm not sure it's going to help me, I feel better when I'm on the Southbank amongst the crowd. I can feel anonymous, yet safe at the same time. Here I feel exposed and vulnerable."

"Why don't you try and come back to the group, you won't have to say anything."

"I'd rather go home now, I'll be here on Wednesday. Do you have these meetings every day?"

"Yes, we try to. You don't have to take part if you don't feel like it, but once you've heard a few people speak it gets easier. In the afternoons we have more structured groups. Lots of topics are covered such as cooking and housekeeping, vocational counselling, art therapy, drug and alcohol counselling, men's health, and woman's issues. Also, you will have a session with a psychiatrist about your illness and your medication, how it works and the importance of compliance. There is a plan for each patient."

He'd been a patient at this day hospital in the past after admissions and found it all very difficult. Once out of the ward he really wanted to forget the ward routine and try and establish one of his own. He did admit that some of the groups might be helpful such as the vocational counselling. He decided to stay. Back in the group, which was really too large, Robert was speaking.

"The week-end has been difficult for me. I didn't see anyone and spent a lot of time on my own in my flat. My mood has been very low and I'm hoping the doctor will suggest some different medication for me. But my brother is coming to see me this evening, so I'm looking forward to that."

Isabel spoke next,"I had a great week-end, my family invited me over for a barbecue. I was able to help with the preparation of the food and clearing up. I did feel as if they were looking at me strangely, though. It felt uncomfortable, and I wanted to shout at them, but I managed to control it. They don't understand what it's like having this illness. I think loads of people stare at me when I'm out and about. You're all staring now, please stop it." She started gesticulating and stood up and walked off. A nurse followed her.

Next up was Andrew, "My wife and I did a couple of long walks which really helped my mood, then we went to a film. The rest of the time I chilled out on the sofa. There are things I could do in the house, but I can't be bothered right now. I'm feeling lazy and have no motivation."

Clare could not speak, she appeared to try but no words came. She broke down, and one of the CPNs took her aside. The group disbanded and some went to look at a notice board where the various group activities were listed.

"You sign up for the ones you want," Andrew told him.

He signed up for art therapy and vocational counselling.

At lunch he found himself sitting next to Isabel, who had clearly been crying. They ate in silence. He had no idea what to say to her. Then she suddenly turned to him."You seem different from all the others. They're all in it together you know, watching me all the time, worried I'm going to do something. What's your name?"

"Ian."

"Well, Ian, you can be my friend, I need a friend with all these enemies I have to deal with."

"Do you live with anyone, Isabel?"

"Yes, my boyfriend, Mark, but he drinks a lot so is out of his mind most days. My family are good, but they don't understand what I have to go through, and I think some of them are in league with the others. This place is all I have. I come here for lunch and the art. I love the art."

"Well, I'm doing the art group this afternoon, so we'll be together there."

"Good," she said, and went to clear her plate. Most of the patients were outside having a cigarette so he joined them. It was a depressing little courtyard with a few dead plants in plant pots and three brick walls. He was looking forward to seeing Jack on Wednesday. It would be good to have someone he knew to talk to.

Back inside Hazel called him over." The psychiatrist is coming to see you in ten minutes to go through your treatment plan, I'll let you know when he arrives."

A besuited man in his fifties with long grey hair called him over.

"Mr Soames do you understand your drug regime? "

"Well, I know I'm on an antidepressant and a mood stabiliser."

"Exactly, good. It's very important that you continue the mood stabiliser for the long term. You have been prone to recurrent bouts of severe depression and without this drug you will undoubtedly suffer again. We may be able to withdraw the antidepressant in the future but must taper it off very gradually, it should never be stopped suddenly. Do you understand? '

"Yes."

"Are you having any side effects from the drugs?"

"Well, when I started them I felt nauseous and very sleepy, but these seem to have worn off, and I'm sleeping very well at night."

"Excellent. What do you hope to get from the day hospital?"

"To be honest, the fact that it's giving me a focus for three days a week is the main thing. Filling my day is the toughest thing, especially when I don't have much energy or 'get up and go'."

"Yes, a lot of patients say that. You seem to be doing very well. Hazel gave a good report of your activities over the weekend, so I don't think you will need to be here for too long, maybe a month or so. Most patients are here for several months."

"Good, that is good news."

"Well, I'll see you sometime next week to see how you're progressing and what you've done here, OK?"

"Very good."

The doctor went back to the office, and he went to find the art therapy group.

Isabel was already painting a bright abstract painting in acrylic paints. The therapist, a young woman who wore a highly colourful blouse introduced herself as Sheila and showed him the materials. She was a warm woman with sensitive eyes. He immediately took to her.

"This is a free for all session. I have a still life set up over there and some photographs. You can use any of these or work on your own composition. Next time you're welcome to bring any object or image from home you might like to paint. It doesn't matter if you mix the paints or not, but I can give you some advice on colour mixing if you want."

He chose an image of a lake with mountains and a wooded area at the shoreline. He'd no idea where to start, so Sheila took a sheet of paper and showed him how to roughly mark out the areas of colour.

"Try to focus on dark and light, and warm and cool tones. Let me show you how to mix the colours."

She spent some time telling him about primary and secondary colours and how to tone down a colour with its complimentary colour. It was a lot to take in, but he was keen to get going. Soon he was completely absorbed. First of all he mixed a variety of greens and then he did a wash of pale green all over the paper. He then came in with different greens. Then he mixed some purples for the mountains and sky. He was enjoying this. Isabel looked over at his painting.

"That's jolly good, you must have done this before."

"No, it's my first time."

"You're getting some great colours."

He came in with some dark blues and greys and decided on a streak of yellow just on the horizon. It worked.

"I can see that the problem is knowing when to stop."

"Stop now," said Sheila, "that is just perfect as it is, well done."

He started on another painting, but a bell rang which signalled the end of that session and a break for tea. Isabel had painted two very bright abstract works which were difficult to look at. He fumbled for words to say to her, and it sounded all wrong,

"They're interesting and very bold."

She turned away mumbling under her breath.

He headed out for another cigarette and found Robert, who was pacing up and down. "What session were you at just now?" he asked.

"Alcohol counselling," Robert replied, looking down and taking a long draw on his cigarette.

"Any good?"

"Well, I have a problem if that's what you mean and I have to do something about it," he replied curtly. He looked dishevelled and morose and walked away, clearly not wanting to talk. Isabel came out and lit up.

"Sheila was very impressed with your painting you know, you should take it up. At least do it every time you're here. I just don't seem to progress, I think Sheila's given up on me."

"I don't think it's about the end result but just the process. You get lost in the process and have no sense of time. That's what's good for you."

"I guess you're right. Well, I best go to my next session."

"What are you doing?"

"Housekeeping and cooking, more things I'm useless at."

"I could do with that too, but I signed up for the vocational counselling. I've no idea what that will entail."

When he joined the session a man in the group was talking to the social worker about his previous employment.

"My penultimate job was as a gardener in the municipal parks, that lasted two years, but I had to pack it in because I was ill. Then after that episode I had a very brief spell working for a small private gardening company, tidying old ladies' gardens, that sort of thing. Then I got ill again and here I am."

The social worker, Max, was reclining in a low chair looking as if he was only half listening. He had a big bushy beard and round spectacles.

"You've done really well to keep up your employment record, Steve. Do you think that small business would take you on again?"

"Well, the boss didn't seem very sympathetic towards me when I started to go downhill. I was late for work and didn't pull my weight as I was so slowed up. I will get in touch with him again, but I don't hold out much hope."

"With autumn approaching these small gardening firms often take on extra labour, I'm pretty optimistic you'll get something else soon. What have you done besides gardening?"

"Years ago I worked as a school janitor, I had the same job for fifteen years. It was great, I loved the contact with the kids. Then I had my first major breakdown and I never got back to the job, just picking up casual labour, you know."

"Well, I suggest we look at yellow pages and ring round a few firms asking if they need anyone this autumn. You've got the experience. Let's do this next week, shall we?"

Steve nodded, looking pleased.

"Now, Ian, isn't it? Tell us about your previous jobs."

"Well, I did evening classes in computing after school and started working for the Post Office. First of all I was a regular postman and then I started in the sorting office, working my way up to being the manager. I enjoyed the job on one level, it was steady and undemanding. I don't manage change very well, so I didn't think about looking for anything else. The Post Office HR were very good about my breakdowns and kept my job open for me, but this time I just don't feel well enough to go back. I know it's early days, but being responsible for ten people fills me with dread. I hope I shall qualify for some sort of pension, seeing as I've worked for the Post Office for so long."

"We'll have to look into this for you Ian. Meanwhile looking for something quite different is what we have to do for you. What skills do you have?"

Ian wracked his brains. This was the problem, he didn't have many.

"My computing skills are out of date, I'm sure, and my people skills have taken a knock from my loss in confidence. I'm not a practical man, so unlike Steve would be useless at gardening. I love libraries and would love to work in one, but I guess you need qualifications for that?"

"I think we should both look at the ads in the local paper and see if anything seems appropriate and discuss next week. Meanwhile you could ask in your local library whether there is any scope for volunteering, say in the coffee shop if there is one. Just being in the library environment may be good for you."

"OK, that's helpful, thanks."

It was time to go. He helped Sheila tidy away the art materials.

"You must keep coming to my art session, Ian."

"Oh, I will, it was great. I'll try and find an image to bring along next time."

It had stopped raining and the afternoon sun was still warm when he left the building. He saw Isabel walking quickly away, looking furtively over her shoulder. Andrew's wife had picked him up. He was rather relieved no one was at his bus stop. He suddenly felt exhausted. Altogether, though, he'd quite enjoyed his day. The support staff were excellent, and he had a plan for looking for work. He would go to the library tomorrow before Paul picked him up for lunch.

The meeting with the GP went well. He was efficient and interested. He explained what the NHS could offer in the way of physio, occupational therapy, and community psychiatric nursing.

"Having her sleep downstairs until she can manage the stairs seems the best option. Of course she will need someone with her at all times, so you may want to contact one of the private nursing agencies, if you need relief, George."

"My brother has already contacted an agency and we're meeting them this afternoon," Abigail said.

"Good, well I suggest you contact me the week before you plan on getting her home and I'll mobilise all the relevant people to visit her as soon as she's back in the house, OK?"

"That seems fine. How long do you think she'll be in St Mary's?"

"That depends on the GP who looks after her there. If you like I could give them a ring and explain the home situation and that you're keen to get her home in the near future."

George looked animated, "Oh that's wonderful, I can't wait to get her home."

Back home Abigail briefed the others. Helen and Greg were sitting expectantly at the kitchen table.

"It looks like the ball's in our court," Greg said, in his business-like manner.

"We must be sure she's safely mobilising with the Zimmer, and we must ask about toileting. I still think we must have a nurse in fulltime for the first few weeks at least."

George reluctantly agreed.

"I'm afraid we'll all need to get back to London soon and back to work, Dad. I think realistically she's going to be in St Mary's for another three weeks or so. Can you manage here, visiting her every day? One of us will be down every weekend."

"Of course, I can't expect anything more. Do you think we should interview a nurse from that agency you've contacted Greg?"

"Yes, I can set that up for when I come down next. We'll also have to plan where she's going to sleep. Thank goodness you have a downstairs bathroom."

Greg left that evening and Helen and Abigail the following day. George looked forlorn as they drove off.

"I'm glad I managed to put some stuff in the freezer today," Helen said, "I'll do some cooking to bring down next time I'm here." It was easier thinking about the practical issues than feeling the emotional strain of Dorothy in that place crying to come home.

The next few weeks saw each of them trying to juggle home, work, supporting George and planning for Dorothy's discharge home. Helen felt very guilty that she had so little time for the children, but Mat was very understanding and, because of his teaching job, could manage most after school runs and juggle the activities.
Abigail was shattered and found little support in James. Many evenings they hardly talked. She was sleeping badly. She found great difficulty sympathising with her patients when they presented with minor ailments. She knew she was nearing burn-out.

Greg went back to his clients and their clubs. He and Julian resumed their fast lifestyle of eating out and gallery viewing. Julian was independent but understanding. The perfect partner at a time of great stress.

One evening the phone rang.

"Hello, Helen, Dad here, the practice rang me just now to say that they plan for her discharge next week. Maybe we all need to meet up this weekend to sort the furniture etc."

"Yes, of course I'll let the others know. That's good Dad, isn't it?"

There was a hesitation," Yes, it is." She could tell he was apprehensive.

All preparations were in place by the Sunday. The agency nurse could start the day Dorothy came home. She would prepare her meals, wash, dress her and toilet her. Effectively George would be free to read to her and play simple games. He would have no responsibility for her direct care. They all wondered if it would work.

They each phoned him to offer help.

"We should get a collapsible wheelchair," Greg suggested, "maybe the physio will be able to advise next week Dad?"

"Yes, I'll certainly ask her."

"I'll take Wednesday off and come down Tuesday evening," Abigail volunteered.

"I'll come down Friday after work and check everything's going OK," Helen offered. "Dad, you won't be tied to the house you know, we can take you out for a meal, and to shop."

"We'll see how it goes."

As planned discharges go this was a good one, Abigail decided. Everything in place, the family all getting along, nothing should go wrong.

But nothing could prepare them for Dorothy's reaction when she entered the house. She had no idea where she was and started shouting, begging to be taken back home. It was impossible to calm her. She was struggling up onto her Zimmer all the time and trying to walk lifting it off the floor, it took two of them to help her back into a chair. The nurse, Paula, was a young German girl, who had been very impressive when Greg had interviewed her but now seemed totally out of her depth.

"Are you planning to toilet her regularly?" Abigail asked.

"Yes, I guess so. How often do you think?"

"Well fortunately the practice has delivered incontinence pads, but I think we should take her to the bathroom every four hours minimum. We should do that now."

The nurse explained it to Dorothy who obliged by standing up unaided and walking lifting the Zimmer properly this time. Abigail helped the nurse in the bathroom but left them there to see how she'd manage getting her back to her chair.

"It's hard work you see, Dad, you'd never have managed her on your own."

"You're right Abigail, I'm so lucky you're here today, too."

Over the next few days, a routine emerged. Paula's confidence improved and she managed to develop a good rapport with Dorothy. Whilst Paula prepared meals, George sat with Dorothy, and they looked at old photo albums or watched a mystery on the TV. She slept a lot. The physio got her going up a few steps and the occupational therapist suggested various aids for the bathroom. The night routine took a while and the night nurse liked to settle her by nine o'clock. The first few nights she had called out, but the nurse had managed to settle her. There was a sedative prescribed but only to be used when all else failed, and Abigail was, of course, very reluctant for it to be given. It was clear this was going to be life now, it was for real. George just had to accept it. When the others were staying he felt guilty leaving her and was always agitating to get home.

"But Dad, she's fine, don't worry," the walk will do you good," Helen said one weekend.

It was nearly Christmas and they planned to decorate the house. The hope was that all the family would be down for Christmas lunch, which Abigail and Helen would prepare together.

"Don't you think it will be too much for Dad, having us all in the house, not to mention poor Mum." Greg was on the phone to Helen.

"I think we have to try being all together, it may be the last time we manage it."

Preparations were in full swing. Presents were wrapped, the decorations were up, the stuffings were made. The children were as high as kites. Helen had finished work and was free for two weeks. There were neighbours in for drinks, carol services, pantomimes, all the trappings of the festive season. Meanwhile Dorothy sat and tried to recognise the faces in the book. She tried to tell someone she needed the toilet. She tried to understand what the kind man was saying to her and do what the pretty young girl wanted her to do. She had become placid and easy to care for. She was settled. It was a huge relief to everyone.

"More turkey anyone?"

"No, I'm absolutely stuffed."

"Me too, shall we delay the pudding and open a few presents now?"

"Pass the wine will you Dad?"

"Yes, presents!" shrieked the children.

"What is happening?"

"It's Christmas Day, Mum, so we're going to open some presents. Do you want any more water?"

"No, I want to sit down."

Paula helped her to the bathroom while the table was cleared.

They sat around the roaring fire while the wind howled outside. There were a few snowflakes falling.

"Oh dear, we all have to drive home tonight," Greg said.

"Well, if it gets heavier you'd better go sooner rather than later, but remember I have three spare bedrooms so some of you can stay if you prefer."

"Oh Mummy, let's stay, please."

"We don't have anything with us, and it's too much for you, Dad."

"Look, I've spare toothbrushes and I'm sure you can make do, just for one night."

"Let's wait and see what happens with the snow."

Presents were handed out, there were whoops of delight from the children and guarded appreciative noises from the adults. No one had had much inspiration this year. Dorothy seemed to be enjoying the commotion, she laughed out loud at random, but quite appropriately when Mat opened his boxer shorts. Helen gave her a new album with all the photos annotated with names and where the photo had been taken. She also had some very sweet-smelling soap for the shower.

"It smells lovely, Mum."

"I can't smell, you know," she said.

The snow was getting heavier.

"I think we should go," Greg stood up and signalled to Abigail.

"Yes, we have to get back Dad, I'm sorry."

George looked disappointed but resigned.

"Well, I'm glad you could make lunch, and I hope to see you both soon."

It was hard to drag themselves away from the scene, the glowing embers, the twinkling Christmas tree, but they bundled their gifts up quickly and left kissing Dorothy on the cheek.

"Are you going now?" she asked. "Will you be back for lunch?"

"Are we staying Mummy?"

Helen looked at Mat, "Yes I think we'll stay. You'll have to sleep in your pants and T-shirts."

The children were playing with Bobby.

George breathed a sigh of relief, he wouldn't have to say goodbye to all of them this evening. It had been a splendid day. He was relaxed, the lines in his highly coloured face seemed to have disappeared. He had his arm round Dorothy, enveloping her in his alcohol-fuelled exuberance.

"Who'd like a sherry?"

The next morning he had a text from Cathy to say she had managed to get three tickets for the concert on Thursday. He was delighted. The library had a good selection of CDs and he managed to get both the Mahler and Shostakovich symphonies. He always enjoyed concerts more if he had listened to the music recently. His phone buzzed as he was checking out the CDs, it was Hazel, his CPN.

He called her back,"How are you doing Ian, I hear that you've recommenced medication. Dr Grove contacted me and asked me to get in touch. I'd like to meet up with you sometime this week."

"I'm doing well thanks, I'm working in the Mind shop every day part-time, but can meet up when I'm free."

"Great news, how about tomorrow afternoon 3 p.m. at your flat?"

"That should be OK, see you then."

She rang off.

I don't really think I need much input at the moment, he thought. However, past experience had taught him that it was always a rocky road and to accept all offers of help. He decided to pick up some paint and brushes and a roller on his way home. He would paint his living room a light colour. In the hardware shop he was very indecisive but eventually chose an off-white he thought would do. He had the stuff for preparing the paintwork in the flat. Best not to start painting 'til after Hazel's visit, he thought.

"Hi, Phil," he said as he entered the shop. Phil grunted a greeting and went back to sorting some books that had just been handed in.

"Shall I go on the till?"

"Yes, if you like, I've got several jobs to do out the back."

"I really enjoyed yesterday evening."

"Good." He turned away. He looked flat and despondent, Ian thought, it would be difficult to get much conversation this afternoon.

An elderly gentleman struggled in with two large bags of clothes. He looked tired and drawn.

"These are my wife's clothes, I've just lost her." He was trembling and fighting back the tears, hunched over the sacs. He seemed reluctant to part with them.

"I am so sorry to hear that. Thank you so much, do you gift aid with us?"

He clearly didn't want to linger and turned and left the shop. Ian took the bags through to Phil, they were heavy as if laden with grief. By the time he was back at the till there were three more people in the shop. One was a smart young woman who seemed extraordinarily out of place.

"I'm looking for some clothes for a fancy-dress party." She seemed to have to make an excuse for being there. She didn't volunteer what costume she wanted, and he didn't have the courage to ask. He watched her intently. She wore a navy suit that hugged her neat figure and red high-heeled shoes. She clutched a red handbag under her arm as she worked her way through the rack of clothes.

"Oh, just what I was looking for," she said, pulling out a short black skirt. "May I try it on?"

"The changing room is right there, it's a bit cramped, I'm afraid."

He could see her wriggle out of her skirt through the gap at the bottom of the door.

"Excuse me, may I buy these?" A middle-aged woman had placed two items of bric-a-brac on the counter. Why anyone would want to buy these items he had no idea. The woman had a coarse tremor and great difficulty getting coins out of her purse. He offered to help.

"No, I can manage well enough thank you," she retorted.

"Did it fit?" he asked the attractive young woman.

"Perfectly, now I just need a top, but you've nothing here that's suitable."

The third customer was an elderly man with a walking cane. He was hunting through the DVDs and books and clearly wasn't in any hurry.

Phil came through, "Do you want to pop back for a cuppa? I'll take over."

He gratefully accepted. There was not much space to sit in the back due to the hoards of clutter and clothing. An overwhelming musty smell made him quite nauseated. The smell of hundreds of old cupboards. He glanced at a pile of books that Phil was pricing, there was a PD James, an Ian McEwan, an Ian Rankin. He put all three to one side.

Phil popped his head round the door:"OK, do you want to come back?"

"Yes, I'll take these three once you've priced them, OK?"

"Just have them, it's the perk of the job."

"No, I insist on paying for everything I take."

"Please yourself, I'll let you know the total cost."

I don't think I'll ever get to know this guy, he thought. He had such difficulty forming friendships, and it looked as if Phil did too. He thought back to Jack. He had just begun to know him when... He pushed the thought to the back of his mind. He didn't often think of him, but last night's session with the card games reminded him of the day hospital they had both attended. He was having trouble with this memory, it kept coming back. Fortunately, the rest of the afternoon was busy and took his mind off it, but as he left the shop he again found himself picturing Jack's face that last afternoon on the South Bank, his pained expression, his features immovable. He'd looked lost, but resolute. Ian just couldn't reach him. He felt his mood dipping as he walked amongst the crowds. He wondered whether the young woman had found the rest of her outfit. A party, he would never again go to a party. He couldn't possibly interact with people. He was a misfit, a failure. He hadn't saved Jack, he wouldn't save himself. Entering the flat he saw the tins of paint and thought, this is what I will do tomorrow, it doesn't matter that Hazel is coming, I will paint.

The next session at the shop went better, he was definitely getting the hang of it, now. Rushing back to the flat he moved all the furniture into the middle of the room and covered it with some old sheets. He couldn't remember the last time he had painted anything, but he hoped he'd remember. It would be good to get rid of the nicotine stains on the ceiling if nothing else. He balanced precariously on a chair as he rollered the ceiling. The smell overpowered him. By 3 p.m. he had done most of the ceiling. The doorbell rang.

Hazel was the motherly sort, jolly, rotund and tactile. She wore a tweed jacket and ill-fitting trousers and carried a voluminous handbag from which she dragged out Ian's file.

"So, what made you see Dr Grove and ask to go back on your medication?"

"Well I began to spot some tell-tale signs such as difficulty reading and concentrating, panic attacks, being suspicious of people. You know the symptoms.

"But you've been well for so long, do you know what triggered this?"

He felt the beads of perspiration on his forehead and hesitated before he spoke.

"Although I helped in the library coffee shop and took regular walks, I was lonely. You've no idea how long-term loneliness destroys the soul. Some people are alone but never lonely. They are to be envied. I craved human contact. So, when I was walking, I singled out someone, usually a young woman, someone who was alone and walking with a purpose. I would follow them, from a distance, often to their destination, usually work but occasionally on the train home. It gave me some solace, made me feel more alive somehow."

"How long was this going on?"

"Probably a year or more. I forget, possibly longer, on and off. It was like a compulsion."

"Did the people you followed ever notice you?"

"No, I don't think so. I became adept at keeping a distance. I often lost them in the crowds. It didn't matter, I would always find someone else. I didn't do it every day."

"You presumably knew this was wrong, almost sinister, and if reported could lead to prosecution, possibly a jail sentence. Why are you telling me now?"

"Things came to a head recently. Yes, I knew I shouldn't be doing it, but it became a compulsion. I needed it to keep my depression at bay. It was a defence if you like."

"How did things come to a head?"

"Well, I followed the same woman on her way to and

from work for three days in a row. On the last morning I lost her leaving the train, but came across her at the top of the escalator where she appeared to have fainted. I stayed with her until the paramedics arrived and then walked with her to her work as the paramedics wanted her accompanied."

He looked down.

"Go on," she said.

"We spoke a few words, I asked her what her job was, and she asked me about mine. I think she said she'd lost her mother recently. She thanked me and that was it."

"The last you saw of her?"

"Yes, but the first day I'd followed her all the way home and I was scared I'd do it again. I felt too close to her and knew I had to stop."

"Ian, your need for human contact runs deep. I can understand your desperation. However, you need to channel this need into a healthy contact with people."

"Yes, I suppose so, a very pleasant elderly lady has recently been talking to me in the library and we've had the odd coffee. The staff are friendly, too, but I don't help out very often there. Of course, my new voluntary job in the Mind charity shop is a good opportunity."

"Absolutely, these activities are bound to distract you from your obsession. I must say that having told me about it, I feel duty bound to run it past Dr Macintosh who may well want to see you, I suspect."

He felt the weight of the past year bearing down on his shoulders and the tingling limbs of impending panic. How could he explain himself? He only knew that it was best this was out in the open. He knew it had been coming to a head and who knows what might have happened?

"Recently I've been dwelling on the death of a friend of mine, I met him on the ward last time I was in hospital. His name was Jack, and he took his own life."

"Tell me about him."

"There's not much to tell, I didn't know him well, but we shared the same interests, classical music and art. He was also of the same political persuasion as me and had been a member of the Labour Party. He had a brother and a niece who visited him rarely. He seemed incredibly fond of them. I was worried about him at the Day Hospital after our discharge, he didn't seem well. There was always something secretive about him though, as if he carried a huge burden. We met for lunch the day before he died. I was so shocked to hear of his death and would have liked to go to his funeral, but it was for family only. I wrote to them but didn't have a reply. It was hard to keep attending the Day Hospital after that, and fortunately I was discharged soon after."

"Have you had any recent suicidal ideas?"

"No, I haven't. I met my sister the other day, the first time in ages, and she told me that her husband is terminally ill. He has no choice. I have a choice, why would I throw this away? Although I don't feel worthy of it sometimes."

"How are you feeling now you've restarted the tablets, as you were trying homeopathic treatment at one point, weren't you?"

"I know I need them at the moment, my life feels at a crossroads. I want to be in control of this relapse, if it is one."

"I understand. Now with your permission I will e-mail Dr Macintosh about our conversation today and hope that he will see you soon. I shall be in touch next week to see if he has made contact, and we'll meet again very soon. What are your plans for the rest of the day?"

He always hated that question.

"You can smell the paint? The walls I think, the ceiling has had one coat."

"Excellent it will freshen up the room and make you feel so much better. I'll be on my way, then."
She buttoned up her jacket, stuffed his notes back in her bag and was gone.

He sank back in his chair. What had he done? He'd told Greg and now Hazel and no doubt he would have to tell Dr Macintosh. Where would this lead? He put the Mahler CD on loud and took up his paintbrush.

Greg was running late so they met him at the flat in Tunbridge Wells. He had the particulars from the estate agent. George was looking morose.

"Now, Dad, we're just having a look, we don't have to commit to anything today."

They had arranged to be shown round by the Manager who, they had been informed, came in five mornings a week. Mrs Aikman was a pleasant cheerful bespectacled woman in an olive-green suit who introduced herself and shook their hands.

"They call me a warden, but I'm not strictly a warden. I'm not on call for the residents. They each have their on-call buzzer and pull-cords to use if they need help when I'm not here. This is the communal lounge. We have coffee mornings twice a week and sometimes themed evenings. Someone's relative came in to show his photos of his trip to Africa, for example. All the residents seem to get along, but they like to keep themselves to themselves. Some are older and frailer, whereas some, like yourself," she said addressing George, "are very fit and active for their age."

They walked along the corridor.

"Here is the laundry room and there is a small library, though I don't think it's used much.

They climbed the stairs.

"Of course there's a lift, but you all look fit enough to climb stairs. George had flashbacks to Dorothy's last fall. This was torture for him.

"I don't want to see people's holiday snaps," he muttered under his breath.

"Shush, Dad," Helen said.

They were entering the flat now. It was pokey, even without furniture. There was a kitchenette, a living/dining area, small bathroom, and single bedroom with a walk-in cupboard.

"Where will I put all my books?"

"That's what everyone says, downsizing on this scale is very hard. That's why this walk-in cupboard is handy, there are boxes on the top shelves in most flats. I forgot to say that there's a guest bedroom on the ground floor, bookable in advance, but lots of people have a sofa-bed in the living room for emergencies."

"Well, thank you for showing us round, we'll be in touch," George said perfunctorily.

"Are there any questions?"

"Do you allow family to have keys?"

"We allow one per family and that is the person that is first to be contacted if the emergency cord is pulled. I forgot to say there's one in every room, I'll show you. The centralised community alarm is based in London, and they have contact details for each resident and can call an ambulance if it's deemed appropriate."

"Why would I need an ambulance?" George retorted. "I'm not coming here to die, you know."

"Right, we'd better be off, thank you very much for your time Mrs, what did you say your name was?"

"Well, I don't want every busybody knowing what I keep in my wardrobe," George said as they drove off.

"I thought it was very nice, Dad," Helen said trying to placate him. "And it would be company for you."

"I don't like coffee mornings. I will just wait until you come down to visit me."

"Talking of coffee," Helen pulled into a car park near the centre, Greg following behind.

"Well, I think that went very well," Greg announced when they were seated in the tea-room.

"I'm afraid I'm not moving, and certainly not there." He seemed adamant.

"I think we should all sleep on it," Abigail said sensibly.

"Dad, you said the other day you thought the house was too big for you. You've got all that garden to look after not to mention the house. I know you've got Mrs Watts in twice a week,"

"She could come more often, and maybe cook for me," he interrupted.

"Yes, of course and we could get gardeners more often, but it's not the same for us as knowing you have a back-up system should you fall ill."

"I'm not doing it to make your lives easier you know." This conversation was going nowhere. It was time to change the subject.

"Look Dad, you know we spoke about Scotland? I wondered whether you'd like a trip up there in a few weeks. The autumn colours should be lovely - they're always later than us here in Kent. We could have some good day trips as we discussed. I've found a very nice-looking hotel in the Trossachs, I'll show you when we get home."

This seemed to do the trick, he was smiling now.

He was silent all the way home. Greg was picking up some things for lunch.

"Would you like a few days up with us in London before we fly up to Scotland?"

"That would be great Helen, I could do with a dose of those children of yours."

"That's settled then, we'll book flights and hotel when

Greg gets back. I take it you'll come up as well, Abigail?"

At times like these, families don't need to get along, Abigail thought, she had had plenty of experience of crises when an elderly parent left it too late to move and regretted it. There again, if they wanted to die in their own home why shouldn't they? All these discussions needed time and patience. Helen was worried that she would have to work out her notice before the trip North, maybe Abigail and Greg could take him. It would be too late in the year otherwise. Over lunch, they talked about the plans. Abigail and Greg agreed they would go, as they had the time. Greg could take leave.

"It's all settled then," said George. He went to get his guidebook.

"Of course Mum and Dad had that holiday in Scotland just before she was diagnosed."

"Damn, I forgot that. Still, he seems happy with the plan, and if it goes well, then Spain in the spring." Helen was pleased with her efforts, she had booked return flights for two weeks' time and was in the process of checking out the hotel."

"There's just one problem," Greg said, "I've a client who's a bit precarious at the moment, I'm a bit reluctant to leave him. However, he knows Paul, my colleague, so hopefully Paul can step in for a week."

"Let's hope so."

It was all working out. They were holding his grief, easing his passage, keeping him close. He needed them as much as they needed him. Once a matriarch dies the offspring must find a way. They were finding theirs.

Summer 2000

They got off the Tube at Leicester Square.

"It's only a short walk to the restaurant." Paul had one in mind. Tourists were thronging the streets. It was drizzling.

"Mind how you go," Paul shouted over his shoulder. The crowds were getting denser, Ian was feeling a panic rising in his chest. At one point he lost sight of Paul and he almost stopped in his tracks, but then he saw his head bobbing along and rushed to catch him up.

"Thought I'd lost you then," he panted.

They reached the restaurant, garish red lanterns were strung all up the stairs.

"They do excellent Dim Sum here, a classic Chinese lunchtime dish," Paul said. The restaurant was warm and claustrophobic, but the smell was enticing, and he was hungry.

"I'm very happy for you to choose from the menu." He was relieved to be out of the noisy streets.

"We'll have the selection of Dim Sum, please, and two Jasmine teas. Is that OK for you, Ian?"

"Perfect."

There were lots of Chinese families and groups of businessmen in the dining room. Always a good sign, he thought.

The meal was delicious, the best he'd had in ages.

"Thank you so much for suggesting this, you must let me pay for you."

Paul refused to allow this, and they settled the bill between them. The atmosphere was getting very stuffy, he longed for some fresh air.

"Would you like to walk back to the Embankment?" Paul said.

"That sounds like an excellent idea."

Once they were away from Leicester Square the crowds thinned.

I must suggest this restaurant to Jack, he thought. He was looking forward to seeing him.

The sun was coming out, giving the afternoon a welcome warmth.

"What do you fancy doing next week?" Paul asked.

"Going for lunch somewhere around Hampstead would be good, then a walk on the Heath."

"Sure, just a few more stops on the Northern Line. I should have time for that."

"Well, somewhere closer if you prefer?"

"No, Hampstead is fine. I'll be in touch. I may let you make your own way back now, I have another client to meet near here."

They parted at the Embankment, and he crossed the river to walk along the South Bank.He stopped for a cup of tea outside the Festival Theatre. Once again, he watched everyone intently. There was a smart businesswoman sitting near him, drinking a mineral water. She wore a striped jacket and a short grey skirt. He couldn't take his eyes off her. He quickly paid and stayed sitting, wondering when she'd leave. After about fifteen minutes another woman joined her, and they started an animated discussion. He strained to hear what they were saying but he couldn't make it out. Their conversation seemed to be getting more heated, he thought. Suddenly the smart woman got up to leave. He also stood and set off in the same direction. She was easy to follow in the crowd with her bright red shoulder bag. She quickened her step and he had to almost run to keep up with her. He was sweating now, a heat rising in his body. He needed to stop and catch his breath.

Fortunately, at that moment she stopped to answer her mobile phone. He drew back. They were on the bridge heading back to the Embankment. Then she was off again. He kept his distance watching all the time for her noticing him. If she did, he would disappear into the crowds and walk in the opposite direction. He planned to follow her to her destination. She took a right turn off the bridge, down the steps and along the river. He was struggling now but he wasn't going to give up. They reached Somerset House and she entered by the lower door. He was close behind. She held the door for him.

"Thank you," he said. Then he went with her in the lift up to the central foyer. He could hear her breathing, smell her scent, it was intoxicating. From the foyer she went into the Courtauld Gallery speaking to the guide at the door. He paid for a ticket and followed her in.

It was dim inside after the bright sunlight and his eyes took a while to adjust. He looked around but couldn't see her anywhere.

The paintings were by Andre Derain, and there were some wonderful works of the Embankment and other views of the Thames. He calmed himself by looking at the bright colours. Then he saw her, sitting on a chair by a portrait of Matisse, reading a book. He stopped to gaze at the painting, the light and shade on Matisse's face, the thick red beard, the pipe, the blue shirt, the soulful expression. How had he got the features with such bold brushstrokes of pink, red, green, and purple? It was hard to drag himself away.

"What a wonderful painting," he said to her.

"Yes, I just love his work."

A tingling sensation crept down his back.

"How long is the exhibition on for?" he asked.

"Another month or so."

"Well I'll come back I think, these are worth seeing more than once."

She smiled.

As he emerged into the bright sunlight he wondered how Derain had seen all those colours in the river and the buildings around him. He thought he would try and take the inspiration to the Day Hospital tomorrow when he had another chance to paint. He would call into the library on the way home and see what art books they had. If there was one on Fauvism he would read it in preparation. The image of the portrait of Matisse came back to him on the train. It truly was the best portrait he had ever seen, it communicated so much. The pensive, melancholy expression. He should like to go back to the exhibition soon, it would give him a chance to see her again while she still remembered him.

There was a book on Matisse in the library, so he sat and flicked through the pages. It was a visual feast. The pinks and greens complementing each other. The doves and the sailing boats. He remembered he had said he would find an image to take tomorrow. He must get back home and search through his photographs. He took the book out as he wanted to gaze at the prints and remember the exhibition. Art sustains, he thought, and sustenance was what he needed just now. He found an old holdall containing holiday snaps and searched for an image he could paint. At last, he found a scene of a river with green fields and trees, rocks and a fence. He looked at it for a long time. The greens became blue, the river green, there was red in the rocks, the fence was orange. How could he make sense of what he was seeing? Art is best done from life, he knew. But that was impossible just now. He put the print aside and went back to the book. The genius that was Matisse just jumped from the pages, the cut outs were spellbinding.

His phone rang.

"Hello, Ian? It's Jack here, just checking that you're going to be there tomorrow."

"Yes, definitely, look forward to seeing you."

"Great, 'til tomorrow then."

He looked forward to it indeed.

They heard her calling out in the night. "George, save me, I'm falling, falling. Where am I? Help me, help me."

Helen got out of bed and went into their bedroom, George was holding her. She was shaking and lashing out.

"Dad, what can I do?"

"Nothing, she's often like this, it will pass. Go back to bed."

The night nurse was on annual leave, they had managed to get her upstairs to her bedroom. It seemed like progress was being made, but nights like these drained them all of energy.

"No, I think you need a rest, Dad, why don't you sleep in the spare room, and I'll sleep with her."

"OK then, if you're sure you can manage."

Helen got into bed by her mother and held her tight.

"It's me Mum, Helen, now just relax, let go, it's time to sleep." She stroked her mother's hair, tears streaming down her face.

At last, the tension in Dorothy's body relaxed and she drifted off into a deep sleep. Helen on the other hand couldn't let go of her and lay awake for the rest of the night. She wanted her father to have a deep sleep too. It was the least she could do for them. How the tables are reversed in time, she thought.

Boxing Day dawned bright, the snow lay gleaming all around. Bobby was barking downstairs. The children clattered down to see him. They were desperate to get outside.

"Did you manage to sleep, Dad?"

"Yes, thanks. How was she after I left?"

"Eventually she slept, she's still sleeping now."

"I must go up and see her. The nurse will be coming to get her up and washed soon."

He disappeared.

"Can we build a snowman?"

"Of course, have your breakfast first."

Mat appeared and took over. "You look shattered, did you get any sleep?"

"Not really, I think I'll have a bath and a nap now, if that's OK?"

"Of course."

"I don't know how long this is sustainable here. I think Dad is emotionally drained. I think we should be thinking of St Mary's long term."

"I think you're right."

Painful though it was Helen was reconciled to her mother ending her days in a nursing home. Her father needed space. He had coped for so long, longer than most people do, she thought. It was the lashing out that was so difficult, witnessing the fear and agony in her eyes. It was as if the familiar was too frightening, the strange would be more comforting. But today was about fun, and fun they would have. She would get her father's old walking boots out and they would go for a walk in the snow. They would have cold turkey for lunch and build a roaring fire. If need be they would stay another night. This was about George, easing his passage to accepting life without Dorothy at home. Later she would speak to her father, ask him whether he felt he still needed the night nurse.

The snow was sticky, perfect for building. They soon had a snowman, and fetched coals and a carrot for his face. The children were exhilarated, George was enjoying himself. He popped his head around the back door.

"The nurse can stay with Mum, Helen, why don't you come on the walk too?"

"No, I'd rather stay and prepare lunch."

They left down the lane, leaving a trail of fresh footprints. The snow underfoot was sparkling in the sunshine, and lay on the branches of the trees, it was a perfect scene.

Dorothy had managed to come downstairs and was drinking a cup of tea. Paula was holding her hand.

"You know, your father is heartbroken and finding it harder every day," she said.

"Yes, I know. What can we do to help him?"

"From what my colleagues tell me the family cope for so long, then the patient goes into care. It's heart-breaking I know, but it's what happens. Sometimes there's a crisis but sometimes it's planned."

"But things seemed to be going so well, I don't know why she's become so agitated. Maybe we should get the GP to assess her."

"Sometimes the excess stimulation unsettles them, everyone here for Christmas and all."

"But it's been happening for weeks now, her crying out at night and even with the night nurse here it's distressing for my father."

"I think the GP should have an input, maybe a light sedative would help."

"My sister is adamant she shouldn't be sedated. She says it only worsens confusion."

"Oh dear, that's a problem then."

Helen built a fire and then went into the kitchen to prepare lunch. A few moments later the rest of them returned, George laughing. He'd obviously been hit by several snowballs.

"That was great, it's just beautiful out there," he said, "shall I light the fire?"

"Yes, go ahead, lunch won't be long."

"I think I'd rather stay tonight and give Dad a hand if he needs it. You go home with the children, you could come down in a couple of days with some stuff and we could stay over New Year," she said to Mat.

"OK, if you think that's best."

"I think the roads should be OK by now."

She was feeling exhausted and emotionally drained. She really couldn't imagine how her father must be feeling. Her mother was sleeping now and Paula came in to see if she could help. Helen asked her to prepare a salad. It must be strange for her too to have the house full of people, she thought. They probably could have managed without Paula over Christmas, but the toileting and washing was something she was reluctant to do unless she had to. Paula was singing to herself under her breath. Her East German background gave her that efficient image, yet she was delightfully chaotic in her approach to the salad. Helen smiled. When the family leave, she told herself, I will speak to Dad. Try and find out how he's coping. Let him know that we're behind any decision he makes.

"There, is that OK?" Paula said.

"Perfect, let's call everybody."

Dorothy had to be woken and helped to the table. She was clearly disorientated and started putting food on her table mat. This was painful to watch. The children were giggling, more from embarrassment, but Mat gave them a strict reprimand. George was upset. Everybody felt uncomfortable. Paula came to the rescue, serving Dorothy and clearing away the mess.

"I love these Boxing Day meals, all the trimmings from yesterday with lovely salads. Did you make this one, Paula?" Mat asked.

"Yes it's a typical one from Germany, Karrottensalat, with lemon juice, ginger and sugar. You can have a different dressing with orange juice, wine winegar and dill. There are lots of wariations."

Dorothy was already tucking into her meal. George sat beside her prompting her. He poured himself a large glass of Rioja. His eyes looked sad, as he gazed at her. He was remembering past Christmases when Dorothy was in full command. Hearing her voice as she sang along to the Christmas carol CD she always played. Hearing her laugh at the cracker jokes. Seeing her there holding the turkey. This was too painful, he snapped back to the present.

"Here, have some more meat, Dad, and try some of Paula's carrot salad or Karrottensalat to be precise."

"This looks good for me," he exclaimed

They all liked Paula, she had a sense of humour and never complained. She efficiently changed Dorothy when she had an accident without making a fuss, so that no one knew it had happened. She blended in with the family.

"When are you managing to get home to Germany, Paula?" Helen asked.

"Oh, not until the end of January. My family are used to me not being there for Christmas. They have my younger brother and sister, so they're OK. I have to confess, I get good pay over the festival so it's worth it to keep working."

"When does the night nurse resume?"

"When you want her, I think."

"I think we'll manage 'til the New Year."

"I can tell the office."

"Paula, what is German food like?" Polly asked.

"Well, we eat a lot of sausage and salami and ham and bread. We also have a potato salad called Kartoffelsalat which is delicious. At Christmas we don't have turkey but rather goose or duck or rabbit or another roast with apple and sausage stuffing and red cabbage. But the main difference is that in my country we exchange presents on Christmas Eve."

"What about Santa?"

"Well, that's complicated. Santa brings his presents earlier too, and in some parts of Germany as early as the 5th or 6th of December and leaves them in the children's shoes."

Polly and Ben didn't seem very impressed by this.

"You wouldn't fit our presents in our shoes," said Ben.

George laughed. Dorothy suddenly started laughing too. Helen was sure it was a reflex given the jollity of the conversation. Her mother couldn't follow it, she had no idea what they were talking about these people, but it was funny all the same.

"No, I think you get bigger presents from Santa in this country," Paula said.

"That doesn't seem fair to the children in Germany," Polly said thoughtfully.

"Talking of presents can you two gather all yours up and decide if you want to leave any down here for when we come back in a couple of days. We'll take the rest home."

"I want to take them all home," Ben said defiantly.

"Well, it's up to you, I suppose we can bring them back down with us."

Mat went to pack, it was time to get on the road before it started freezing again. Dorothy was still at the table, George holding her hand. It was as if he didn't want to let her go. Paula was helping Helen clear up. She hummed a tune as she worked.

"Let's go through and sit in front of the fire, love." He helped Dorothy up and got the Zimmer. Her feet didn't move, and she swayed backwards, losing her balance. George managed to support her and called for Paula to help.

"We couldn't manage without you, Paula," he said.

Together they settled her into an armchair by the fire. Soon she fell fast asleep, her head back, her mouth drooping open. George, too, went off to sleep, the warmth of the Rioja coursing through his body. The family played a game Polly had been given, which involved acting out a word to the opposite team, a bit like charades. They roared with laughter as Ben tried to act the word 'space-station'. George woke up and thoroughly enjoyed watching them. He would miss the children when they left. Still, there was that bottle of Rioja open, he and Helen could finish that once Dorothy was in bed.

"Train, fast, flying, firework?" They were struggling to get it.

Later, when they had left, Helen sat next to her father and holding his hands looked into his eyes.

"Dad, do you think Mum should have another spell in St Mary's. It's awfully hard for you here, even with Paula. She's soon not going to be able to manage the stairs, and it really takes two people to mobilise her. I can understand you want to keep her at home for as long as possible, but we see you getting more tired and frail every time we visit, and we're worried about you."

"Oh Helen, you may be right. It has been hard these past few months. Let's see how it goes in the New Year. I'd like to wait 'til the spring and she can see the bulbs coming up. It was always her favourite time of year."

"That seems like a good plan," although she knew that once spring came he would be likely to change his mind.

Paula came back from walking Bobby. She woke Dorothy and, when she had come to, took her to the toilet.

"I think we should try and keep her awake now as she'll not sleep tonight otherwise, and I worry a bit about you having to cope with getting her up."

"I don't plan to get her up. I think if you change her in the morning that should be OK, unless she soils of course."

"No, that's OK"

They passed the afternoon peacefully, watching an old film. Paula helped them take her upstairs and get her ready for bed. She was difficult now, tensing her limbs and hitting out.

"I'm OK, don't do that," she shouted as they removed her clothes.

"Where's that man. Who are you? Leave me alone."

Skilfully, stroking her arm, Paula managed to get her nightgown on.

"I think I'd better stay with her until she falls off to sleep," Helen said.

"I'd better be going, the roads will be bad, I'll see you in the morning."

Helen rather dreaded the night. Maybe it had been all the excitement of the past two days that had unsettled her mother. A quiet few days with more of a routine might help.

Secretly she had her doubts.

The next morning he woke to the overpowering smell of paint. He lay in bed planning what he was going to do. He had the second coat on the walls and the skirting, door and window to do. He wouldn't get it finished today. It was a reason to get up, he had four hours before he had to be in the shop. He had a quick breakfast and checked his messages. There was one from Cathy, asking him if he wanted to have a bite to eat before the concert. He replied saying that that was an excellent idea. The morning passed quickly, and he was very pleased with his work. The living room was transformed. Walking to the Mind shop he felt a lightness, a calmness and a sensation of peace such that he hadn't experienced for as long as he could remember. He'd listened to the fifth symphony of Shostakovich and been transported. It was arguably his greatest work, especially the gut-wrenching third movement. He couldn't wait for the live performance.

The shop was busy when he arrived, there was a group of middle-aged women perusing the books and three people searching the clothes rails. He liked it when it was busier.

"How much is this blouse?" A young woman asked.

"Oh, I think let's say two pounds fifty, for you two pounds." He surprised himself with his forwardness.

"OK, I'll take it, and this please."

She was wearing a low-cut T-shirt and tight jeans. He tried to focus on the task in hand. The next customer was in a wheelchair, his carer leaned over him to get his purse. His voice was thin and staccato like, his hands weak and flailing. He was buying some thriller and gangster movies. Ian gave him his change smiling warmly.

"It's getting cold out there," the man said, wrapping his coat around him tightly.

"Hope to see you in here again soon," he said, as the carer wheeled him out.

One of the middle-aged women came to the counter next. She was wearing a green padded jacket that was too tight for her and had her grey hair tied back in a ponytail.

I'm looking for a book by Elizabeth Strout, Anything is Possible. We're doing it in our Book Club. If you see it coming in, can you put it by for me?"

He didn't think this was normal practice, but he decided to accede to her request.

"Can I have your name and telephone number, please?"

She gave him her details and left.

It turned out that two more women were also looking for a book by the same author.

"Are you in a book club," he asked.

"How did you guess?" came the reply.

"Well, someone else was looking for a novel by Elizabeth Strout for her book club."

He was glad when his shift finished, he was tired from his painting, and he had to get home to get ready to meet Cathy and David.

They met at the Festival Hall restaurant, where Cathy had booked a table. She and David were already there. He was shocked to see David. He was gaunt and there was a yellow tinge to his eyes. He gave him a warm handshake, his was weak in return. His jacket was hanging off him. He wore a red cravat. He'd made an effort, he thought. Cathy was looking great in her cream blouse and pearls. She was commanding the situation.

"Let's have some wine, shall we? Red or white?"

They poured over the menu. David was clearly having difficulty deciding what he could face to eat.

"You could have that consommé soup as a main, maybe?" she said.

The views over the Thames were superb. The atmosphere in the restaurant was buzzing. It was a real treat for him, this. The waiter came and they placed their orders.

He thought he would be direct: "David, I was so sorry to hear of your illness."

"Well, I don't want to talk about it this evening, I trust Cathy has put you in the picture. In brief I have to make the most of the next few months."

There were tears in his eyes.

"Do you know the programme this evening?"

"I borrowed the CDs from the library and have been listening to them while I'm painting the flat. I particularly like the Shostakovich, which is new to me. Mahler's second is a favourite of mine."

"Yes, it should be good, especially with the Maestro conducting."

"I can't wait to see him."

Their wine arrived. David poured himself a large glass.

"Do you think you should have so much with your medication, darling."

"I bloody well will, I'm in charge, so shut up."

The atmosphere became tense.

"When did you last come here, Cathy?" he asked.

291

"Oh, a couple of years ago. We've been lazy about going out really, but now David wants to go to everything. He's been started on steroids recently and it's given him a bit more energy."

"I wondered if you fancied going to the theatre, maybe the Globe? Although the seats may be a bit uncomfortable for you, David."

"Yes, I think they would be. But the theatre, yes, if it's not a depressing play."

"I could look at what's on and let you know. Maybe a West-End farce. We must definitely go to more concerts too."

The food arrived.

David took one spoonful of his soup and grimaced.

"Everything tastes foul just now, I'm hardly eating anything.

It was difficult to eat in front of him. He refused to taste either of their meals. He poured himself another glass of wine.

"What about the bread?"

"Too dry. Maybe I'll try some ice cream in the interval."

Cathy looked anxious. Watching loved ones waste away must be torture, he thought. You are helpless as the cancer marches on relentlessly. It's often the only thing you can do, offer food.

It was time to settle the bill. "I'll get this," Ian said. Cathy gratefully accepted and they made their way into the foyer to buy programmes. There were crowds of people milling about and the usual hum of anticipation. David looked quite lost and strained.

"I think we'd better get to our seats," Cathy said, clearly worrying about him and wondering how he would sit through the concert.

But when Sir Simon Rattle came on stage David's face lit up. He was transported by the atmosphere. This is what he should be spending his last months doing, Ian thought.

Ravel's Mother Goose Suite opened the programme, followed by the Mahler symphony. It was a fantastic performance. Cathy bought ice creams in the interval. David ate his, they were relieved to see, but he was obviously getting uncomfortable in his seat.

"Did you bring any painkillers with you?" she asked him.

"I've already taken one, so I can't take one for four hours. Don't worry, I'll be OK. I'll just get up and walk around for a bit."

Cathy followed him, anxious not to let him out of her sight. The orchestra were coming back on stage, the tuning up of instruments taking over from the murmurs in the auditorium. David looked hunched and haggard as he settled back down in his seat.

"Can you make it through the second half?" he asked him.

"I wouldn't miss it for the world."

The audience roared with approval as Sir Simon Rattle came back onto the platform. He stepped onto the podium and raised his baton. All eyes of the orchestra were on him as the first chords of the Shostakovich soared into the air. Ian let himself become completely absorbed in the music, closing his eyes and banishing all thoughts. It was as if the notes led him on paths to infinity. The opening movement was so conflicted and unsettling, but by the time it came to the sensitive and sublime third movement he was calm and accepting. The notes from the flute rose into the auditorium, the soft strings following on behind, stirring into a climax.

The oboe soared, accompanied by high strings, and followed by the clarinet's plaintive melody. Then the strings came in with a stirring section with repeated notes and minor cadences. The sensitive playing of the first violins brought tears to his eyes. What was the composer thinking about when he wrote this movement? The composer, writing in the Stalinist era, was treading a fine path between artistic composition, subversion and conforming with the regime. The sublime harp playing was followed by two chords softly played by the strings. At the end of the third movement there was complete silence in the hall for several minutes and no movement in the orchestra as if the players were frozen in time. The huge final movement was an assault to the ears, especially the last section with all the brass and percussion playing with full force.

At the last beat of the drum the audience was on its feet, there were shouts of appreciation and huge applause. The atmosphere was electric. David was standing whooping with delight, his pain forgotten, his illness denied, his defiance palpable, his acceptance strong. He was defying suffering and using music to face death head on and with full vision and understanding. Cathy was gazing at David with admiration, she caught his eye and smiled.

"What a terrific performance," David said.

Sir Simon Rattle was coming back on the stage for the fourth time, bringing all the sections of the orchestra to their feet in turn.

"We should go now before the rush," Cathy said.

Ian didn't want to leave the hall with its safe cushioning. Facing the uncertainty of the future seemed harder now. He was unsettled. He wondered how many of the grey-haired audience felt similarly. They were carried along by the crowds, Cathy supporting David who seemed even weaker now. At the entrance to the foyer, they stopped.

"Thank you so much for inviting me and getting the tickets, Cathy. I hope we can do this again soon."

"Yes, we definitely will, I'll be in touch."

On the Tube back to his flat he thought of the powerful emotions he had felt that evening. His rising affection for Cathy and David, his fear for what the future held for them, his joy at finding the beauty of live music again. He would continue to borrow CDs from the library and keep an eye on the Festival Hall programme. He felt relaxed and strong as he turned the key to the flat. The healing power of music was having its effect and would continue to do so.

Autumn 2005

The trip to Scotland went well. George had apparently thoroughly enjoyed the whole experience, especially the visits to the distilleries. They had spent four nights in the Trossachs and two nights on Skye before returning to Edinburgh. George had become rather subdued on Skye, remembering the last time he'd been there with Dorothy.

It was only four weeks to Christmas and Helen had had her leaving do. They had all gone to the pub opposite the office. Calum had been ingratiating, it had been a painful affair. She spent the next two weeks cleaning the house from top to bottom and making lists. The children were delighted to have her home when they came back from school. She was already thinking of the next trip she planned to make with her father. Nerja, that was the name of the place in Spain that Greg recommended. She would look up flights and accommodation. Maybe March would be a good month to go.

"Hi Dad, how are you?"

"Not too bad. You know, I've been thinking. Maybe moving to that flat is not such a bad idea, I wonder if it's still on the market."

"Golly, Dad, that's a turnabout. I'll check and let you know. By the way, I'm looking at Spain. Do you fancy going in March? I could book it all up just now. I'll need to give Abigail a ring to see if she'll come with us."

"Great, thanks love. Are you coming down soon, and what are your plans for Christmas?

"You must come here, Dad. I'll see if the others will, too, it would be good to be all together, especially this first Christmas."

"That's right."

"I'll try and pop down in a week of so for a night, I'll have to see what's going on with the kids."

"Good, I'll hear from you then?"

"Yes, bye Dad."

She texted Greg. *"Dad has changed his mind about the supported flat. We should strike while the iron's hot."*

"Leave it with me," came the reply.

"By the way, Christmas at mine?"

"We'll see."

She got her laptop and typed in Nerja hotels. After a few minutes she found a small three-star hotel that looked good. She needed to check dates with Mat. He was late back from school. This was the third day in a row he'd been late. Maybe, as she was home, he could do his preparation there, without rushing back for the children. She trusted him completely.

"Sorry love we had a staff meeting," he said, coming into the kitchen.

"I'd like to speak to you about dates for taking Dad to Spain in March. I guess the kids could go to after-school club again."

"Let me get my diary. Remember it was your Mum's birthday in March, you'd better avoid that date."

"Of course."

"Anytime in March should be OK."

"We'll go at the end of the month then, maybe for a week, if that's OK?"

"Perfect."

She texted Abigail the dates. Abigail had been better lately and was talking of going back to work.

"I'm not sure if I'll be able to get that time off, of course, but if you book a double and a single room and flights we'll hope for the best."

"Are you up for meeting for lunch tomorrow, say Portrait Gallery at one?"

"Sounds great, see you there."

"Just remembered that the BP Portrait Award Exhibition is on, shall we do that first, say at eleven thirty?"

"See you in the exhibition."

She tried to see it every year, it was so inspiring. She was thinking of enrolling in a life drawing and painting course at The New School of Art.

A text came into her phone, *"Flat still available, second viewing arranged Friday, can you make*?"

"Yes, what time?"

"Eleven."

"I'll stay with Dad on Thursday and bring him."

"Good, see you there."

She was pleased, things were moving in the right direction. She hadn't missed her work, had more time to cope with the family, nuclear and extended, and for herself. She called her father and let him know the plans.

"OK, I suppose I'll have to make up my mind on Friday then."

"Not really, but soon after."

Abigail was already looking at the portraits when she arrived. The winner was a huge canvas of broad-brush strokes in muted greys and browns, oranges and purples. The eyes were vivid. It was of a woman, and her expression was soulful and pensive. Helen loved it, so did Abigail. How the artist had crafted the features with such large strokes she couldn't imagine. The runner up was in a completely different style, a fine cameo-like painting in relief. Most unusual choice, Helen thought.

They spent a full hour in the gallery and then made their way to the restaurant.

"I've booked the flights and the hotel," Helen told her.

"Good. Oh, Greg phoned about Friday. Unfortunately, I've got a GP's appointment then and I'm hoping he'll let me go back to work. I feel ready now."

"Don't worry, you must go to that, we'll manage Dad. Let's hope it all goes ahead now."

"Yes, fingers crossed."

After lunch they walked down to the Embankment.

"I'd best get back for the children. Good luck on Friday."

"And good luck for your second visit!"

It was lovely to spend a night with her father on his own. They watched Fawlty Towers, George bellowing with laughter. There was no mention of the letters. Best forgotten, Helen thought.

The visit to the flat went well. George was much more civil to Mrs Aikman, and as he was leaving told her he would be placing an offer.

Greg and Helen were delighted.

"I think we should celebrate," George said. "Let's go to the Black Bull."

"I'm afraid I have to get home, Julian has invited people round for dinner. I'll have to leave after coffee."

"Have you decided about Christmas?" Helen asked him.

"Yes, we'd love to come, just for lunch though."

"Great, I forgot to ask Abigail. Incidentally, I've booked a hotel in Nerja for a week at the end of March for Abigail, Dad and me. I guessed you'd be happy not to come on this trip."

"Yes, I think I'll look at taking you somewhere else in this country, Dad, say Stratford for a weekend."

"Sounds terrific," George said, "it's great to have some things to look forward to."

"I think I'll stay another night if that's OK, Dad?"

"Perfect."

They grabbed a coffee at a garden centre and Greg left for London.

"Lunch at the Black Bull then? Shall we take a taxi, and we can have a glass of champagne?"

"Sounds good Dad if you're sure."

"Cheers, Dad, we've got a lot of work ahead of us."

"Yes, that's what I'm dreading."

They followed on their champagne with a glass of Rioja that went perfectly with the roast pheasant. Helen was sure there would be a hitch, it was all going too smoothly.

"Now, Dad, maybe after a snooze we could go through one of your bookcases and decide what you really want to keep. Then there are all your CDs." Her Father was passionate about the classical repertoire, particularly opera, he had piles of CDs all over the house.

"I guess we have to start somewhere."

They were sitting with piles of books all around them, George had been more indecisive than she had expected. This was not going to be easy.

"Now Dad, are you realistically going to read these Agatha Christie novels, you know they were Mum's favourite."

"That's just the point, they remind me of her. Many a night we would be reading opposite each other by the fire, and she would exclaim as the murderer was announced."

Helen smiled, "but Dad, everything you throw out will have memories, I'm afraid."

"OK, let's pitch them," he said.

Next were several political biographies, many of which looked as if they'd never been opened.

"Henry Kissinger, are you going to read his biography? I can always borrow a copy from our library for you."

"OK, out it goes."

"Tony Blair, George Brown, Anthony Benn's memoirs, John Kennedy, I think they should all go to charity. You will only have room for a small bookcase in the flat, and we have to find room for the albums."

"I wonder if the photos can be scanned, so I just have a digital copy."

"That's possible, but very time consuming. I'll investigate whether we can pay to get that done, shall I?"

"Yes, good idea."

After a couple of hours the pile of books to keep became even smaller. Helen was pleased with their work.

"I think that's enough decisions for today, don't you? Let's have tea and watch a bit of TV. I'll take these into our local charity shop when I get home tomorrow."

She loaded up the car before he could change his mind about any of them. They spent a very pleasant evening watching a couple of films. As he was going to bed, he turned to her, "Oh I think I should have kept the Benn diaries, Mum gave me those."

"They might be at the bottom of a bag, I'll look tomorrow."

Great, she thought, I'll probably have to go through every damned bag to find them.

All was quiet when she crept upstairs, he'd remembered to turn his radio off.

Suddenly she was woken in the night, she heard a ruffling of papers.

"Dad, what on earth are you doing? It's two in the morning."

"I have to find something, it must be here somewhere." He had the whole contents of the bureau on the floor.

"What are you looking for?"

"Mum was compiling a family tree before she took ill, I think she will have put it in here. She knew more about the family than anyone, I must find it."

"Not tonight, you won't. Now I'm going to get you a glass of milk, and you get back to bed."

It was hard to believe she had just said that. By the time she got back upstairs he was in bed reading a letter.

"Here you are, Dad. It's best not to read anything just now, why don't you listen to BBC World Service."

She put the radio on and switched off the light. She couldn't sleep, it was five o'clock before she drifted off, dreaming of wading through piles of rubbish, putting it in black sacs.

The next morning, she found George at the bureau again frantically going through papers and envelopes. Eventually he found what he was looking for. She was afraid to look at it.

"Look, here you are," he said, "Helen Jane, first born of George and Dorothy. That's settled, it's official."

She gave him a hug. That was all he needed to see. The rest would be easy.

Jack was walking towards him as he approached the Day Hospital. He looked pensive and sad. His jacket was grubby, and his hair dishevelled. He hadn't shaved for several days.

"Good to see you," Ian said, "how are things?"

"Oh, pretty good, I'm glad to be out of the ward, I can tell you." He managed a weak smile. Ian wasn't convinced, he saw a great change in him.

They were greeted by Paul and Greg, who were arranging tables.

"What do you two fancy doing today?" Paul asked.

"I'm going to concentrate on my art, I think, I've brought in a photo of a landscape."

Jack looked vacant, expressionless, frozen.

"Jack, you will be seen by the doctor and your CPN, so there won't be much time before coffee break, but maybe you'd like to do some art or craft work after that."

It just felt like the ward all over again, there was no escape. He found it difficult to concentrate on his painting this time, he kept wondering how Jack was. Robert was painting the still life Sheila had set up in bright reds and greens. He could smell the alcohol on his breath.

He held the photograph up to the light. The colour changes he had seen yesterday seemed to escape him. He tried to remember the works by Derain and Matisse, their vibrancy and passion. Gradually, by applying layer on layer, he could see a way to transcribe the image into a vibrant colour study. Once again, the blues of the fields merged with the purples of the sky and the river in the foreground ran green and grey to the edge of the canvas, the shadow of a cloud giving way to rays of sunlight. He heard no sounds, lost in his world of colour and light.

At coffee break he looked for Jack. He found him hunched over his coffee mug, head in hands.

"Do you fancy meeting for lunch tomorrow, we could meet at the Globe Theatre and get a meal around there?"

"I think that would be very good, I need to get out. Meeting halfway is a compromise."

Jack lived in Islington. He'd described his flat as a bachelor pad, cold but practical. He too lived a lonely life, but did see his family from time to time. He hadn't told Ian much about his immediate family. It was as if it was painful to talk of them.

"Shall we say twelve at the Globe?"

"Fine, I'll see you there."

Ian spent the rest of the morning working on his painting. He was dreading the group meeting. which was scheduled for two o'clock. What would Jack say? There was no doubt he would come across as still deeply depressed.

Clare spoke first. "I had to leave the meeting on Monday as I was upset, but today I feel strong. I've managed to get out to the local shops, which is a first for me for a long time. I'm feeling panicky right now, but I'm going to stay here."

Greg smiled at her,

"That's really brave, Clare. Just take your time, there's no need to say anything else. Robert, did you want to say anything?"

Robert grunted, "Well, I just had two beers last night and I'm not going to buy any more whisky. I too feel stronger for that decision. I know that drinking lowers my mood. I just have to find something to replace it with."

"Yes, that is the challenge, but you've insight, which is good. Maybe we can chat later this afternoon. Jack, have you anything to say?"

"Hello, I'm Jack and I've just been discharged after seven months on the ward. This is all new to me and it's very difficult to talk." His voice faltered. All eyes were on him.

"Don't worry, it will get easier. We just encourage everyone to tell the group what they've been doing, what seems to have helped them, what things have been difficult to do and so on. That way you can see that others maybe have the same problems as you and give you ideas about how to overcome them."

"Well, tomorrow Ian and I are going to meet up for lunch, which I'm looking forward to."

"Good. Ian, what about you?"

"I'd like to tell you about an art exhibition I went to yesterday. It was of works by an artist called Andre Derain in the Courtauld Gallery in Somerset House. The paintings were so bold and vibrant with extraordinary use of colour. I found the whole experience so uplifting. I want to go back. There is an admission charge, that's the only thing. But remember that there is loads of art in London that is absolutely free and waiting for you to view it. I have felt inspired by Derain in my painting today."

"Excellent, Ian," Greg said, "thank you for sharing that with us. Art and music are powerful tools that can aid recovery from a relapse. Maybe we should start up a noticeboard of what's on and organise a trip or two. How does that sound?"

There was a murmur of agreement. Isabel piped up, "I

prefer going to galleries on my own, but I would be up for a group trip if others were keen."

Ian felt pleased that his contribution had led to this suggestion. He would go to the library and print out lists of exhibitions.

The rest of the afternoon was spent in the cooking and housekeeping group. Patients discussed their difficulties with budgeting and planning meals, and guidance was given on healthy diets and balanced meals. A menu was drawn up for preparing at the next session on Friday. Ingredients were to be brought individually. Ian wasn't quite sure how it would work with one small cooker, but he was keen to take part. This was something he could benefit from.

"See you tomorrow, then, Jack."

"Yes, thanks, Ian."

He watched him scurry away to the train station, his collar turned up against the howling wind. He was a pitiful sight, weak and vulnerable, he thought. He hoped tomorrow he would learn something of what troubled that poor man.

He slept a fitful sleep, the hours passed slowly, he didn't understand why he could not let go and drop down through the layers of the night. He eventually slept only to wake to the wind and rain lashing against the window. It wasn't looking promising for a walk along the river with Jack. He hoped he'd turn up. He took some time before leaving the warmth of his bed. Padding through to the kitchen he thought he would call into the library on his way to meet Jack. He would see what exhibitions were on and arrange to go to one with him. His arm felt numb, he must have slept on it awkwardly. He rubbed it and slowly it returned to normal. He felt alive and positive.

Jack was waiting for him at the Globe. The rain had stopped, the grey clouds moving quickly across a threatening sky.

"Let's walk through the market, there's a little restaurant at the other side that does good seafood."

Jack was silent, his features fixed.

"How are you?" he asked.

"Not great, I'm afraid. I feel detached from the world as if I am an observer."

He knew how he felt.

"Have you felt worse since you left the ward?"

"Probably. It's difficult to tell. There are things preying on my mind."

He didn't want to pry but hoped that Jack would open up over lunch.

Once again, the bustle of the market lifted his spirits. The colours and smells together with the noise of the vendors shouting stimulated all his senses. There was plenty of material here for his art, he thought.

"Do you want to buy anything?"

"Not now, maybe later."

He noticed that Jack was shaking, unsteady on his feet.

"Are you sleeping?"

"No, hardly at all. I lie awake all night thinking of my daughter."

"Where is she, do you see her often."

"She's here in London, but no, I'm not really in touch with her these days."

"So sorry to hear that.' They reached the restaurant, he followed Jack in, and they were shown to a table. "Would you like wine?"

"No, not at lunchtime, just water please." The waiter disappeared.

"I recommend the scallops, they get them from the market, they're so fresh."

Jack looked down at his lap.

"I hope I'm not prying but could you contact your daughter and try and see her?"

"I don't think it's possible, you see she doesn't know."

The waiter arrived with the drinks and took their order.

"She doesn't know I'm her father." The emotion this obviously aroused in him was overpowering. He was tearful and unable to make eye contact. Ian didn't know what to say.

"She's my brother's child, you see. My elder brother. I couldn't tell them. Her mother, my sister-in-law, is the only person who knows."

Ian wondered how a secret could remain hidden for so long. How a heart could be broken for fear of hurting others. It seemed such a sacrifice. How could you move on from that? This poor man had shouldered it for years.

"They visited me on the ward, my brother and Helen his (my) daughter, you may have seen them. She's a beautiful woman, just like her mother, Dorothy. Oh dear, what am I going to do, I feel I can't go on like this."

"You need to talk to someone about all this," he replied, "and soon. Did you mention it to anyone on the ward?"

"No, I've resisted telling people. You're the first person I've spoken to about it."

He felt a huge burden fall on him.

Their food arrived. Jack picked at his.

"I'm afraid I can't eat," he pushed his plate away.

He was worried now, should he get help? Jack's GP would surely see him if it was urgent.

"Look, I think you need to see someone today, you're not eating or sleeping, and I'm worried about your mental state. Would you mind if I called your GP surgery?"

"Oh no, that's not necessary, I'm really OK, I just had a particularly bad night. You see, yesterday was Helen's birthday. Don't worry, I'll be better in a few days."

"I'm sorry you can't manage the scallops, what about a dessert?"

"Just coffee, please."

There was an awkward silence.

"I always remembered her birthdays, I was her Godfather you see. It was a happy time for me when she was young. I saw a lot of the family. Dorothy and I were always close. But as Helen got into her teenage years we grew apart. I was busy with my job and there were these crises to contend with. My brother suffers as well, I'm afraid. The years we have lost. You as well, I guess. It's a cruel illness. I've just about had enough."

"You can speak to your CPN tomorrow at the Day Hospital and she may get the doctor to speak to you."

"There's nothing anyone can do. My life has been ruined by one simple event, but one that led to great joy, though joy I could only occasionally taste."

"After coffee let's walk, I find walking clears my mind, just looking about and out from myself."

"Yes, but I see Helen in so many people, young girls, young mothers, smart businesswomen. She haunts my waking day and my night. I just want to tell her, but I can't."

They emerged into the grey afternoon and walked back through the market to the river.

"Do you want to go into the cathedral, it's calming, especially if there is music."

"OK."

Inside the cathedral there was a stillness and a silence so pure it was deafening. They sat in the pews. Jack was weeping. Suddenly the organ struck out, its thunderous chords almost tangible. What should he do, he thought. Jack was clearly in a crisis but wouldn't accept help. Should he accompany him home, should he offer to put him up tonight? Neither of these options seemed feasible, he was bound to refuse. The best thing was to take him on a long walk and try and get him to eat something. He looked calmer after the music, he thought, and walked with a brighter step.

"I'm concerned you haven't eaten anything," he said.

"I'll get something when I get home, I'd better get back."

"Would you like me to come and spend the evening with you?"

"Oh no, I've things to do, arrangements to make."

He couldn't imagine what he meant but he seemed strangely resigned, as if he had found some inner peace. They walked along the South Bank, people were passing laughing and chatting vigorously.

"Well, thank you for taking the trouble to meet me, you've been very kind and I'm sorry if I have burdened you with my sorrows."

"No, I only wish I could help, I'll see you tomorrow." Jack shook his hand, turned and left.

He watched his shrunken figure until he disappeared into the crowds. I shall be glad when he's seen the CPN tomorrow, he thought. Something inside him gnawed away, he couldn't get the story out of his mind.

That night he felt he was falling, down through the strata of sleep, but always there were more layers. He dreamt of reaching out to someone, but that person was falling down below him into the darkness. However far he stretched he or she was always just out of reach.

He woke in a cold sweat. He had to get to the Day Hospital early. The traffic was heavy, the journey tedious, he felt his anxiety rising.

Jack wasn't there when he arrived. He was restless, should he tell anyone about his concerns? More people began to arrive, but still Jack didn't appear. By mid-morning he was frantic. He spoke to Greg, "I saw Jack yesterday, he's not at all well, you know. Should we get in touch with him?"

"I already have, he's not answering his mobile or his landline."

"Should we alert the practice, I'm worried about him."

"Maybe, if you're right and he was expressing worrying thoughts yesterday."

Greg went off to make the call.

"Someone is going to go round to check on him. That's all we can do for now."

The rest of the day passed in a bit of a haze. Somehow, he got through the cookery practical and out the other side and was relieved when he could leave. He tried Jack's mobile. It went straight to answerphone. He left a message.

He had a sinking feeling, he hadn't been able to reach out to him. He knew it had been Jack in his dream, Jack was the one who was falling.

Early Spring 2005

Gradually she deteriorated, it was a slow process. Come the spring, Helen had been right, George wouldn't hear of her going into St Mary's. He struggled on, getting thinner and thinner, until one night the phone rang.

"It's Mum, she's completely off the legs and she has had a fall on the stairs. Fortunately, she hasn't injured herself this time. Paula thinks she may have a urinary infection. She's quite delirious, we're going to call the GP."

"I'm on my way," Helen said reassuringly.

The GP arranged admission to the acute receiving ward. There they confirmed a urinary tract infection and put up a drip.

"She's very dehydrated," the junior doctor explained, "she should be better in a couple of days."

But she wasn't. Her confusion got worse, and she had to be managed with sedatives. They all accepted that the time had come to admit defeat.

George was beside himself.

"Does that mean she won't be coming home?"

"For now, she must have a spell in the nursing home, Dad."

"She won't see the roses coming out, oh Dorothy."

It was for the best they told themselves. She wouldn't know, she hardly recognised them. Their Father could visit every day.

He did for the next four months. When she could no longer feed herself he spooned a sloppy meal into her patiently, waiting for each swallow. He never failed. She must eat, he told himself. It was the least he could do for her. Sometimes the tears would drip from his chin as he fed her. Driving home he would only think of the next time he could see her. His love for her knew no bounds. It was a love that had surpassed all love in its forgiveness. He forgot old wounds, they were together in their suffering.

One night the phone rang at eleven: "I think you should come in George, your wife has suddenly taken a turn for the worse."

There was no time to call the children, he rushed to get dressed and drove at breakneck speed to St Mary's. He found her peaceful, but her skin was clammy and her breathing very irregular. He held her, whispering into her ear. There was no response, she was sinking fast. The nurse on duty popped her head round the door.

"Do you want a break, George?"

"No, I'm fine, I don't think it will be long now."

He was looking at the photo of all of them at the beach in France on the bedside cabinet. When he looked down at her she took a deep breath and was still. He was holding her as she went. He was too numb to cry, too hollow to feel, too anguished to let go. He couldn't leave. They made him tea. He sat and stroked her arm. Before he left he placed the photo of them on their camping holiday in France under her hands. It would go with her in the coffin. Happy memories.

By the time he got home it was a bright sunny day. The sun drained him, he needed a dark room, somewhere where he could weep and shout.

He called them all.

"She's gone." The words resounded in his head. He couldn't breathe. "Can you come? Mum's dead."

Winter 2005

The winter was a cold one. There was frost most mornings and a dump of snow the week before Christmas. David had rallied and they had been to several shows in the West End and more concerts in the Festival Hall. This evening they were meeting at Southwark Cathedral for a candlelit carol service.

"You'll come to us for Christmas Day, I hope," Cathy asked him.

"Thank you, yes."

He remembered Christmases past when he'd sat alone in front of the TV, imagining families all getting together. The pain of loneliness was so acute during the Festive period. He thought of Jack and how tough it must be for his family. "Christmas is a hard time for so many," he thought.

The service was enthralling, the choir ethereal, the organ thunderous. The smell of the candles and incense took him back to his childhood. The dark corners of the Cathedral were illuminated by candlelight and sound. He wanted to stay for a long time after the last note flew up. He couldn't leave. He had found such solace in music. David, too, was clearly immensely moved. He was wasted yet his abdomen was swollen. He struggled to stand but his spirit was not diminished.

They emerged into the dark, snowflakes illuminated by the streetlights, the smell of roasting chestnuts floating to them. It was magical. He was, for the first time in many years, almost happy. He had a sister who cared. He would in turn care for her. He felt pangs of guilt experiencing this warm feeling. How could he feel this when David was so near death?

Christmas Day was a strain. David was in bed, he had taken a turn for the worse, and couldn't eat anything.

"I shall have to call the doctor, he's in such pain."

"I'll stay tonight if that would help?"

"No need, I'll manage. If you could just clear the table, I'll go and check on him."

Over the next few days his condition deteriorated, and he was commenced on a syringe driver. The nurse came twice a day. Cathy felt well supported. Their daughter, Juliet, flew home from South Africa. They were waiting at his bedside. His gasps grew feebler. A cloud was descending. He called each day, she didn't want him to come. He sat at home in a daze, as if life was ebbing from him and not David. He wished he could be of more help.

The sun came out, the snow melted, traffic came back. He walked. He thought of Robert, Clare, and Isabel, how were they getting through the festive week? At a time when everyone is supposed to be happy the struggles are magnified. The struggles to get up, to get through the day, to go to bed facing another day. Only those who have been there can understand. It's as simple as that, he thought. He couldn't wait for the week to be over, to go to the library and help in the café. He was making progress. He was walking in the centre. He was alive. But still the image of Jack falling came back to haunt him. How tenuous one's hold on life is. He'd been on a knife edge before. But the calmness of Jack, that's what he remembered. The look on his face as they left the cathedral. He had been comforted. Think on that, he told himself.

He went round to see David; Cathy was holding his hand. He was yellow, his eyes were sunken.

"It's not long now," she whispered.

He made tea; she didn't drink it. She couldn't leave his side. He sat at the foot of the bed.

"What can I do?" he asked.

"Just be here," she replied.

David was drifting in and out of consciousness, his breathing was irregular, his skin clammy.

It seemed as if someone was calling from afar, telling him to let go.

Juliet came in, "Mum, go and get some rest please."

"OK, just for ten minutes, but call me if there's any change."

The smell in the room haunted him. Juliet was crying.

"I should have come back earlier," she said.

"Don't worry, you're here now, for your mother, that's what counts," he said.

The stillness in the room was restful. Juliet put on some music, Chopin's Nocturnes. "His favourite," she whispered.

Cathy came back into the room when, suddenly, David took a long gasp and grimaced and was still. His face was peaceful and relaxed. He was away. No one spoke. The piano kept on playing, lifting them with him. He got up to leave. "Don't go, stay a while with us," Cathy said.

Juliet was weeping but Cathy gazed dry-eyed at David's face and planted a kiss on his forehead.

"Sleep my love, sleep now."

After a while he got up and left the room. Downstairs he made tea and sat at the kitchen table hunched over his mug.

Who would be with him at his last breath, easing his passage, he wondered.

The GP was called and then the undertaker. It seemed all wrong to have to deal with these practicalities.

Meanwhile Chopin played on, filling the room with melancholic but uplifting chords, and David lay, peaceful and in harmony with his life.

There was a strong bond between them now, he felt, one that would last. He would support her, as she had him. He would have a role; one he would cherish.

Christmas 2005

"Can you just move a little to your left, Dad?"

Mat and Helen were lifting in the Christmas tree, the children were hunting in the box for decorations, eager to get going. There was an enticing smell coming from the kitchen. It was so good for him to be here, George thought, the build up to Christmas must be spent with children. He suddenly thought of his brother and how lonely he must have been. They used to include him in their plans, but towards the end they drifted apart. He felt guilty and immensely sad. Dorothy was always in his thoughts, too, but he tried to remember her in her prime, hosting Christmas, which she did so capably.

The children's school concert was held three days before Christmas Eve. George roared with laughter at the moment when Mary and Joseph fought over the baby, grabbing it from each other. The children were besides themselves with excitement.

"Let's build a fire and toast crumpets when we get home," Helen said.

George tried to make himself useful.

"There's nothing worse than being in the way," he said.

"Just go and sit in front of the fire and relax, Dad."

"I'm always relaxing, can't you give me a job."

"Choose a game to play with the children." He went with Polly to the cupboard and pulled out a couple of board games and they sat at the dining table.

What would he do without the family, he thought. They were always there for him. Pulling him back from the abyss that is grief. On his own he felt he was wading through treacle. Here in this warm glow his whole body felt lighter, he had a reason to live. He thought of Jack again and the guilt came back even stronger.

"I'll be green, you be blue Granddad. Ben will you play?" Ben reluctantly put down his i-Pad and joined them in a game of Ligretto.

"Anyone for a crumpet?" Helen placed a steaming plate of crumpets covered in lashings of butter on the table.

"Only two more sleeps 'til Santa," Ben said.

George was very quiet on Christmas Day. He hadn't expected to feel like this, so empty and vulnerable. Even the children's excitement wasn't enough to rouse him. The sherry and wine accentuated his feeling of being on the edge of things. He kept wanting to leave the room, to be on his own. It was so unlike him. Every empty chair had Dorothy sitting in it. Sitting, smiling at him. He longed for her. She was all he wanted.

Even when she had told him about Jack, all those years ago, he had wanted her. He forgave but he would never forget. He battled to eat the meal. Everyone was making the most of it, realising he was struggling.

"Dad, don't worry if you can't finish it, it was a huge plate."

Relieved, he pushed it to one side, "I'm really sorry, I think I need to go and lie down."

He got up to leave and suddenly fell to the floor. Abigail rushed over, "Dad, Dad, can you hear me?" He had a ghostly pallor, and his breathing was laboured. Abigail was checking his airway and pulse.

"Should we call the ambulance?" Greg asked, the panic obvious in his voice.

"No, I think he's coming to," Abigail replied.

George opened his eyes.

"Where am I?" he asked.

"You're at Helen's, we've just had Christmas lunch and you had one of your fainting dos. Don't worry, we'll get you over to lie on the couch and you'll soon feel better."

"Oh I'm fine now, I'm sorry to be such a nuisance."

He tried to get up but needed Greg's support.

"Come on. Dad, do as Abigail says and lie down. I think you knew this was coming on."

"Yes, I remember now. I was feeling very hot and full and a bit nauseous. Still, it was a delicious meal, Helen."

"Oh Dad, don't worry, everything's going to be OK." She wasn't sure of this but had to tell herself. He was clearly going through a terrible time, and it was taking a toll on his physical health. There is no way to speed up the grieving process, she thought, and it hits everyone differently. So often a spouse dies soon after being bereaved, she could see this happening to her father.

Her father, she too had been thinking of Jack and his last few days. If only he had reached out to them. She put the thought to the back of her mind. Just remember the happy Christmases we spent when he joined us, he was always so generous with his presents, she told herself

"Shall we leave the pudding 'til after the presents?"

"Presents!" the children shouted.

They stacked up the dishes then crowded round the fire. They felt a warm bond between them, all united in their loss but looking to the future.

"Here Granddad," Ben handed George a present. It was a guidebook on the South of Spain.

"Great, thanks Abigail, I'll have a good read of this before our trip."

Helen was secretly apprehensive about taking him away with his fainting spells and increased frailty. Abigail would be there, of course, that was reassuring. George gazed into the embers.

"Put a log on the fire, will you darling?" it was Dorothy's voice, as clear as day.

He turned to see Mat bending over to get a log. It sizzled and cracked as it met the searing heat. Flames shot up the chimney, lighting Mat's face. Candles were lit, the Queen gave her speech. It was the same in houses up and down the country. People missing loved ones, seeing them, hearing them.

A game of charades was played, the pudding was eaten, more sherry was poured. It was time for the others to leave. Julian had to go and see his parents on the other side of London.

"Thanks, Helen, that was great, shall we see you for a walk on the Heath tomorrow?"

"Yes, text me, hopefully Dad will make it, too."

"Don't push it, he'll be tired after today," Abigail said.

"I can't leave him, not at the moment, whilst he's like this."

"He'll be OK, but see what he's like in the morning. I could always come over and stay with him."

"That won't be necessary." George came into the hall, "I'm perfectly fine to go for a walk."

Helen looked up to the ceiling and smiled at Abigail.

"Well, we have to get you fit for Spain, Dad," Abigail said.

Abigail, Greg, and Julian left and George flopped down again in front of the fire. He was looking very flushed in the face.

"You know how hard it is for me just now."

"I know, Dad, you're doing so well. It will get easier."

"Part of me doesn't want it to. I'm frightened of forgetting her face, her laughter, letting go of the memories."

"That's natural too. If you want to have some space just go to your room, I can bring you tea."

"No, I'm better off here with the children."

Mat was in the kitchen clearing up.

"Dad's really struggling today."

"Can't say I'm surprised, are you?"

"No, I guess not, I just thought we'd be able to distract him."

"It's hard to distract someone from their grief," she sighed.

It was very dark outside, but the candlelight and flames made for a warming sight. George had his head in his hands.

"Dad, how about a film, something upbeat."

"Like Mamma Mia you mean?"

"Exactly that."

All weekend he worried about Jack. He left countless messages on his answer phone. He paced in his flat and walked miles across Hyde Park and Green Park. He needed to keep moving. He wondered if he should go to Jack's flat. But something stopped him. He was frightened, he had a bad feeling.

On Monday he spoke to Greg as soon as he arrived.

"I've been trying to get hold of Jack all weekend. Have you had contact with him?"

Greg looked down, "I'm afraid it's not good news, Jack's dead. He took his own life on Friday morning."

The words resounded in his head, he reached for a chair. Jack's gaunt face flashed before him. "I have arrangements to make." He was planning it then. He should have listened more carefully; he should have stayed with him. How could he have let him go alone to his flat in that state?

"Oh my God, Greg, I should have called someone on Thursday. I should have known. How can I live with this burden?"

He felt the walls crowding in on him.

"No, you shouldn't blame yourself. You weren't to know, and you were offering him friendship and support. I'm going to make an announcement to the group. There will be some fallout. Jack was a popular man; patients knew him from the ward. He was always polite, a perfect gentleman. If you want I can get the CPN to talk to you. People have all sorts of guilt reactions after a suicide, it's quite natural."

"What about his family, his daughter?"

"Jack was a bachelor. His only family was a brother, I think."

He remembered the information he had in confidence; he must keep it to himself.

At the group meeting Greg announced the news. There were gasps, and Clare burst into tears. It seemed as if their tenuous hold on life was shaken to the core by Jack's act. It was difficult to hold the group together after that, but Greg skilfully managed by bringing up a possible outing to the Tate Modern. No one seemed keen though, they were all so shaken. It could have been any one of them missing in the group. The empty chair, left when Clare fled from the circle, drew everybody's attention. Greg got up and moved it.

"I think we'll wind this up if no one has anything else to say. I think Jack's funeral will be private, but I'll let you all know."

Most of the patients went outside to have a cigarette. Ian found himself next to Andrew.

"Well, he was an odd, quiet sort of a bloke. You couldn't imagine him opening up to anyone. It's tragic. It's hit us all hard."

"Yes." He was lost for words.

The rest of the day passed in a blur. He didn't know what to do, he found himself pacing around the hall. He had a chat with his CPN, but it didn't seem to relieve him of the huge feelings of sadness and guilt. Guilt that he was still here, guilt that he hadn't prevented this, guilt that he hadn't asked more, guilt that he hadn't picked up on cues. He went round and round in circles until his head felt as if it would burst. He had to walk. Maybe if he walked most of the way home, that would help. He could call in at the library, it was late opening this evening. Maybe he should ask if they needed volunteers in the coffee shop. He set off, it began to drizzle. He didn't have his raincoat, but the water didn't bother him. The drops seemed to make him feel more alive, less numb. At the library he took off his jacket. The coffee shop was closed, but he asked at the desk if there was any need for help.

"Actually, someone has left this week, so there may be an opening. It would just be in the kitchen washing dishes and occasionally clearing tables."

"That would be great, should I drop by in the morning?"

"Perfect."

He sat down and took a newspaper, but the words all seemed jumbled up, he could hardly read a sentence. It was August the sixteenth. Jack had died on the thirteenth. How did he do it, he wondered. What were his last thoughts? Did he leave a note? He would never know the answer to these questions. He sat staring at the pages for half an hour. Maybe an art book, to look at the plates, would be a good idea. He found a large book on Gauguin. The brightly coloured images somehow calmed the turmoil in his head. Then he picked a book of Matisse's paintings and again he found the colour soothing. He had tried to paint that afternoon, but he really couldn't concentrate so had left the group early and asked Greg if he could make his way home. Reluctantly Greg had agreed to release him. Greg was worried about his reaction and how he would cope with the news. He knew Ian had been worried about Jack on Friday.

He would try and paint again on Wednesday, again a landscape in bold colours. He was seeing the colours he would use now, they would be bright, uplifting. Only a little grey and black. Tomorrow he would be back in the library, and hopefully this job in the kitchen would work out. He would have to find a way of working through this, like so many things in the past. No one could help him, it had to come from within. He walked home with a book on Monet under his arm. It had stopped raining. He would look at the paintings and listen to Beethoven. Colour and music would banish those thoughts from his troubled mind.

He tossed and turned that night, he was frightened to let go, to have that dream again, he needed to be awake, alive. It was daylight before he fell into a shallow sleep, one in which he was tossed in waves of black and blue with only the moonlight up above.

Greg drove them all down. They were silent in the car, each with their own memories, each worrying about how they would cope, each apprehensive about seeing their father.

George greeted them in the garden with open arms. He had been crying but his eyes were dry. The lines of grief coursed his face. He had lost more weight.

"Oh Dad, it was sudden at the end, if we'd known we would have been here with you."

"No, I'm glad I was alone with her. It's what she would have wanted, I think."

"Poor Mum, poor you, Dad."

"No, we've been lucky, we had each other, some couples don't make it this far. We had a good life together. The last couple of years have been hell, but up 'til then we had a great time. Don't worry I'll be alright, I've no regrets."

They made their way inside. Abigail fixed coffee while Helen and Greg sat with George.

"She was very peaceful at the end. Suddenly she took a deep breath and sighed, and she was gone. Her eyes were closed, she looked serene."

This description made it easier for them.

"Can we see her?"

"Yes, I'm sure we can arrange that with the undertaker."

"Here, Dad, coffee."

"Thanks, I'd better eat something, maybe some toast?"

"I'll get it."

Over the course of the morning they each had their moments of tears and laughter. It was good to remember the fun times, the quirks and foibles that made up their mother's character. There was strength in their unity.

At two they drove to the undertakers. The dark-suited woman sat in the sweet, sickly smelling office and talked them through the procedures to follow. George wasn't taking it in, he had lost his concentration. One by one they saw her. Helen leant over the coffin and kissed her cold brow, tears falling onto her mother's eyelids. She wiped them away. Dorothy was dressed in her favourite summer frock, one that Helen had bought with her. It was blue with small flowers on it. She was emaciated but as George had said, serene, at peace.

George was in with her the longest, it was difficult for him to leave, Helen had to pull him away." Come, Dad, it's time to go now."

"Oh no! Goodbye my love," he said fighting back the tears.

"I'm glad you've all seen her," he said on the way home," she would have wanted that."

Arrangements for the funeral were made quickly the next day. It would be close family and friends only in the church in the village. She would be buried in the church graveyard.

"I'll still be able to visit her every day," he said.

Helen stayed on whilst the others headed home. She didn't want to leave him on his own.

She tried to walk regularly with him and Bobby. He needed the air and it seemed to lift him somewhat. Mainly, though, he was deep in his thoughts, unreachable, troubled. He'd lost his brother, mother, and wife all within the space of five years. How can someone bear this amount of grief, she thought. The weather was quiet and warm, the sun caressing. It was soothing to be outside in the countryside, she hoped he felt that, too. The smells were invigorating, the bird-song uplifting. Nature is a great healer of the spirit, she thought. They walked past the church, Bobby running up to and around the headstones.

"I can't believe she'll be here in a few days," he said.

"It's so peaceful here," she said soothingly.

She took his arm as they began the walk back to the house.

"Of course, she and I had our differences. After you were born we had a sticky patch."

She wasn't sure that she wanted to hear this.

"And then when Jack died it was difficult."

"What marriage doesn't have its' difficulties Dad? You were a great team, you and Mum, we couldn't have had better parents."

He squeezed her arm. That was all that was needed.

The children came down with Mat the next day, which was a great distraction for George. They took him for long walks with Bobby in the sunshine. Mat had managed to get the time off work on compassionate grounds. Her boss, as difficult as ever, had reluctantly allowed her a week's absence.

"Do you think Aunt Beth will come to the funeral?" Mat asked.

"I think she intends to, unfortunately," she replied.
Beth was Dorothy's younger sister who hadn't been in touch with George all the time he was looking after his wife. This was something that had greatly distressed George, who had needed all the support he could get.

"That'll upset your Dad."

"Yes, but there's not a lot we can do about it."

"What are we going to do afterwards?"

"Oh, I've been in touch with the Red Bull, they are going to put on a sandwich tea in one of their rooms."

"Good, it's all organised then. I hope I've brought down all the clothes you need."

"I'll manage, what I wear is the least of my worries."

He held her tight, she folded in his arms, grateful for the strong shoulders for support. She would need them in the weeks ahead.

Late winter 2006

An appointment came through the post. He hated those envelopes arriving. They always reminded him of his illness, of the need for constant monitoring.

It was an appointment for Dr Macintosh that Friday. The CPN was right, he wanted to question him further.

He'd seen a lot of Cathy since David's funeral. They had gone to galleries and concerts. She was doing remarkably well. He, himself was feeling better and better, the Mind Shop was going well, and the new face-lift he'd given the flat gave him a boost. There would be no problem reporting to Dr Macintosh he thought.

There was no one in the waiting room when he arrived. He sat on one of the plastic-covered chairs and flicked through a magazine. He was soon called in. Dr Macintosh was a stern, elderly man who looked at him with questioning eyes over his gold-rimmed spectacles. It was rather unnerving.

"Well, Mr Soames, how are you doing?"

"Very well, I'm pleased to say. I'm keeping myself very busy, working in a charity shop every day part-time, walking a lot and visiting the library and helping out in the coffee shop there when they're short."

"That's all good to hear. There is something that the CPN reported to me, however, that is concerning. She said you'd been following young women. You volunteered this information but said you realised it had to stop."

"Yes, I haven't felt the need to do this for several months now, so I don't think it will happen again."

"Have you ever had any thoughts of attacking or harming your victims?"

"No, none whatsoever."

"Do you have any thoughts of harming yourself?"

"No, not currently, I have had in the past."

"Do you have any sexual fantasies about these women?"

"No, none at all. Following them made me somehow feel as if I was in the real world and not the detached world I experience so often."

"You see, I would need to contact my colleagues in Forensic Psychiatry if it happened again. This is a very worrying development, Mr Soames."

His eyes began to water, he blinked furiously.

"I can assure you it won't happen again," he said blushing.

"Are you tolerating your medication?"

"Yes."

He asked further questions about the dosage of his drugs.

"Sleeping and eating OK?"

"Yes."

Dr Macintosh asked more questions concerning his motivation and drive. He then spent several minutes entering things on the computer, frowning and muttering to himself. Ian found this all very unsettling. Finally, addressing him with his searching eyes, he summed up the consultation: "Well, I must see you again in a month, and remember my warning, this has to be taken very seriously. In the meantime, I will ask your CPN to keep in close contact with you and report back to me."

He wasn't surprised. For over a year he had realised that what he was doing was giving himself a boost to ward off the depression. Now that he was back on regular medication he felt sure he wouldn't be tempted to follow people. It had scared him feeling so close to the last woman. It was as if he knew her. He left the hospital feeling very downhearted. Dr Macintosh was right of course, but he was a hard man. There was no compassion in him. He would see him punished if he had his way, he thought. Well, he had been warned. He stepped out onto the street where life was going on as normal for the masses. He must stay focussed on his day to day activities and not look at fellow pedestrians. He would stop this compulsion, he had to.

That afternoon he was in the shop with Jean. She was a cheery soul, who chatted away to every customer. He found it a bit wearing doing a shift with her. Somehow he preferred Phil's silence and earnestness. The shop was busy so the time passed quickly, and soon he was on his way home. Young women hurried past him, he glanced back after some of them but checked himself. No, he had moved on.

His phone rang. It was Cathy.

"Hi, I'm feeling a bit rubbish this evening, can I pick you up and we'll go for a Chinese?"

That was just what he was needing too, after today.

"That would be great, on my way home now, see you soon."

At seven his bell rang, Cathy looked haggard.

"I've not slept the past few nights; I think it's finally hit me that I'm not going to see him again."

He didn't know what to say.

"Do you want to come in?"

"Yes, let me have a good look at your new flat. Very nice, much brighter." The smell of paint still lingered.

"You've done a good job. If you feel like painting a few rooms for me I would be most grateful."

"Yes, I'd gladly do that, just give me a shout."

"I thought we'd try that Chinese in Streatham High Street, you know the one?"

"Not sure I do, are we going to drive?"

"Yes, sure, let's go."

It was freezing and foggy outside. The damp fog clung to them. Cathy managed to park near the restaurant, and they were glad to get into the warm interior.

"Have I told you that I'm thinking of going to Spain in March?"

"No, how exciting, where exactly?"

"The South, near Malaga, a small town called Nerja. I wondered if you would like to come with me, maybe for a week."

"I'd have to see if I can get time off work. I'll let you know. In theory I'd like to go with you very much."

He was delighted. He had been worried about going on his own. He should get back in touch with Greg about booking once Cathy confirmed the dates she could get off.

"How's work?"

"Not so great, I'm having trouble concentrating, probably as I'm not sleeping. I keep seeing his face and hearing his voice. The other day when we were at that concert, I could have sworn he was in the audience. I just looked at this poor man for the whole of the first half of the concert. I didn't listen to the music. I was heartbroken when I realised he wasn't David. It's all so illogical. I'm not myself at all."

"From what I have read about grief, these reactions are quite common. They will pass. It's all about not wanting to forget, wanting to keep the image and voice of the person in the forefront of memory, not deep where it is hard to retrieve. Grief is insidious, imposing and demands to be felt, it creeps up on you when you least expect it."

He had read a book on grief after Jack died as it had hit him so hard. He was surprised how long he took to get over it.

"The Macmillan nurse lent me a book which is helpful."

They ordered their food.

"Is there anything on at the National Theatre this week?"

"I think it's still War Horse, we could go if you like?"

"The reviews are great, do you want me to get tickets?"

"Yes, that would be good, not Tuesday, though, as that's the whist club evening."

"Oh, I thought you'd stopped going to that."

"I haven't been for ages, but I think I'll go again for a while. It's good to be busy."

"Yes, I need to find some evening activities now I'm on my own. It still feels so strange to say that."

Their food arrived. The restaurant was nearly full, there was a Chinese family next to them with two small children. They were fidgeting and not eating their meal. The parents were getting exasperated.

"How is Juliet doing?"

"She's struggling too, I'm afraid. It's taken its toll on both of us. To see him go down so quickly."

"Is she coming home again soon?"

"I'd love her to. She wants me to go out there, but South Africa isn't a country I love to visit. I was shocked, when I went that time, to see all those armed response signs on people's homes. It's still such a segregated society. When you live in such a wonderful, relatively safe and peaceful multi-ethnic city like London it's hard to experience that."

"I agree with you, but the change would probably do you good and the climate is fantastic."

"I'll think about it." They ate in silence. They were familiar now; it gave them both comfort. They didn't need to talk. They had never been so close. Being present at David's death had given them a deep bond, one that would last.

He got to the library as it opened. A pleasant woman greeted him in the coffee shop.

"Oh, you're the gentleman who was enquiring about helping out as a volunteer. Yes, we could do with an extra pair of hands sometimes. I'll take your mobile number. It's only occasionally that we're short staffed, so if you can work at short notice that would be great."

"No problem, I'm not working just now, so can help any time."

"Great. Let me see now, Ian Soames, isn't it? I'm Jackie, Jackie Martin." He was thrilled, it was a foot in the door. He just loved the library, its hushed sounds, its smell.

"Of course I will need a reference." I'll ask Greg again, he thought.

"As a matter of fact, I've just had a call from Susan who was supposed to be here this morning but isn't well. Can you stay just now and serve people?

"Gladly."

To feel wanted, that was such a boost. He felt so grateful for the social worker's advice the other day.

Over the course of the next few weeks his life hinged around the library, the day hospital and his walks in the city. He still followed people but not with the same intensity. It gave him a boost though, in what was still an empty existence. He dwelt on Jack but less and less. He borrowed a book on grief and read a few chapters. He tried not to get too friendly with other patients. He was coping.

One day Paul rang. "I'm taking some time off work so I'm handing you over to my colleague Greg, he'd like to meet you sometime soon. Shall I get him to call you?"

"No problem."

"Great, I hope things turn out well for you, take care."

He rang off. He would miss Paul, he had come to like his warm, friendly manner. He was non-judgmental and patient. He hoped he would like Greg as much. He met him at the day hospital. Like Paul he had an open and pleasant face and seemed a genuine and caring young man. They arranged an outing to the National Gallery.

They met at the entrance and immediately he felt at ease. He spoke at length about his distress at hearing about Jack's suicide. It was very helpful to talk.

"Yes, you will have found it very hard and will have grieved for him. Do you know anything about grief?"

He explained that he had read about it but it didn't make it any easier.

"I think it's worse because I've nearly been there myself and probably for similar reasons."

"What reasons are those?"

"Acute loneliness is the predominant one and looking back on a lifetime of relapses which over time appear to get longer and more profound. It's the sense of a life wasted."

"But look how you're doing now. I am most impressed with your art at the hospital and your love of art history. Also, getting involved in the library, in the coffee shop. That takes initiative."

He felt a sense of pride welling up in him. This young man is good, he thought. They were looking at the Impressionist paintings at the national. He had seen them so many times but never tired of them. He loved Cézanne's paintings particularly. Once again the colours transported him. He would love to have a go at life drawing, he thought. Maybe there was an evening class near him, he would look into it. Meanwhile he would carry on at the Day Hospital with Sheila. All the materials were there, it was easy. He had concentrated on landscapes but maybe he would have a go at buildings next time. He and Greg made their way to the exit and walked around to the Tube station. The pavements were crowded with tourists. The evenings were drawing in now, and there was a definite chill in the air.

"I enjoyed that very much," he said, as they boarded the train, "Thank you for coming with me. I find art has really helped my recovery."

They arranged to meet at the Tate Modern the following week. There was a Rothko exhibition on there, a huge contrast to the paintings he had been looking at in recent weeks.

"I think it's good to experience the shock of the new," he said, "although not so new now."

"I don't know his work at all," Greg said.

"He's best known for his colour field paintings, rectangular blocks of bright vivid colours. It's good to see how he chose the colours. They look very simplistic, but you can look at them for a long time and they seem to draw you in."

"I look forward to it, see you there." Greg left the train.

He was helping in the library that afternoon so there would be just enough time to get a snack at a café opposite.

He was managing to fill his days, he felt proud of himself. In the café he was suddenly overwhelmed by thoughts of Jack. Why did these thoughts dominate so quickly? Jack had seemed so calm at the end of their meeting. Was he planning it then, did he have that inner peace that comes, they say, when the decision is made to do it? The acceptance that the struggle is over. Could he have distracted him more? Maybe it had been a mistake to go into the cathedral. He had been over these questions time and time again. He had to stop them. If only he had managed a few more outings with him he might have been able to help his troubled mind. But he knew, though, the downward spiral you could get into with this illness.

The wind had got up as he went outside, the plane trees were buffeted as he felt his mind was buffeted by these unwelcome thoughts.

Inside the library he was quickly distracted, he got stuck in at the café serving customers, greeting them with a cheerful smile. There was a very elderly gentleman in a smart long raincoat with a tartan scarf. He spoke with a strong Scots accent.

"Where do you come from?" he asked him by way of conversation.

"Glasgow. I'm here visiting my sister Phyllis."

At that moment Phyllis appeared, a large woman with a lined face and endearing smile.

"What is the soup of the day, please?"

"Carrot and coriander or French onion."

"I'll take the carrot, what about you Bill?"

"The same for me, please, and water for us both."

He took their order to the kitchen. It was good interacting with the public, so much better than being on his own all day. He hoped he could help in the library itself in due course, but he guessed you needed qualifications for that. He would see if there was a book on Mark Rothko when he finished at three. He doubted there would be, but he could look him up on one of the computers.

He brought them their soup and went to serve a young man sitting on his own at the window. He was immersed in his book.

"Excuse me, are you ready to order?"

"Yes, could I please have the goat's cheese sandwich and a black coffee?"

"Certainly, I'll be right back."

Three o'clock soon came and he went to the art section of the library. There was nothing on Rothko, but there was a book on Jackson Pollock, so he took a seat and browsed through it. Another abstract expressionist, Pollock didn't appeal to him as much as Rothko. He felt uneasy as he looked at the prints. They weren't restful and seemed to symbolise his jumbled, chaotic thoughts. Rothko, on the other hand, managed to create a feeling of stillness, of inner peace, the eyes resting on the pure colours, not darting about as with the cluttered Pollocks. One, 'Stenographic figure', reminded him of Picasso and Miro. He put the book back.

A life drawing class, that was what he was going to look for. He went to a computer and searched. There was one near the High Street with drop-in four hourly sessions, but he would have to take his own materials. He would ask Sheila's advice on what to buy.

Feeling enthused by another project he walked back to the flat. He felt so well, he wondered if he needed his medication. He was keen to try herbal remedies, maybe now was the time to find them. He would pop into the Health Food Store along the road soon and see what they had for nerves. He felt this was a good plan, it would give him more control over his illness, and it was bound to be healthier. He would have to inform Hazel, his CPN, but ultimately it was his decision whether or not he took his medication, he was not on a Section.

The flat was cool and uninviting, he got an extra sweater and put on the electric fire. Huddled in front of it he thought back over the day. A good visit to the gallery, a busy session in the library, looking at the Pollock prints, investigating the life-drawing class. It had been a good day. He sighed and got up to get himself a beer. He figured he'd earned it.

The funeral was small and intimate. George was poker-faced and controlled. Aunt Beth was as painful as ever. Helen and Abigail both gave a eulogy. Afterwards in the pub George was animated, pint in hand. It was as if it had all never happened, the loss of her personality, her inability to recognise him, her physical deterioration. All was forgotten as he circulated amongst the mourners. The low oak-beamed ceiling trapped their hushed voices. Everyone was hot and contemplative.

"She was a great cook," Aunt Beth was telling a neighbour, "her Baked Alaska was famous."

Helen moved away, she found Mat, who was trying to keep the children entertained.

"I need to get away from these people, I need quiet time."

"Yes, I'm sure, but you shouldn't leave before it finishes."

"I can't believe how well Dad is doing."

"I agree, but he'll probably crash soon."

Abigail and James joined them.

"When do you think we can wind this up? Dad's had one too many I think."

"Oh dear, people keep buying him drinks. I think I'll try and have a word with him now."

She went up to him and put a hand on his shoulder.

"I think the landlord wants us to finish soon. Are you ready to go?"

"I guess so, let me just finish this pint."

Walking up the road nobody spoke. It was a cool evening, and Helen was shivering from the emotion of the occasion. It hadn't sunk in yet that she had lost a parent. It brought her own mortality to the fore. The house was cool and dark.

"Let's play a game," Greg suggested.

"What do you have in mind?"

"What about the dictionary game? Mum always enjoyed that."

"Good idea."

Helen made tea, wondering how her father would cope when they all left, and reality started to sink in. She could hear him laughing in the sitting room. He was sounding a bit manic, she thought. But the next minute she could hear him sobbing, deep sobs that took his breath away. She rushed to him.

"Come, Dad, let's go upstairs for a bit." She led him up to his bedroom. There she was horrified to see photos of her mother strewn across the floor and her mother's nightdress on his pillow. His sobs continued, tears, like memories, falling from him. She held him while his chest heaved.

"I want to be with her, I can't go on alone. Let me go to her, please oh God."

"Come now Dad, it's normal to feel like this, but gradually you'll feel better. Let's tidy up these photographs. Oh look, there she is in Guernsey in that lovely summer hat of hers. She looks radiant.

"Yes, that was our silver wedding."

"And that's her birthday party in the garden.'

He looked downcast, and she remembered that was when her mother had announced her illness. She put the photos in a pile by his bed. Gradually his sobs ceased. He lay on the bed.

"Let's go back down now and have tea. Do you feel up to playing dictionary?"

"Yes, sure my love, thank you for all you've done."

They joined the others who had got pens and paper ready for the game.

"Has anyone heard of a girandole?"

Nobody had. Everyone had to make up a definition, and Mat, who had chosen the word, wrote the real definition, paraphrased. All definitions were read out by Mat, and each person had to choose the one he or she thought the most likely to be the true meaning. It usually resulted in some hilarity, especially if a humorous word was chosen. George was looking at his daughters' faces, trying to see traces of Dorothy in them. When he did see a familiar expression he found it strangely comforting.

The evening passed quickly, at nine Greg and Julian got up to leave. George stood and formally shook their hands.

"Hope to see you both soon. Safe drive home. Here, take this. He pressed a photograph onto Greg's hand. It was of him and Dorothy on one of their trips, smiling into the camera, his arm around her.

"Thanks Dad, yes we'll be down in a few weeks, don't worry." His voice faltered.

"I think we should be leaving now, too," Abigail said, aware that he would find all parting painful today.

"You're all staying, aren't you, Helen?"

"Yes, Dad, until tomorrow only. We all have to get back to work and school."

Abigail gave her father a big hug,

"Take care, Dad, don't forget to take one of those sleeping pills the doctor left for you if you can't sleep."

"OK, Abigail, I won't forget."

He started sobbing again but managed to contain it.

"Sorry, it's been an emotional day, let's switch on the TV. Shouldn't the children be in bed by now?"

"Yes, off you go, you two. I'll be up in a minute," Mat said.

Fortunately, the soothing voice of David Attenborough soon calmed them. He was in Borneo with the orangutans.

"He will be sorely missed when he goes," George said.

They agreed. A National Treasure, they said.

"Well, I think I'm off to bed, I'll listen to the radio for a while."

"Goodnight, Dad."

What is a life? Helen thought, when it's reduced to memories and a few photographs. How can it be measured? By good deeds done? By the affection of one's loved ones? By academic achievements? By overcoming adversity?

She snuggled up to Mat.

"What a day it's been."

His arm was secure around her; he was her rock.

"I think we can expect a rough ride for a few months," he said.

"What do you mean?"

"Well, I think your dad will find it extremely tough, and so will you and Abigail. Greg manages to distance himself better from the raw emotion. He's had to learn how to do that to protect himself."

"I guess you're right. Still, we all have to get through this together."

He had much more time on his hands now he was discharged from all follow-up. After a few months he found himself doing it again and again. He couldn't stop himself. He'd take a Tube, focus on someone in the carriage and then follow them when they left. He walked miles, taking train journeys all over London. He didn't realise he was slipping. Beginning to wish the day gone so the welcoming night would come sooner. He'd tailed off and stopped his medication and got a couple of herbal remedies from the Health Food shop. His CPN, Hazel, had stopped seeing him regularly, and Greg, too, had withdrawn his support. He was helping out less often in the library as they were employing more reliable staff. His world was shrinking, and the only way to stop this, as a defence against his impending gloom, was to connect with strangers, enter their world. He began to believe they were there for him to follow, that somehow he was a player in some master plan. There were weeks when he hardly spoke to a soul. His pursuit sustained him. It gave him a feeling of power, of importance. It was only when he heard them speak that he was shocked to the core. It was as if they weren't real until they spoke. They were phantoms of his imagination, visual hallucinations. They were a reason to keep moving, he was running away from himself, not wanting to face up to what was happening to him. He was losing a grip on reality, living more and more in a world of his own.

The seasons came and went, then Christmas, a time when he found following easier. Everyone was wrapped up in their own busy thoughts, there was never a backward glance to notice a lonely man in a raincoat.

He wondered about contacting his sister, but she hadn't bothered getting in touch with him, so he thought better of it. On Christmas day he went to Westminster and followed all the jolly worshippers into the abbey. He watched them singing lustily, shrinking more into his coat, wishing he was them, anyone but himself. They would be going home to hot turkey dinners whilst he sat alone with his steak and ale pie.

The New Year dawned and with it a sense of foreboding. He looked at the bottle of pills he was taking, wondering how many it would take. But he didn't want to die, he just wanted to connect. He carried on, fighting it every day. There was no alternative, it didn't let up. More seasons passed. The summer was hot, London's air was oppressive. He visited galleries, but there were always people there to watch. He was distracted from the paintings. His mood was tumbling. He thought of Jack. How had he had the courage to do it? They say it is more common as you begin to improve after a trough. He was stuck in that trough; he couldn't climb out.

And then he saw her, the woman he would talk to. She was different, she made him feel more alive, more in touch with reality. And then she was fainting right in front of him. He could help her, he had connected. Now was the time to admit defeat, he couldn't conquer this black dog of an illness on his own. He had to get help; without it he would surely succumb as Jack had done.

Early in 2006

There was a message from Cathy:

I can get the last week in March off for the trip. Do you want to book, or shall I?

I'll book, as Greg has said he would help me. We've already found a hotel.

OK then, see you at the Festival Hall at seven. Oh, and try and get two single rooms. X

Will do, see you then. X

He contacted Greg, who said he'd meet him the next day at the library.

The concert that night was Maurizio Pollini playing Debussy and Chopin. It was superb and he gave several encores, all works by Chopin. You could hear a pin drop; the audience was entranced. His nimble fingers just glided over the keyboards like running water. He gave every ounce of himself to the performance.

"What a master," Cathy exclaimed as they left the hall. They embraced in the foyer.

"I'll text you when I've booked it all," he said as they parted.

I must remember to get a CD of Chopin's piano music out of the library, he thought.

The music was still going through his head as he lay back on the pillow, a soothing way to enter slumber.

Greg was waiting for him in the computer room.

"Hi Ian, you're looking well."

"Yes, I'm good, thanks, and my sister has agreed to go on this trip with me, I'm glad to say."

"Excellent, now what date are you planning to go? Let's look at flights first."

Greg navigated the site efficiently and had soon booked flights out and back on the Saturdays.

"My two sisters are planning to take our father to Nerja in March, also on my recommendation. The last time I spoke to them about it they hadn't fixed a date as Abigail is a GP and wasn't sure when she could take holiday."

Once again Ian felt immensely grateful for Greg's help and support.

"Now the hotel, I remember we looked at one before, do you remember the name?"

"I'm afraid not, but I shall probably recognise it."
Greg scrolled down the hotels available for the dates.

"That's the one," he said, "two single rooms - they'll have to be doubles, I think."

Soon it was all done.

"All you have to do is print out the boarding passes nearer the time."

"I expect my sister will do that."

He was working in the Mind shop after lunch so he asked Greg if he would join him for a bite to eat in the café.

"I've been meaning to ask you if you've managed to stop that habit you had of following people?"

"Yes, since I've been busier I haven't felt the need. Dr Macintosh knows about it now and he has taken it on board to follow me up about it. So I have no choice but to comply."

"Good, I'm relieved to hear that."

He felt safe, safe from himself, protected by the normal contact with people he was experiencing. Before, he had been so isolated, absorbed in thinking about whom he could follow. Absorbed in thinking about their imaginary lives. There was no danger of him going back, he had tasted the other life now, the life that normal people led. Free from self-obsession and guilt. He had Cathy now, and she needed him as much as he needed her.

"I don't know why I did it. It frightens me to think of the consequences if the people I followed had reported me."

"Yes, they would be severe. Your life is fuller now, you have no need of fantasies."

"Well, I'd better get going, I have to be at the Mind shop for two. Thank you for all your help"

"My pleasure, I'll be in touch about meeting up again soon."

He texted Cathy the details of the bookings.

Great, really looking forward to it X, came the reply.

He managed to borrow a CD of Chopin's Mazurkas and Nocturnes played by Martha Argerich. She was a completely different artist to Pollini, so it would be interesting to compare the two interpretations. He was tired when he'd finished his shift at the shop. It had been quiet, and Phil had been as uncommunicative as ever. He suggested they go for a drink after closing up the shop, but Phil wasn't up for it. There was no way he was ever going to get to know him, he thought. He made his way home slowly through the bustling crowds on the High Street, feeling a bit detached again. He worried about that feeling. It reminded him of when he was unwell. Maybe the dose of his medication needed adjustment. He picked up a takeaway from the Indian restaurant near his flat. He needed a beer this evening, this was not a good sign.

Climbing the stairs to his flat he felt a bit panicky. The rest of the evening loomed large in front of him. Sometimes being in his own skin was just too uncomfortable. He had nothing to take, nothing to relieve the anxiety. He would have to practice his relaxation exercises, that would help.

He lay on the bed and focussed on his breathing. He worked his way down his body tensing and relaxing his muscles. Soon he felt a calmness, an inner peace. He thought back over the day. It had been a good day, why had he suddenly felt this panic? He remembered Dr Macintosh telling him that panic can strike at any time and to be prepared. There was absolutely no reason for it this evening. He picked up the phone and dialled Cathy's number.

"Sorry to bother you, Cathy, but I feel rather terrible this evening, I've no idea why."

"Do you think you're worried about the trip?"

"I don't think so."

He realised then it had been the discussion about following people that had triggered this anxiety.

"I just needed to hear your voice."

"Do you want me to come over?"

"No, I shall be OK, I'll have a beer and my Indian meal in front of the TV. I'll be OK," he repeated trying to convince himself.

"OK then, if you're sure, I can easily come over."

"No, I'll ring you tomorrow, bye for now."

He rang off, and prepared his meal. The tingling in his limbs had settled, but the tightness in his chest persisted.

He switched on the TV to watch the news.

Gradually he relaxed, he lay on the sofa and shut his eyes. An image came before him, it was of the woman who'd fainted. He'd followed her to her house, how had he done that? How did he think he would get away with it? What would have happened next had he not realised he was ill? The thoughts frightened him. He must distract himself, find something to watch that would absorb him. He flicked through the channels and found a documentary on the Himalayas. Lying back, he practiced his deep breathing again and gradually the panic left him.

That night he dreamt he was on a long journey. He had to get to his destination before he could sleep. He was dragging his feet, his limbs felt like lead, the darkness was enveloping him, he could see no light. But gradually out of the gloom he could see faces. They were faces he recognised, faces from the whist evening, they were all laughing, laughing at him. He woke in a cold sweat, it was barely light. He lit a cigarette and noticed he was shaking. Taking a long drag he remembered his dream, it all made sense now, this journey was his, through his illness. He had to get to the end of it, he had to.

Winter 2005-2006

It was hard to keep the daily tasks going, even showering was an effort, but he knew he must do it every day. He had to keep on going for the children's sake. He longed for her with an aching heart. He stood at her grave and wept. He tried doing the garden, but it was too much for him. He saw her at every turn. He was consumed. He was just treading water and that was where they found him, about to sink. Helen rescued him before he went under.

Grief held him for months and months, and then she gradually let him go. He started to breathe again, to live in the moment.

He began to walk more, to go into the town and have lunch. He could read a book. The children were in constant touch with him, he was so fortunate. They visited more often and took him to see a sheltered flat. Eventually he felt ready to leave the house. The years of memories seeped from every corner, he had to let them go. Helen, Abigail and Greg held him through it, and he was able to move. He kept all the albums including the ones with Jack holding Helen. He found more letters but burnt them, he didn't want any more secrets unearthed. It was time to move on and start a fresh chapter. She was always there though, with her hand on his arm, smiling with her eyes.

Early Spring 2006

The trip was planned, they would fly out to Malaga on a Saturday, returning a week later. The hotel was booked, a small family establishment just on the outskirts of Nerja. The walk into the town was along the cliff. It looked perfect.

In the weeks coming up to the trip George prepared himself as best he could. He ordered his medication early, looked out his old sandals, bought some new summer shirts, booked Bobby into the kennels. He was going to enjoy this holiday.

He had settled into his sheltered flat. It had been very hard leaving the family home, an extra loss which he was grieving for, but he did go back to the village church every week to put fresh flowers on her grave. That helped him. At first, he parked up the lane near the house, but gradually he didn't need to see the house. He would talk to her for several minutes, telling her about the characters he was meeting. It was soothing to talk. Sometimes he would go into the church and then back to the grave.

He did go to the coffee mornings, and found he could have an interesting conversation with several of the residents. They were all in the same boat, missing their homes, and some their spouses. Most of them were struggling to adapt to this, their last chapter. Sometimes he felt he was sinking under the weight of it all, but then he remembered the planned trip with the girls and that buoyed him up.

A week before departure Helen rang. "Dad, I hope your passport is in date, I forgot to ask you to check"

"Golly, I'll just go and get it."

Fortunately it expired the following year. He felt a huge relief.

"Do you want some help before we go about what to take?"

"No, I think I'm organised, I'm going to pack tonight."

She smiled to herself.

"I'll ring on Friday then."

"Great, speak then."

Helen and Abigail arrived prompt at ten to pick him up. The journey to the airport was quick, so they arrived in good time. Helen dropped them off at the terminus and went to park the car.

"It's years since I've been here," George said. "Mum and I had some great trips, you know."

After checking in their luggage and going through departures they found a café selling good coffee.

"I just have to go and get some Euros," Helen said.

"We should all do that."

"Yes, I guess we should. Dad, do you want to come with me?"

He found the crowds of travellers a bit unsettling, he felt a little flushed. Oh dear, I hope I'm not going to faint, they won't let me fly, he thought.

There was someone taking a long time at the cash machine in the queue ahead of them, an older man, about his age. He looked flustered, looking about as if for someone to help him. A woman came up and sorted him out and the queue moved quickly after that. The flight was on time and smooth. He had a window seat and spent the entire time looking out at the clouds, the sun beating down. He dozed for a while, and soon they were landing in Malaga. They had booked a taxi to take them directly to the hotel, it would take just under an hour.

The weather was beautiful as they drove along the motorway. Abigail was in good spirits. Work was going better, and she and James were talking about getting back together. She'd been in a dark place but now the light was streaming down all around her. Helen, too, was relieved to finally be here. She had worried more than Abigail about the journey and how her father would cope. It was all looking good. She fingered her wedding ring, it was getting tight, she'd have to get it enlarged. It would be fifteen years this September they'd been married. They would have to celebrate.

The hotel was charming, and both the bedrooms had sea views. They took lunch on the terrace overlooking the sea. There was a light breeze lifting the gulls as they flew overhead.

"This is magnificent," George said, "Dorothy would have loved it."

"Let's walk into town this afternoon and see how long it takes us."

"If you don't mind, I'd like to rest this afternoon, I'll just take a little stroll along the path there and see you both this evening."

"OK, Dad." They were secretly relieved.

Later as he was passing through the foyer a couple were checking in. Wasn't he the man who was at the cash point in the airport, he thought. He was vaguely familiar, where had he seen him before? He overheard them give their names.

"Ian, Ian Soames."

The date of their departure had arrived. He woke with a mixture of apprehension and excitement. All the preparations were in place, he was meeting Cathy at the airport.

He was shaking when he arrived, the check-in desks were heaving with people. He felt a tap on his shoulder. It was Cathy.

"Am I relieved to see you," he said.

"We are at that desk over there," there was a huge queue.

"Oh golly, I'm not used to this," he felt a panic attack coming on.

"Why don't you get a coffee and I'll stand in the queue."

He gratefully accepted and found himself a seat at a coffee bar not far from the desk.

"Are you travelling together," she asked.

"Yes, can we have a central and an aisle seat, please."

They went through departures and then queued to get currency. He struggled at the cash machine and became agitated; Cathy came to his assistance. He was embarrassed with people looking on. How would he have managed all this on his own, he wondered.

The flight was called, and everyone was jumping up to get ahead in the queue. They seemed to stand for ages before boarding. He felt his palms sweating and his pulse racing.

"I'll need to sit down soon," he said.

"Don't worry, we're moving now," she said reassuringly.

The flight was smooth and on time and they landed in Malaga in glorious sunshine. It was twenty degrees with a slight breeze.

"Perfect," he said.

Cathy had hired a car and they were heading East along the coast.

"There, Nerja is up now, it won't be long."

The little hotel was perched on the cliff, with commanding views. It had a small foyer with fresh flowers. The sun streamed in.

"Let's dump our bags and take a short walk," Cathy said. Their rooms were adjacent, hers had a sea view, his looked over the town. The sea air was so pure after London, he felt better already. "This is fabulous, thanks so much for coming with me, it's made all the difference."

"Well done to Greg for suggesting this place," she replied.

They meandered along the path, the scents of the wild roses and the sounds of the cicadas bombarding their senses. The waves crashed on the shore below, the sea was a deep azure hue, palm trees leaned out from the path over the cliff.

He wished he'd brought his sketch book.

"Shall we turn back now? You'd probably like a rest before dinner."

"Yes, that's a good idea," he said.

He felt at once calm and overwhelmingly relaxed. This trip was going to do him the world of good.

Spring 2006

The walk into town along the cliff was superb. The water was sparkling, the sun high in the sky. The old town centre was small and compact. There were pleasant pavement cafés and a promenade high above the beach. They took a coffee at a café in the main square, then walked on the beach. There were young families playing and couples sunbathing, but it wasn't too crowded. Helen heard German and a Scandinavian language and English spoken.

"I think Dad will like this place," Abigail said.

"I agree," she replied. They paddled in the water. "Not quite warm enough to swim."

Walking back from the beach they noticed crowds in the square.

"Look, there's a wedding at the church, let's go and watch."

Confetti was being thrown all over the wedding party, car horns were blaring, people were cheering. The festive atmosphere was infectious. Guests dressed up in their finery crowded around the married couple. Children searched for thrown sweets. It was a happy scene.

"Mum would have liked to see this," Helen said.

"Yes, she would, Dad too."

"We'd better get back to the hotel."

The sun was going down, leaving a soft auburn glow on the rocks. Seagulls cried overhead. The breeze had dropped, it was a balmy afternoon.

They could see their father reading his book on a bench overlooking the sea as they approached the hotel.

"It's a lovely town," Abigail said, "we saw a wedding at the church on the square."

"Very good, have we booked in for dinner at the hotel by the way?"

"Yes, I said at seven if that's OK."

"Fine, I think I'll go for a little stroll, I'll see you then."

Along the cliff path he passed the couple he had seen in the foyer. He raised his hat and smiled. She gave a warm smile back. The man looked at him quizzically as if he recognised him. George felt a bit uneasy, as if there was more to this brief encounter than he realised. Where could he have seen him before?

Their backs were turned towards them during dinner so they couldn't see their faces.

"That's the couple at the cashpoint in the airport," George whispered, "I was sure I'd seen him somewhere before and I've just remembered. He was a patient on the ward when we visited Jack. At least he looks just like him."

"Well I never, that's a coincidence," Helen said.

"We ought to speak to them."

"We may do in time, but not tonight, I'm tired after our journey."

The couple got up to leave.

Helen glanced up and caught his face as he walked past. She gasped, it was him, she was sure. The man who had followed her and helped her. An irrational thought overwhelmed her. Had he followed her here?

Spring 2006

At dinner they could hear English spoken at several other tables. Maybe they would meet some people, get to know them. This felt normal. What well people do. Then he caught sight of her. It was her, wasn't it? She was sitting next to another woman and an older man. He felt the sweat trickling down his back. What if she recognised him? He couldn't risk being discovered. Something about the man was familiar too. He felt suddenly light-headed. He needed to get away from the table.

"I'm just going to my room to collect the guidebook," he said, leaving quickly. Up in his room he collapsed on his bed, trying to control his breathing. Rationally he told himself that the last contact he'd had with her was positive, and there was no reason to think she suspected him of following her. Gradually his breathing settled. He must get back to Cathy, they were in the middle of their dinner. Grabbing the guidebook, he left the room.

"Are you OK, Ian?" she asked.

"Yes, just tired I think the excitement of the journey hasn't helped, and not sleeping last night." They finished their meal in silence.

They took a coffee in the bar and retired to their rooms. He couldn't sleep. Where had he seen that man before? Was it on the train, or in the ward? His face was so familiar. Suddenly he remembered, he had been the man visiting Jack. The woman must be Jack's daughter. Once again, he broke out into a cold sweat. How had they all ended up at the same hotel? Should he say something to them? I must acknowledge them, he thought. He tossed and turned all night and, in the end, gave up and got dressed. It was dawn and he would go for a stroll. After all those months of following people to end up in Spain staying at the same place as the one person he'd spoken to. He hoped she wouldn't recognise him. He would have to explain to Cathy, and he wanted to forget the past few years. He was starting afresh, putting all that behind him.

He returned to the hotel and took a shower. It was seven and they weren't meeting for breakfast until eight. He tried to read his novel on the bench opposite the hotel, but spent most of the hour gazing out to sea trying to calm his troubled thoughts. At eight Cathy appeared at his side.

"How did you sleep?"

"Oh, not very well, I'm afraid."

"Is the bed OK? Or maybe you were hot, there's no air conditioning here."

"Not to worry, we can have a lazy day, can't we?"

"Of course, reading and lying on the beach is in order, I think."

They went onto the terrace for breakfast.

There they were, sitting in the corner, the man looked up. He caught his eye and smiled.

"Look at all that fruit," Cathy said," We really have struck lucky with this hotel.

They piled their plates high with melon, orange, and mango. Fresh coffee was served with piping hot rolls. The aroma of the coffee was tantalising in the bright sunlight. They could hear the waves crashing below.

"Haven't we met somewhere before?" she was standing in front of him.

He blushed, "No, I think you must be mistaken."

She walked off with the man following.

He thought of Jack.

This was a secret he would keep to himself.

Cathy looked puzzled.

"She seemed to be certain she recognised you."

He hesitated before replying,

"No, I'm sure this is a case of mistaken identity. Let's get ready for the beach."

He had had his chance to connect. But he didn't need it now, he had Cathy and the warm sun of Spain to envelope him. Then he would return to his life in London and talk to people. He got up and walked over to the cliff edge. The gulls were crying. In the past he would have thought their cries were mocking him. Many a time he would have felt the urge to jump. But now he felt the warm breeze embrace him. He was climbing out of this. He would survive.

George was down in the foyer before the others. The English couple were talking to the receptionist. Once again, he glanced at the man. Maybe he was the patient who Jack had confided in, and who sent them the letter after he died. He would tell Helen over dinner. She had recognised him from there. It all made sense.

The full moon was reflected in the sea. The evening was balmy, the noise of the cicadas was calming. Helen looked a bit on edge though, George thought, after he'd told her about the man on the ward. She was lost in thought, and hardly spoke during dinner.

It was him; she was sure. But he had been so kind when she fainted. She would speak to him again.

As they got up to leave she walked over to his table.

"We *have* met somewhere before, I'm sure."

"I don't recall."

"I'm sure you kindly helped me when I collapsed on the way to work a few months ago. You walked with me to the office. Your name is Ian, isn't it? Ian Soames."

"Yes, and yours is?"

"Helen and this is my sister Abigail and my Dad George, Jack's brother."

"I think you were on the ward with my brother five years ago. We had a letter from you after he died so tragically. I'm sorry we never replied, we were so very distressed."

"Would you like to join us for a coffee in the hotel?" Helen asked.

He was shaking now; this was too much to take in.

"Oh, I'm sorry, this is my sister Cathy. Yes, it would be very good to join you, thank you. We'll be in in a minute."

"What a coincidence," Cathy gasped. "That you helped her when she fainted, and they recognised you from the ward."

Ian was silent. He had no idea what to say. How was this going to end? He had a bad feeling.

They joined the others in the spacious sitting room. Coffee was ordered.

"What made you choose Nerja?" Helen asked them, "our brother Greg recommended it to us."

Ian froze. No, it was inconceivable that Greg was their brother. Hadn't he mentioned that his father and sisters were coming here? He was horrified at the number of threads that were weaving to connect them. He felt trapped in their web. He felt their lives were inextricably linked. To extricate himself he must speak the truth.

"Funnily enough it was a friend, also called Greg, who recommended Nerja. He is my befriender." As soon as he had said this, he regretted it. What if Greg had mentioned to them that a client of his was following women? No, client confidentiality would prevent that. He wasn't thinking clearly.

"Is this Greg, your befriender?" Helen held out her phone showing a family group photo.

"Oh my God, yes that's him. He's been so supportive to me over the past few years. I don't know what I would have done without him."

"We know very little about what he does." George said.

Abigail and Cathy were talking about the walk into town. They seemed to be getting along well. It was late, and Ian got up to leave.

"Well, it's been very good to talk to you. We look forward to your company tomorrow."

"Yes, sleep well."

Ian lay awake for hours, however, thinking of Helen and following her. What if she thinks I followed her here?" he thought irrationally. How was the week going to pan out? Did Helen have any idea about Jack's secret? Did he leave a note for her? What did George make of all this? He tossed and turned, his limbs aching, his palms sweaty. Sleep just wouldn't come. It didn't seem as if this holiday would be the relaxing break he'd so desperately craved. He had a lump in his throat. He felt as if he was sinking again. He tried to picture the beach and the waves crashing on the shore, and gradually his limbs began to feel heavy, and he drifted into a troubled slumber.

Helen, meanwhile, in a room above, was also wide awake. Her mind was tormented by questions. His kindness when he helped her had dispelled any thoughts she'd had about him following her, but now she knew why he had looked vaguely familiar. What could Jack have told him? How close were they? What had he told Greg? Her disturbed mind was racing around these questions. In her drowsy state she couldn't come up with any reassuring thoughts. She was plagued with anxiety and desperation. Maybe the best thing was to act as if none of these links existed. As if their lives hadn't crossed at all. Yes, that was the best plan, she thought. She turned over, the moon's light was seeping through the curtains, and she could hear the waves. Counting them she let herself be taken onto the sea, floating, until her thoughts dissolved into the deep below.

Spring 2006

The dawn colours were spectacular. Orange, pink and crimson laced with blue and yellow. The sun was rising on a new day, one that would bring rest for them all. Rest from the questions, rest from the past. The healing power of the sun was what they all craved.

Helen was the first downstairs. She stepped out of the hotel and was greeted by the smell of the sea. Glorious blooms of mimosa billowed in the breeze. The sky was a deep blue. She sat down on the seat overlooking the sea and closed her eyes. The swell of the tide and the crying of the gulls, together with the smells of the vegetation, crowded her senses. She let her mind be blank. Suddenly she was aware of someone sitting next to her.

"It's so beautiful here, isn't it?"

It was him again, the man she thought had followed her, Ian. He had a kind face and looked somehow vulnerable. How could she have suspected him?

"Do you fancy a stroll along the cliff before breakfast?" he asked.

"Yes, why not."

They got up together and made their way to the path, both lost in their own thoughts but fighting for the present to overcome them. It would be hard, but maybe they could reach out to each other, make some space, ease the tension. This must be the way forward, Helen thought. Ian was the closest link she had to her real father, Jack, to his last few weeks. She mustn't shun him, she must welcome him, get to know him. There was a lightness to her step as they meandered along the cliff.

From a distance George could see them, Cathy was by his side. Two bereaved souls searching for companionship.

"Shall we catch them up?" she asked.

"No, let's just take our time."

Abigail appeared, bleary eyed, her mobile in her hand. She looked towards the town and saw two couples making their way along the cliff. The breeze ruffled her hair, there was already warmth in the sun. She had just spoken to James. All was well.

I would like to thank my sister, Maggie, and my friends Sue and Carol, for their helpful suggestions whilst writing this novel.

Also, my grateful thanks go to Christopher for all the time and effort he put in to proofreading the book.

Finally, I thank my husband, Rick and family for everything.

INDEX